"HAVING SOME SECOND THOUGHTS?" HE ASKED

John studied her eyes as Kathryn mouthed a silent no.

"So what would you like me to do next?" he asked seductively.

"I don't know," she replied, blushing.

He frowned, stroking the swell of her cleavage gently. "What about when you've been with a man before. What did you like best?"

"I've never . . . ever . . . I've never been with a man before," she whispered, avoiding his gaze.

"Never?"

She tried to turn away, but he restrained her with his body.

"You're still a . . ."

"Yes," she murmured. "It's almost a dirty word in today's world, isn't it?"

He studied her intently, then asked softly, "You're not joking, are you?"

When she replied, Kathryn's voice was tinged with bitterness and she fought tears. "Sometimes, John," she said quietly, "I think my whole life until now has been nothing but a joke."

ABOUT THE AUTHOR

After completing her four-book Montana
Superromance series, Sally Garrett was ready for
a new challenge. So, with her helpful husband,
Monty, in tow, Sally headed off to research the
world of the lumberjack. The result is this tender
story of the romance between a middle-aged
schoolteacher and a divorced logger, *Until Now*.
A former accounting manager, Sally is now a very
successful full-time author.

Books by Sally Garrett

HARLEQUIN SUPERROMANCE

Sally Garrett

UNTIL NOW

Harlequin Books

**TORONTO • NEW YORK • LONDON
AMSTERDAM • PARIS • SYDNEY • HAMBURG
STOCKHOLM • ATHENS • TOKYO • MILAN**

Published August 1986

First printing June 1986

ISBN 0-373-70225-6

Printed in Canada

To Eileen Pearsoll, Kathryn Scott and Ann Tripke:
Three special women who were my former
co-workers in Phoenix and have
remained my friends across the miles.
I still miss our talks,
the crying window and the good times at GCC.

ACKNOWLEDGMENT

The logging life was new to me when I conceived this story. A special thank you to: James Lee Robinson, whose cartoons show more than words can tell; Steve Duthie, who took me on the ride of my life; Bernard Ball, who patiently explained the working tools of a logger; Wilma Barnes, who introduced me to people I would not have met without her help; my husband, Montie, and his son, Bill, who shared their personal experiences in the woods; Liz Codoni, whose articles in the St. Maries *Gazette-Record* were so informative; and especially to Dave McKim at Marble Creek, who discussed the logging environment from many viewpoints.

John, Kathryn and Chris are from my imagination, but without the friendly help of many people in the St. Maries area, they would not have come alive nearly as easily as they did.

CHAPTER ONE

"BUT YOU HAVE TO, Daddy. I told everyone you were making me one and we'd have it in the parade." Chris Brasher's eyes shone like wet emeralds.

"Maybe you should check with me before you boast like that, Chris," his father replied. "Making it is one thing, but having it in the parade..." John Brasher grimaced as he studied the logging truck he had been constructing for his son. The cab was large enough for Chris to sit in, and the trailer carried several small logs ranging from three to six inches in diameter.

John had built the vehicle to scale and had taken unexpected pride in the project he'd started during the spring thaw. Logging operations had come to a halt as they always did then. It was a time when the ground turned into boot-deep mud that could suck a piece of equipment down like quicksand.

During the wait for the ground to dry out and firm up, he had moved from his cramped trailer in Avery to his sister's home forty-eight miles away in St. Maries, Idaho. Spending a few weeks with his young son had been rewarding, but now that the summer logging season was in full swing, John was back in the woods, running a small logging company and seeing his son on as many weekends as possible. Building the truck had definitely brought him a better understanding of Chris, and he regretted he hadn't known his son earlier.

Not learning about the boy's existence until three years after his birth had been a jolting experience. But having full custody thrust upon him four years later had caused a full-scale upheaval in John's life. They had been together for eight months now and had recently celebrated Chris's eighth birthday with a full day of boating on nearby Benewah Lake.

Gradually they were working out the kinks in their relationship. He was especially grateful to his younger sister, Natalie, whose care gave Chris a sense of security and whose three children provided Chris with much needed companionship.

Chris tugged at his father's pant leg. "But it's almost finished," he said.

"I know, but . . ." John ran his fingers through his thick dark hair, adjusted his red suspenders and peered down at Chris. Realizing that he must look like a giant in his son's eyes, he knelt on one knee and tried to reason with him. "How would you move it?"

Chris tucked his thumbs in his own suspenders and stuck out his chest. "You could put in a motor, like the one in Aunt Nat's lawn mower."

"You guys leave my lawn mower alone," Natalie insisted, shaking her dark head as she stepped back over a pile of scrap lumber and touched the machine's handle. She frowned at Chris. "Your Uncle Cal already has enough excuses for not mowing the lawn. Don't you dare give him another."

Chris grinned up at her. "I didn't mean that one. Daddy can buy one just like it."

"I've spent enough on this truck as it is, young man," John warned. "You'll have to think of another solution." He covered his wide mouth to hide his own grin. At times like these, he sensed that, other than his son's green eyes, he was looking at his own replica.

"Well," Chris said, nodding his dark head, "we could get a goat or a big dog to pull it." He motioned with his hands to indicate the size of animal he thought would be strong enough to move the three-foot high logging truck.

"And who has the goat?" John asked.

"Billy Bates has a billy goat, but he's mean," Chris said. "But Andy Overstreet has a big dog. Andy says he's part Saint Bernard and part wolf!"

John shook his head no.

Chris's small shoulders fell, and his chin touched the front of his red-and-blue flannel shirt. John waited, trying to maintain his stern demeanor. Slowly he took his pipe from his shirt pocket and filled it with fresh tobacco. After several draws the garage was filled with the aroma of cherry tobacco. He watched his son slide into the seat of the cab and begin to imitate the sounds of a powerful engine.

He's such a bundle of endless energy and so easy to love, John thought. Sometimes he still felt wonder and disbelief that the small boy was his son. "I'll tell you what, Chris. Between you and Aunt Nat, you come up with a solution this week while I'm gone, and I'll certainly do my best to make the truck work. Next weekend is Paul Bunyan Days, and I'm letting the men off early. I'll be back in town Friday night, and we'll have two days to work out the details. I wouldn't want you to be embarrassed in front of your friends."

Chris's eyes shone with renewed hope. "You promise?"

John drew on his pipe. "I promise," he said and extended his large hand, which quickly swallowed his young son's. "My word is good."

"Hey, fellows," Natalie said. "I have an idea, only it would take both of you to carry it off."

"Tell us, Aunt Nat," Chris called from the cab. "What is it?"

A peculiar smile played across Natalie's attractive face. "Your father might not go for it," she said playfully, and she swung her attention to her handsome older brother.

"Of course he will," Chris replied. "He promised he would do anything we decided on. What is it? Tell us!"

Natalie smiled at John. "Are you game?"

John shrugged. "Sure. I'll keep my word. What is it?"

"You could be his power."

"What?" John asked, scowling at her.

"You could be his power. He needs an engine. You can be it."

"Are you crazy?" John said. "You always did come up with some strange ideas when we were kids, but this one is beyond anything I've heard before. Please explain yourself."

"Well," Natalie said, glancing from John to Chris and back to John again, "Chris can ride, and you can pull the truck with a rope or cable—give it logger power. Sort of like the old steam donkeys Granddad used to move the logs. Only instead of a downed tree at the end of the cable, you'd have a scale model truck and your son."

Chris bounced with excitement. "That's great, Aunt Nat. Just great! Oh, Daddy, will you do it? Boy, that fat Raymond Crosley will really be jealous now. And when

Billy and Andy see my truck, they'll want to ride in it, too.'' He grinned mischievously. ''This fall when I'm in Miss Keith's third-grade class, I can charge a nickel to anyone who wants to sit in it. Boy, I'll be rich!''

John choked and his pipe lost its fire. As he busied himself relighting it, he tried to think of a way out. *Damn Natalie.*

''Well, John?'' Natalie asked.

''Yeah, Daddy, will you do it? Will you do it?'' Chris chanted.

''You promised,'' Natalie reminded, her blue eyes twinkling.

''Yeah, you promised, and a man *never* breaks a promise, does he?'' Chris asked.

John ran his hand up and down one red suspender, but still didn't answer.

''Well, John?'' Natalie taunted, grinning.

He stared into his son's upturned face. ''Oh, hell,'' he mumbled, knowing he was trapped by his own words. ''Okay, I'll pull it in the parade.'' He frowned at the truck, trying to estimate its weight. ''For forty years I've managed to avoid being in a parade. I suppose it's about time I took the plunge.''

THE TUBA PLAYER'S off-key notes drifted back to John as he gallantly pulled his son and his seven-foot long logging truck down the town's main street. The community's Labor Day Parade had brought most of the St. Maries-area residents into town to line the parade route. This was going to be the longest mile walk of his life.

He had listened with half an ear to his son all weekend as Chris told of his plans for the coming year in the third grade. By Sunday evening John had heard more glowing stories about the fabulous teacher named Miss Keith than he could stomach. His son obviously had a crush on the woman. John had asked him to describe her.

"Well, she's old, but she's still pretty."

"What color is her hair?" John asked, trying to gauge the woman's age so he could develop a strategy if problems occurred.

Chris shrugged. "I don't know. Dark, maybe."

"Is she fat or thin?"

"In between," Chris replied.

"Tall or short?"

"Tall."

John studied his son, wondering what tall was to an eight-year-old. "As tall as me?"

"Gee, Daddy, no one is as tall as you."

Recalling the conversation, John grinned, then spotted two of his employees and friends from Avery in the crowd.

"Hey, Daddy, there's Swede and Mugger," Chris called, waving frantically to the men.

"Way to go, boss," one of the men called. John waved back, and the man gave him a thumbs-up sign.

Suddenly Chris shouted and bounced up and down in the cab, throwing John off stride.

"Daddy, look! There's Miss Keith!"

John glanced over his shoulder at his son and tried to follow the boy's pointing finger into the crowd of parade watchers.

"Did you see her, Daddy?" Chris called.

"I'm not sure," John admitted.

"There, Daddy, by the Cook Shack. See her?"

John peered at the crowd standing in front of the restaurant where he took Chris to breakfast most Sunday mornings and tried to spot the illustrious Miss

Keith. He had no idea which one of a dozen women she might be.

"There, see, she's looking for me," Chris called. As John looked over his shoulder again, he saw his son waving excitedly. He turned back to the crowd in time to see two gray-haired women waving at them.

"Hi, Chris," the more attractive one called. He recognized her as Chris's second-grade teacher, Mrs. Watkins, who had had a habit of writing him notes about Chris's lack of progress in completing his classroom assignments. John had had the best of intentions but had missed the spring conference appointment because of equipment problems. He had received a terse scolding a few days later in his mailbox in Avery. He had wanted to remind the woman that what his son did in the classroom was the teacher's concern and what he did at home was John's, but Natalie had warned against antagonizing her.

"Then you go see her and explain why I can't always drop everything and come at her beck and call," he had insisted. Natalie had interceded, and the notes had stopped coming.

John glanced again at the two women and shook his head. If the other woman was Chris's idea of a pretty woman, he had better have a talk with him. She looked at least sixty, with pursed lips that probably hadn't smiled in years. Why would such a prune-faced woman want to teach a classroom of energetic eight-year-olds? he wondered.

He tugged the rope as he thought about what the new school year would probably bring. He was already aware that Chris was no angel, that under his engaging smile was a troubled little boy and an overactive bundle of energy. His son was a child filled with insecurity and doubts, who needed a stable home, something John could only provide through his sister Natalie. There were certainly plenty of adults to share the blame for his son's problems, but the responsibility of his son's welfare was now his and his alone.

"Hey, Daddy, do that again," Chris called, giggling loudly.

John grimaced, wishing the parade was over. His shoulders were getting tired of towing the heavy truck. In spite of the conditioning of hard work in the woods, this exercise was testing muscles he normally didn't use. He glanced up and saw the parade disbanding a block ahead. The ordeal would soon be over. He gave the rope one last tug.

"Get a horse," a teenage boy shouted from the curb and gave John an obscene gesture when he glanced his way.

"Yeah, get a horse or a jackass," a husky younger boy at his side shouted.

"Shut up, Raymond," Chris called back and gave the younger boy at the curb a loud raspberry.

John slowed his stride and was about to scold Chris when the older boy on the curb called back, "He already has a jackass."

Before John could react, Chris jumped off the truck and darted toward the boys. The two boys disappeared into the crowd with Chris in hot pursuit.

"Chris, come back," John shouted, but his son continued to chase the other boys. *I had better rescue him,* John thought, *before he finds himself in deeper trouble than he can handle.* He cut through the crowd at the end of the block and parked the handmade truck behind his pickup, hoping it would still be intact when he found Chris and returned.

He felt a tug on his belt and turned to find Chris standing behind him, sweaty and flushed from his chase, his green eyes shining with excitement. The boy was grinning from ear to ear.

"What happened?" John asked, frowning heavily.

"I got him," Chris said proudly. "Can I help you load the truck?"

John squinted at his son. "Sure." Soon the bulky vehicle was safely loaded on the pickup. He grew puzzled at his son's continued grin. "Just how did you 'get' him?"

Chris puffed out his small chest. "I picked up a rock and pow! I got him right in the back," he boasted.

"Chris, haven't I warned you about fighting?" John said, reaching for his son's shoulder. "It only makes things worse."

"I aimed for his head, but his back is good enough," Chris explained. "He cried. He didn't want me to see him crying so he ran home. I didn't cry when he tripped me last spring on the playground at school."

"What is this? A grudge match?" John asked, giving his errant son a boost into the cab.

"What's a grudge match?" Chris asked, twisting around to make sure the truck was safe and secure in the bed of the pickup.

"Oh, never mind," John said. "Just try and stay away from him. Please, Chris. I can't come into St. Maries every time you have trouble with some bully from school, and sometimes I suspect you start the battle. So cut it out, understand? I received enough nasty letters from Mrs. Watkins last year. I don't want the same kind of letters from that old lady Keith this year. Do I make myself clear?"

"But, Daddy, Miss Keith isn't—"

"That's enough, Chris," John warned, glaring at his son. "No fights, or I'll have to punish you myself."

"Gosh, would you spank me?"

John sighed again, weighed down by the still unfamiliar responsibility of raising his son alone. Would he ever get the hang of it? "No, Chris. I don't think spanking would solve anything, but don't get overconfident. I'll think of something—something you'd really hate to miss or do without."

"How about making me miss a week of school?" Chris offered.

"Oh, Chris," John said, laughing. Impulsively, he reached for his son and gave him a hug. "Let's get to Natalie's place. She has fried chicken and homemade biscuits for dinner, and then we'll go to the fair one last time."

"Are there more lumberjack events?" Chris asked excitedly.

"Afraid not," John replied, ruffling his son's hair. Chris giggled and moved away.

Minutes later they pulled into Natalie's driveway. Her husband, Cal, helped them unload the logging truck and roll it onto the patio behind the house.

"We heard over the radio that you two won the award for best walking entry," Natalie said. "Four dinners at the Cook Shack."

"Great," Chris shouted. "Now Dad will have to come in every weekend and take me to breakfast."

John shook his head. "Sorry, son, but that won't be possible for a few weeks. I have to go check out a site that's coming up for bid. It's north of Sand Point. When I get back, I'll be working seven days a week for most of September. I've explained how it is. These hoot-owl hours don't allow much time for me to get into town." He explained the problems again to Chris. "I'm up at three in the morning, and when we stop in the early afternoon, there are always repairs and maintenance to do. I'm working when you're asleep and in school. I sleep in the evenings when you want to play."

He watched his son's posture slowly sag.

"It won't last long, Chris," he promised. "When the first three-day weekend comes along for you, I'll come get you, and we'll spend it together, up in the woods. You can ride in the cab of the loader with Swede, and we'll scout the creeks for signs of beaver. Fair enough?"

"You promise?" Chris asked, his lower lip still in a pout.

"Sure, son. Don't I try to keep my promises?"

"I guess so," Chris replied, "but I wish I could be with you all the time. If you had a mom—I mean a wife who could be my mom, then we could all live together, and we could—"

"You have a mom," John reminded him.

"But she didn't want me," Chris said, his lower lip in a trembling pout. "And she was mean, and Leo never would let me call him dad. I'm glad now. You're my only dad. Leo always said I was a—"

"That's enough, Chris," John warned. "Sometimes it's just hard to understand why grown-ups decide to do what they do. Your mother loves you. She just can't take care of you now. You're with me because I love you, too. It's my turn to have you now. Try to understand."

"Okay," Chris replied begrudgingly. "But if it's your turn now, why do I have to live with Aunt Nat and Uncle Cal?"

John wished he had an answer.

CHAPTER TWO

"YOUR DAD'S A GYPO!"

"He is not!" Chris insisted. "He's a logger." He shook his small fist at Raymond, who had been taunting him since school had begun several weeks earlier.

"A gypo!"

"A logger," Chris shouted. "And he's the best in the whole state of Idaho, too," he added.

"He's a cheat. He steals jobs from the union men and doesn't pay his bills. My dad says so," Raymond said, his rotundity giving him an edge in the argument.

"Your dad is a liar."

"My dad says your dad cheats at the scales, too. He—"

Lowering his head, Chris lunged at the other boy. Their sizes were a mismatch from their first scuffle, but Chris's light weight gave him speed the huskier Raymond hadn't considered.

They separated for a few seconds, each breathing hard, their faces flushed and sweaty. Suddenly Chris lowered his head and charged the other boy again, hitting him in his soft, rounded stomach and knocking the wind from him. Furious, the fatter boy regained his breath and doubled his fist, connecting with Chris's slightly upturned nose.

Blood spurted out, darkening Chris's T-shirt and blending with the dust from the play yard.

Suddenly a woman's hand grabbed the back of Chris's blue-and-white short-sleeved soccer shirt, and he was pulled away from his opponent.

"Christopher Brasher, stop this fighting immediately!"

"But . . . but . . ." Chris wiped his nose on his forearm, and the blood smeared across his face. "He said my dad was a—"

"I don't care what Raymond Crosley said," the woman replied. "While I'm on playground duty, there will be no fighting, period." She looked sternly at the other boy as well. Raymond was being restrained by Pete Busbee, a fourth-grade teacher.

"Yes, Miss Keith," Chris said, his eyes downcast.

"We'd better get them both to the nurse's office," Pete Busbee suggested.

"No!" Chris hissed and tried to pull free.

Kathryn Keith tightened her hold, determined to keep the upper hand on her wriggling captive. "You take Raymond," she said, her voice soothing yet confident. "I'll take care of Chris." His body went lax. Together they watched Mr. Busbee marching a bloody, sobbing Raymond off toward the school offices. Ray turned once and sent a loud raspberry back toward Chris. Chris stiffened and lunged forward, but Kathryn's grip was too strong to break.

"Stop it, Chris," she said. "Everyone is looking at you. Don't be foolish. I want to help."

Gradually he became more pliant as she took his hand and led him to the boys' rest room. The room quickly emptied. Kathryn Keith squeezed water through a handful of stiff paper towels and helped Chris wash the blood from his face, arm and shirt.

"Now, Chris, come with me to our classroom," Kathryn said. "We'll talk about this."

The dark-haired boy lagged farther and farther behind as she marched into the brick building and opened the classroom door.

"Come, Chris," she said briskly, motioning to him as he dragged his scuffed canvas shoes slowly toward her. She waited at the door until he made his way into the room.

Kathryn took her place in the chair behind her desk, but when Chris ambled toward his own desk near the middle of the room, she motioned him to join her at the front of the room. His eyes grew round with uncertainty. She beckoned again with her hand and reluctantly he joined her. She lifted him up onto the edge of her wooden desk.

"Now tell me what that fight was all about, Chris," she said. She smoothed the pleat in her plaid woolen skirt and adjusted the ribbing on the pale-green cable-knit sweater that enhanced the green of her eyes.

He stared at her face. Seldom did he get a chance to be this close to her. He thought she was very pretty, and he wondered if anyone else in the classroom realized that her hair color was exactly the same as his.

"Well, Chris?" She smiled encouragingly.

"He—Ray—he said..." His eyes began to tear, and he looked down at his jeans.

She handed him a tissue, and he wiped his face.

"He said my daddy was...a gypo...a cheat, but he's not, Miss Keith. My daddy is a logger. He's the best logger in the whole state of Idaho. I know because Swede told me so. And I got to work with him last summer. He's stronger than any of the men who work for him. They said so. And he let me ride on Swede's loader twice when Swede said it was okay, and he let me...he's a logger." But his confidence faded as tears filled his eyes again and ran down his flushed cheeks.

"It's okay, Chris," Kathryn Keith said, patting his knee. "Why don't you blow your nose? Here's another tissue."

He blew his nose and wiped his eyes several times. "I just wanted . . . Ray can't say mean things about my dad. He can't!" He wiped his nose again.

She smiled. "Every boy wants his father to be the best."

"But my dad really is. He's hon—hon—"

"Honorable?"

"Yeah, that's the word," Chris replied. "Aunt Nat says it, but I forget."

"Do you know what honorable means?"

"Sure, that he don't cheat."

"Doesn't," Kathryn cautioned. Chris nodded, but didn't repeat the correct word. "Chris, do you know what the word gypo means?"

"Course, it means a guy cheats to make a living and—"

"No, Chris. A gypo is an independent logger who hires other men to work for him. He sells to the mills. It's a very honorable profession, and I'm sure the timber industry couldn't get along without men like your father."

"But Raymond says—"

"Raymond is behind the times," Kathryn explained. "In the early days, when the unions were very powerful, some men tried to buck them by going into business themselves, and they had a difficult time making it in such a competitive business. Some cut a few corners at the scales, in the woods, and avoided the checkpoints when they overloaded their trailers, but actually they were just trying to make a living and to feed their families. Logging country isn't the easiest place to live, and these men were fiercely protective of their families and—''

''That's what my dad says, that he's just trying to feed his family, and his family is me!'' Chris beamed.

''But don't you live in town with your aunt?'' Kathryn asked. ''She's the one who came to the parent-teacher conference.''

Chris's boastfulness wilted. ''I have to stay with her for now.''

''How often do you see your father?''

''I go to his trailer every weekend, Miss Keith. It's up at Avery in the mountains.''

''Why don't you go to school there? Avery has a two-classroom school. You'd be with first through fourth graders and in a smaller class with only about twelve children. I would think your father would prefer to have you close to him.''

Chris's voice quavered. ''We tried that, but one day when my dad was late getting to the trailer, I tried to cook supper, and I couldn't get the propane burner on the stove off, and the skillet...these big flames shot up and the grease...it caught on fire and...'' His face turned pale.

''What happened?'' Kathryn touched his hand, frightened for the young boy as she thought of all the tragic possibilities.

''Mrs. Boren from the café was walking by, and she smelled the smoke. She came in and put out the fire and made me stay with her until my dad got home.''

''What did your father say when he got home?'' she asked.

Chris frowned as he recalled the near tragic experience. ''My dad, he wasn't even mad. I thought he would spank me for sure and all he did was hug me—so hard I couldn't breathe.''

"I'm sure he was very concerned," she said.

"He and Mrs. Boren talked about what happened for a long, long time," Chris continued, staring at the swinging toe of his shoe. "That's when my dad talked it over with Aunt Nat, and now I stay with her."

"Do you like it there?"

"It's okay. My dad says he wants me with him, but he says I got to go to school. I told him I could skip a year, but he said, 'Ab-so-lute-ly not!'" The boy bobbed his head with each syllable. Chris took a deep breath. "So I stay with Aunt Nat until my dad comes and takes me to the woods. He comes every Friday...almost." Again his eyes darkened and his young voice faltered.

"Almost? When did you see him last?"

"During Paul Bunyan Days."

"Goodness, Chris, that was almost two months ago," Kathryn said, straightening in her chair. "Why has he stayed away for so long?" She wondered what kind of a father would neglect his son for so many weeks. She glanced at her watch. Lunch break would end in less than five minutes. There was no time to ask more about his home life, but she knew the only way she could meet the emotional needs of this special boy was to learn more.

She had first noticed Chris the previous January when he had been enrolled in the second grade. His scrappy nature had become the center of conversation in the teachers' lounge, with his new teacher vowing she was adding gray hairs daily trying to reach him.

"He's a troubled child," Mrs. Watkins had said. "He's always on guard, afraid, but I don't know what he's afraid of."

Kathryn had established a rapport with Chris one afternoon in early April as she walked to her rented house on Jefferson, a few blocks away from the elementary school. She had found him sitting on the curb, arranging sheets of torn paper in a none-too-neat stack and wiping his nose on his sleeve. She suspected he had been crying.

"Can I help?" she had asked.

He had shaken his head and busied himself with his task.

"What happened to your take-home work?" she had asked.

"That fatso Raymond grabbed my worksheets and tore them apart," he had mumbled, sniffing once.

"I've seen you in Mrs. Watkin's class," she had said. "I'm Miss Keith."

"Yeah, and you teach the third grade," he had said, grinning shyly.

Kathryn had nodded. "What's your name?" she had asked.

"Christopher Brasher," he had murmured.

"Do they call you Chris?"

He had nodded.

"Well, Chris, why don't you come inside with me, and I'll help you repair those pages? I live right here."

She had helped him gather the torn sheets and he'd tagged along behind her, shuffling his feet.

"I have a kitten you can play with while I find the mending tape," she had suggested.

He had brightened. "I want a kitten, but my dad says they're a nuisance."

"They are, but I like the company," she had said as she'd unlocked the door and entered the quiet house.

Within minutes Chris had been playing with the three-month-old calico kitten while Kathryn had taped the torn pages.

"Don't you have kids?" Chris had asked, looking up from the kitten.

"No."

"Are you married?"

"No."

"Why not?" he had asked.

She had shrugged, unwilling to explain her marital status to an inquisitive seven-year-old.

Soon she had sent him on his way with neatly repaired papers to show his aunt. In the weeks that followed she had often had a companion to walk home with, but he had always declined her offers to play with the kitten.

"Aunt Nat says I gotta go straight home."

When the school year had drawn to an end and next year's classroom assignments had been given out to the teachers, Mrs. Wills, another third-grade teacher, had complained.

"I refuse to have Raymond Crosley and Christopher Brasher in the same room. Those two have been archenemies from the first day that Brasher boy enrolled in January. Who wants one of them?"

She had surveyed the other third-grade teachers. One had ducked her head. Kathryn had thought of her encounters with Chris. He had slipped under her skin without her being aware of his charm. In spite of his impulsive temperament, she suspected he was bright. If only he had a father who cared more about his welfare, she had reflected.

"I'll take Chris Brasher," she had volunteered, raising her hand. "We get along."

Now, as he perched on the corner of her desk, she had no regrets. She handed him another tissue.

"The other boys and girls will be coming in any minute, Chris. Would you help me pass out these papers?"

"Sure," he beamed, jumping light-footed to the floor and extending his hands.

She gave him the work sheets, and soon each place held a single sheet, neatly centered on the desktop.

"Thanks, Chris," she said, and he grinned at her, his eyes sparkling. The door burst open and the room was filled with excited third graders, anxious to finish the day's classroom activities so they could return to their play in the fresh air of a warm Indian summer day.

KATHRYN ADJUSTED the tagboard turkey on the bulletin board and took several paces backward to evaluate the Thanksgiving scene.

Pretty good, she thought, smiling privately at her artwork. Part of the focal point was missing. Tomorrow she planned to have the children make suggestions for completion. Then they would divide into small groups and make some three-dimensional figures to complete the theme of giving and sharing.

The large wall clock read six in the evening. The day had been long and busy, made longer by the fight between Chris and Raymond. Darkness was quickly falling, and she knew the temperature would be quite cool. Perhaps she could stop at a restaurant in town, rather than eat alone again. No, that would be a waste of funds. She might as well use up the leftover casserole from Sunday.

Kathryn slid into her long coat, grabbed her purse and left the room, checking once to see that the door was locked. The emptiness of the building brought strange sounds to her sensitive ears, and she smiled. She'd probably lived through too many years of listening to imaginative eight-year-olds tell of their nightmares and daydreams.

Running a slender hand through the waves of her shoulder-length dark hair, she sighed. She had been teaching for a long time, maybe too long. On graduating from the University of Arizona in Tucson a month before her twenty-first birthday, she had taken a teaching position in a suburban school and stayed there for ten years, enjoying her work until a new principal had changed everything.

His overtures had quickly become entangled with her career, and her refusal to become involved with him because of his marital status had affected her ability to give her full attention to her students. One evening, very much like this one, he had accosted her in her classroom, and except for the unexpected knock on the door by a janitor, the visit might have ended in sexual assault.

Her request for a transfer to another school within the unified district had been approved. Two years ago the principal of her former school had received a transfer to the same school, and his pursuit had resumed with renewed vigor.

Not wanting to bring attention to her situation, she had tendered her resignation at midsemester rather than file a complaint. Two of her close teaching friends had chided her for her passive way out of the problem, and she had conceded that they were right. Her record for bucking the establishment and asserting her rights was embarrassing at best. But Kathryn hoped that focusing her attention on her students would heal any nagging doubts about the significance of her accomplishments over the years.

Now, at thirty-five, a new dissatisfaction had begun to stir within her. *Thirty-five years old.* As she left the empty building, she thought about herself analytically. Her body was still as trim as ever. Weight control had never been a problem for her. Her breasts were still firm, even if they weren't as high as in her youth. *But who needs high breasts, and what good are breasts unless you have children to nurse . . . or a husband . . .*

She quickened her pace, tugging at the belt of her beige coat. Recently a first-grade teacher had made Kathryn's waist a topic of discussion in the teachers' lounge.

"No one your age should still have a teenager's waist," the matronly woman had teased.

Kathryn had tried to ignore her.

"That's the difference between having five kids and none," Pete Busbee had interjected. "I can remember when my wife looked as sexy as Kathy, but not anymore."

"Don't call me Kathy," Kathryn had retorted.

"Sorry," he had said, smiling. "How about Kitty? Are you like a kitten? Soft to the touch, but feisty when cornered?"

"This is a disgusting conversation," Kathryn had said, rising from her chair. "My body and personal life are of no concern to you, only how I teach my students." She had left the room, shutting out the laughter that had followed her exit.

She shook off the unpleasant memory as she stepped off the curb and crossed the street a block from her house. Why should a woman's body be a subject of discussion by her peers? And what would they think if they knew hers had proven to be an 'unfulfilled vessel'? She chuckled aloud over her archaic choice of words. Couldn't a woman be fulfilled in ways other than physical?

Of course. Some women were meant to live a celibate life—only she had always thought it would be by choice, motivated by some deep spiritual conviction, not because she had never met the right man, a man who found her... exciting. Maybe there was something wrong with her. Some flaw in her emotional makeup. *Otherwise,* she thought cynically, *why had God given her a body without the opportunity to use it?*

The night breeze blew strands of her hair across her face, and she shook her head to toss it back, slowing down. The breeze gusted again, and she whipped the strands behind her ear. The scent of a fall storm filled the air, promising perhaps the first heavy snow of the season. She had grown to love this northern climate, so different from her native desert.

Glancing ahead, she saw a small figure huddled on the steps of her porch. She peered into the dusky shadows.

Chris Brasher? This late?

"Chris," she called, quickening her pace once more. "Is that you?" He rose as she started up the steps. "Your aunt must be frantic."

"Probably," he mumbled.

"Why didn't you go home?"

"That fatso Raymond Crosley is waiting for me."

"Ray? After all this time?"

Chris stood ramrod straight on the porch. "He said he and his big brother would be hiding on Washington Street, but I don't know where. I'm not really afraid of them, but...it got dark and I couldn't tell where they were. I saw them once up ahead...in the bushes, but they probably sneaked to a new spot. Raymond says he—I need to tell my dad, but he's still up in the woods." He peered up at her through the darkness.

She shook her head. "Why don't you come inside and call your aunt from here?"

"I keep forgetting her number."

"It's in the phone book," she reminded him. "We'll look it up." She unlocked the door and switched on a light. Dropping her purse on a chair and shedding her coat, she hurried to the phone desk in the dining room.

"Chris, come in here and I'll show you how to look up your aunt's number."

Chris ambled through the door, the half-grown calico kitten draped over his arm. He leaned against Kathryn as she explained the method of sorting through the alphabet. The kitten mewed. Chris leaned a little closer. Kathryn put her arm around him and unconciously stroked the kitten's fur. Chris snuggled closer.

"Why don't you push the buttons on the phone, Chris?" she suggested.

"I can't."

"And why not?"

"I'm holding Patches."

She glanced down at him, and he motioned to the purring kitten.

"My cousin Ronald has a book. He's only three. It's a baby book, but it's all about this kitten named Patches. She looks just like yours, Miss Keith, so I named yours Patches, too." He looked up at Kathryn. "Is that okay?" His straight dark brows furrowed. His nose was still slightly swollen from the fight earlier in the day, and he looked so lovable she felt herself slipping under his spell.

Kathryn squeezed his shoulders and smiled. "Sure. I never got around to giving the kitten a name, Chris. We'll call her Patches."

He sighed. "I wish I had a cat like Patches."

"We'd better call your aunt," she said. Unwilling to suggest he put the cat down and dial the number himself, she placed the call. On the first ring the phone was answered.

"Natalie, this is Kathryn Keith."

"I'm glad you called. My nephew Chris is missing," Natalie Wright cried. "We've looked everywhere."

"I found him on my steps when I got home," Kathryn said.

"Oh, thank God! We were about to call the police." Kathryn sensed the mingled relief and concern in the other woman's voice.

"Chris has been giving us some problems lately," Natalie said. "I just don't know what to do. John is gone so much of the time, and I know he needs his father, but we try to give him a stable home life until John can . . ." The woman sniffed. "Sometimes I feel so inadequate. I want to reach him and give him love, but so often he's suspicious and withdrawn. Then he changes and is so rowdy and mischievous. He's different from my own children."

"I understand," Kathryn said. "It's okay now."

"It's so late. He must be starved," Natalie said. "I'll come and get him."

Kathryn looked down at Chris. "She's going to come for you."

"Can't I stay and play with Patches?" he asked, his speech still slightly slurred by the split in his lower lip.

She studied his upturned face. An internal warning sounded at her involvement with him. Usually she avoided entanglements in her students' lives. "I'll ask," she said. "Natalie, could he stay and have supper with me? I worked late at school. I'm hungry, too."

"I don't want him to be a bother."

"No trouble," Kathryn replied. "I was just going to heat up some leftovers, a ham-and-broccoli casserole from Sunday. Chris can play with my kitten. I'll bring him home in an hour or so."

Chris's face beamed with delight as Kathryn replaced the receiver. "Don't you have hot dogs?"

She frowned. "Yes, but I would prefer the casserole. It has scalloped potatoes in it, too, and it's delicious."

"But it's got that yucky green stuff in it," Chris insisted.

"You mean broccoli?"

"Yeah," he confirmed and he shuddered.

"Tell you what, Chris," she said, smiling as she went into the kitchen. "You can have hot dogs if you'll eat a serving of tossed salad as well. Hot dogs alone aren't good for you."

"My dad calls them junk food, but I think they're the best food in the whole wide world," Chris replied.

During the meal Kathryn watched him finish one hot dog and ask for another.

"You can have another hot dog after you've finished your salad. A promise is a promise," she reminded him.

Chris wolfed the greens down and eyed the second wiener on a saucer in the middle of the table. She slid it toward him and offered him a bun.

He concentrated on giving the hot dog a liberal dose of catsup, carefully spreading the red sauce along every inch.

"Why don't you live with your mother?" she asked.

"I lived with her until last Christmas. My dad says I was his Christmas present."

"Where is your mother?" she asked.

He cocked his head as he chewed a big bite of hot dog. "In Oregon."

"Do you have brothers or sisters?"

"Two sisters, but they're a lot older than me. Debbie got married, and I got to be in the wedding and Sherie was a bridesmaid. I had to wear this fancy suit. The bow tie choked my neck," he explained, making strangling sounds to prove his point. "But my mom said I had to wear it."

"Is Sherie living with your mother?" Kathryn asked.

He shook his head. "She moved in with her boyfriend."

"How old is she?"

He shrugged. "Eighteen."

"So you were alone with your mother?"

"Oh, no, Leo was there," he replied.

"Who's Leo?" she asked, knowing she was prying.

"He's my dad's old partner."

"Oh?"

"Yeah," he said. "My dad says they deserve each other." He took another bite of his hot dog. Kathryn waited.

"My dad says she moved away with Leo before I was born. He says I was a surprise to my mom and Leo. I was born after they moved to Oregon."

"Oh?"

"Yeah," Chris replied. "My dad said I was her catch colt, and he knew I was his little boy the minute he saw me. What's a catch colt, Miss Keith?"

Kathryn suppressed a smile. "I think he means you were...unexpected, unplanned for. Maybe when you're older, he can explain it again. How old were you when your father first saw you?"

"I don't remember it, but he said I was three years old. He wanted me then, but he says my mom took him to court and got a bunch of money instead." He wiped his mouth with a paper napkin, flinching when he touched his swollen lower lip. "Do you have any ice cream?"

She studied his handsome face, trying to digest this story of his early life.

"Do you?" he asked again.

"Oh...no, but I have some cookies. Will they do?"

"Sure!"

She prepared a small plate of oatmeal chocolate chip cookies, left over from the previous week's classroom party, and offered it to him.

He took a big bite of a cookie. "These are from our party, aren't they?"

She nodded.

"How'd you learn to make such good cookies, Miss Keith?"

"Sometimes I have trouble getting homeroom mothers," she explained, "so I learned to bake them myself, just in case my students' mothers couldn't find the time to help."

"Well, these are great." Four cookies disappeared in quick succession along with a glass of milk.

"Do you like living with your father?" she asked.

"Sure, but Daddy lives in Avery in a trailer, and sometimes he camps out where his crew is working. The trailer is really neat. It has a bedroom and a living room, and my dad made me a bunk bed with a door and everything so I could bring a friend sometimes. He moved the sofa and built it right into the end of the trailer. Boy, is my dad smart." He giggled. "You oughta see the kitchen. It's so little that my dad and I have to turn sideways to pass. He says when I get bigger, we'll have to put in a traffic light."

"It sounds . . . cozy," she agreed, wondering how anyone could live in such cramped quarters.

"Daddy lets me make the toast when we have breakfast. There's no television so I can't watch cartoons. My dad says we can read, but sometimes he lets me go to Swede's trailer. He lives right next door."

"What else do you do when you visit him?"

"We explore," and he wiped the milk from his lips. He winced and held the napkin to his mouth. Red seeped through the paper.

"Oh, Chris, your lip has started to bleed again," Kathryn exclaimed. Without much thought, she went to the bathroom and brought back a cold wet washcloth.

"Put this to your mouth. I'm surprised you were able to eat the hot dogs with catsup. Didn't it burn?"

He smiled in spite of his swollen nose and split lip. "Course not. My dad says I'm pretty tough."

"Maybe too tough," she remarked.

"My dad says when men live alone without women," Chris said, assuming a derisive tone, "they have to be tough to get along."

Kathryn grew increasingly skeptical about this father who was filling his son's impressionable young mind with such attitudes. "Tell me about your explorations," she said.

"We go along the creeks and the river and find things. We count the birds and squirrels." He bounced on his chair and grinned. "Once he took me way beyond where he was working, and we hiked up to a pond and found a moose, a real moose, Miss Keith! He was in the pond, and it was filled with water lilies, and he would put his head underneath the water and then come up with green stuff hanging out of both sides of his mouth. He was eating it! Have you ever seen a real live moose, Miss Keith?"

"Just in the zoo, Chris," she admitted. "It must have been very exciting."

"Gee, it was, but we had to be very quiet, or my dad said it would run away and hide in the trees." He grinned. "He was right. I stepped on a stick, and the noise scared the moose away, but we saw it, really saw it! That fatso Raymond never saw a moose."

"Not every boy gets to see a moose in the wild, Chris. You're a lucky boy. But you've got to stop calling Raymond fatso."

He grimaced. Finally he mumbled, "Okay."

Her curiosity grew about his father. "How do you get back and forth to your father's trailer?"

"He comes and gets me on Friday nights and brings me back to town on Sundays...when he can." He sighed deeply. "He has to be back logging early every Monday, and sometimes he works hoot-owl hours."

"What are those?" she asked.

"He gets up in the middle of the night and goes to work so the truckers can get as many loads to the mills as they can. Once I got to ride in a logging truck. Sometimes they can't saw during the day because they might catch the woods on fire."

"Is your father a sawyer?"

Chris puffed out his chest and grinned. "No, ma'am, he owns the whole damned company."

"Chris! You mustn't use words like that."

"My dad does."

"Well, good little boys don't."

He stared back at her defiantly, but slowly the fire left his eyes.

"When does your father rest, sleep?" she asked, wondering about this logging superman.

He shrugged. "Sometimes in the evening. That's why I can't stay with him Sunday nights." He looked forlornly at Kathryn. "I wish I could."

"You must love being with your father," she said.

"I do. That's why that fats—stupid Raymond is wrong when he..." He stopped when she held up her hand.

"You can't win an argument with your fists, Chris. If another fight happens, I'll have to write your father a note and insist that he come to the school and talk to me and the principal. Would your father want to do that?"

Chris's dark head moved slowly from side to side.

"I thought not," Kathryn said, smiling warmly at him. "What's your father's name?"

"John. John Brasher. He says if he had known about me when I was born, I would be John, too. My Grandpa Brasher is John and that would make me John the Third. I didn't have a middle name, just Christopher, so my dad went to court, and now I'm Christopher *John* Brasher," he said proudly.

"Well, Christopher John," she said, and he grinned at her, "no more fighting. Promise?"

"Promise," he said, holding up his hand and displaying the proper number of fingers. "I'm in Cub Scouts now. I'm gonna be a Wolf pretty soon."

"Good for you, Chris. Now we'd better get you home. It's probably bedtime for you soon."

When she returned to her house, she thought of Chris. "John Brasher, father of Chris, why aren't you with your son?" she said aloud to the empty house. "He loves you. Do you know that? Give him more of your time, before it's too late."

CHAPTER THREE

JOHN BRASHER STAYED away from the St. Maries school activities over the next few months. He even missed the community Christmas program in which Chris portrayed Joseph, his cowlick plastered down obediently with hair spray by his aunt Natalie.

After Chris had yet another fight with Raymond, Kathryn sent a note to John's address in Avery, requesting a conference, but received no reply. She wrote another letter, this one stronger, but it, too, was ignored.

Spring parent-teacher conferences were scheduled, but Natalie appeared in John Brasher's stead.

"He's in Oregon," Natalie said. "Chris's mother has been trying to get him back. John says she just wants the child support money, but she says he doesn't provide a stable environment for her son."

"Poor Chris," Kathryn replied. "Does he know?"

"A little, but we've tried to keep him out of it."

"Chris seems so unsure, so... it's hard to put a finger on it," Kathryn said. "But I have no doubt he loves his father very much. He would be devastated if he had to leave him."

"You've never met John, have you?" Natalie asked.

Kathryn shook her head. "Chris insisted that I saw him in the parade last fall, but I was talking to a friend, and apparently I didn't see Chris wave at me. Now I'm sorry. I've tried to understand why a father wouldn't try to spend time with his son if he wants to have custody, but frankly I can't. Couldn't he change jobs?''

Natalie smiled. ''You don't know the men in our family. My father was an independent logger until he was hurt a few years ago. Mom convinced him they were rich enough to retire. They live in Yuma, Arizona, now. We don't see them much anymore. Dad was a bull bucker before he saved enough to buy a skidder and strike out on his own.

''My grandfather was a donkey doctor for years, and before him my great-grandfather worked as a river pig for years. In 1908 he and the other log drivers on the St. Maries River struck for higher wages. Can you imagine? They were getting three dollars a day and asked for a fifty-cent-a-day raise. He taught my grandfather to ride the booms, but Grandfather Brasher always said the good Lord made men to stand on firm ground.''

She laughed. ''Grandma Brasher asked him once why then, did he insist on climbing up those tall trees. He said trees are in the ground so they're part of God's plan for loggers.'' She became somber again. ''John has never done anything but logging.''

''I don't understand all the terms of logging,'' Kathryn admitted. ''Sometimes it's as if loggers speak a different language, but still, I think Chris's father would want to spend more time with his son. Is a job more important than a son?''

''You don't understand,'' Natalie said. ''He's trying. He's looking for a hooker to give him some relief so maybe he will have more time soon. A good hooker is hard to find.''

''I'm sure,'' Kathryn murmured, wondering how Chris's father had managed to rationalize such an immoral solution to his problems with his son. Already she was too involved in this bizarre family. "Well, just tell your brother he has a very sweet son, but the older he gets, the more he will try to solve his problems with his fists, if his father doesn't teach him . . . something."

She rose from her chair. "How John Brasher solves his problems is of little concern to me, unless it affects his son's conduct in the classroom. Please tell him that."

A WEEK LATER Chris and Raymond came to blows again. Kathryn mailed another note to Avery, but as Easter break approached, she had received no response.

"What are you all going to do during the break?" Kathryn asked her students the day before Good Friday.

"We're going to visit Grandma," one girl said.

"We're going to church," another girl replied. "My mom says that's what you're supposed to do at Easter."

Kathryn nodded without commenting. "Anyone else?"

Chris's hand shot into the air.

"Yes, Chris."

"My dad's coming for me right after school, and we're going to Avery. We're gonna hike way up," and he lifted his small body off his chair, "way up to a lake my dad found last month. My dad says it's too muddy to work so he's taking a week off to be with me!"

"That's great, Chris," Kathryn replied. "I hope you have a good time."

"What are you going to do, Miss Keith?" another boy asked.

"Spring housecleaning," she replied, and the class groaned.

Later that day, Kathryn gave the classroom one more survey before leaving. *A week of freedom,* she thought, *to do anything I choose, without the pressures of a dead-*

*line or disciplining someone else's child and only a few
stacks of papers to grade.*

As she approached her house, she saw movement on her
porch. Coming closer, she recognized Christopher
Brasher. He was sitting by the door, his chin resting on his
knees. Kathryn sensed trouble.

"What's the matter, Chris? I thought you'd be in Avery with your father by now."

"He can't come."

"Why on earth not, after promising?"

"He's working on his truck," he said, sighing deeply.
"He called from the restaurant up there and said he didn't
know when it would be running again. He said his hooker
had left earlier so he didn't have a ride in."

Kathryn was shocked to think that John Brasher would
discuss his relationship with such a woman with his young
son. Anger filled her as she unlocked the door and invited Chris to come inside with her.

"You must be very disappointed," she said, hanging
her jacket in the closet.

She turned to him when he didn't answer. He sat cross-legged on the floor, holding Patches tightly in his arms.
He sniffed, then his shoulders began to shake as his crying
became more audible. Fury at John Brasher's insensitive
actions coursed hotly through her as she ran to Chris and
scooped him off the floor. She carried him to the sofa and
held him in her arms while he sobbed out his disappointment.

"I want-want-wanted to be with my dad," he hic-cuped. "I just wanted to be with him . . . jus-just for a
while. Raymond gets to be with his dad all the time." He
sniffed and Kathryn handed him a tissue to wipe his face.
"He woulda come for me if that dumb old truck hadn't
broke down. I know he woulda."

"Was that his only excuse?" Kathryn asked.

Chris nodded his dark head.

"I'll tell you what, Chris. If it's all right with Natalie, I'll drive you to Avery myself."

He wriggled out of her arms and looked at her, his green eyes shimmering with new tears. "Really? Would you really drive me all the way to Avery? It's a long, long way," he warned.

She smiled. "I know, but I think it's time your father and I met."

She and Chris went to Natalie's home, from which she called the restaurant in Avery. A good-natured waitress offered to go to John's trailer to find him. Several minutes later a brisk male voice spoke.

"Listen, Miss Keith, if you want to bring my son to me, that's fine, but don't expect me to take time to socialize. I'm behind schedule as it is, and I have no time to entertain some lonely old-maid teacher who has nothing better to do in an evening than to drive fifty miles to antagonize some parent."

"Why, you selfish, insolent..." Kathryn huffed. "If it weren't for Chris being so disappointed at your broken promise, I would save my gas and my time. My schedule is just as busy as yours, but at least I take time to give your son some attention. Don't worry, Mr. Brasher, I won't stay any longer than it takes to see that Chris is safely at your trailer. Please don't clean up or do anything that might put a strain on your egotistical pride."

"You can count on it," he promised gruffly.

Kathryn suppressed the comment on the tip of her tongue. "We'll be there in an hour, an hour and a half at most. I'll expect you to be ready for him."

"I'll be ready, but don't expect tea and cookies," he warned.

"With a person like you, hardly. Goodbye," she said coldly, slamming the receiver down. She turned to Natalie. "That man is unbelievable!"

"There must be some mistake," Natalie said. "You don't understand. John tried to get here, but his hooker couldn't wait around."

"There's no mistake, and I intend to tell him just what I think of his idea of trying," Kathryn promised.

"ARE YOU MAD AT MY DAD?" Chris asked as the small automobile sped through the darkness.

Kathryn mulled over the boy's question before replying. True, she had never met John Brasher, but his avoidance of his parental responsibilities concerning Chris's school progress said more than a few shallow words or token appearances. Still, he deserved a chance to explain, if he could find time in his precious schedule to talk to her. She didn't relish the encounter looming ahead.

"No, Chris, I'm not mad at him."

"What did he say that made you mad?"

"I told you I'm not mad," Kathryn insisted, but her rising pitch belied her words. She wiped her palms on her lavender-and-black pleated skirt, wishing she had changed to comfortable jeans and walking shoes.

Chris twisted sideways in his seat belt. "You sound mad. I wanted you to like my dad."

She sighed. "I don't know, Chris. Sometimes people just don't get along. But I'll try."

"Promise?"

"Sure, as long as he's courteous to me."

"Great." Chris peered out the side window. "It's dark out here," he said. "Sometimes I'm afraid of the dark . . . unless my dad is with me. That's the only thing I

like about living with Aunt Nat. I have a streetlight outside my bedroom window.''

They drove past the bar and trailer park at Marble
Creek. The road wound through the mountain valley,
following the St. Joe River as it flowed from its source
high in the Bitterroot mountain range near the Idaho–
Montana border.

A shiver of apprehension weakened Kathryn's confidence as the miles passed. Maybe, she thought, she should
have offered to take Chris tomorrow when the sun would
have made the driving easier. Mountain roads still frightened her, especially on a moonless night such as this one.
Chris was right. ''It's very dark, but we're together, and
I'll see that you get safely to your father. You deserve to
spend this holiday with him. I'll be as polite to him as he
is to me.''

''Great! He didn't like Mrs. Watkins,'' Chris volunteered. ''He said she was a busybody who didn't know
how to keep rein on second graders.''

''Really?''

''Yeah, she used to send him notes all the time, and he
would get mad at her. He said he always got them a week
after she wanted to see him.'' His young voice lowered to
a whisper. ''Don't tell Mrs. Watkins, but he decided to
throw them away. Sometimes he didn't even open them.''

''Is that what he does with mine?'' she asked.

''Not yet,'' he assured her. ''He called you old Prune
Face once, but he says you don't write as much as Mrs.
Watkins.''

''Old Prune Face?''

''Yeah, but I told him you weren't a Prune Face.'' He
grinned. ''I think you're pretty.'' Quickly he returned his
attention to the darkness outside.

"Why did he call me Prune Face?" she asked, knowing she should let the subject drop.

"He said he saw you once."

She touched her cheeks, searching for a crease that might be noticed by a man. Was she showing her age more than she was willing to admit? How dare this man, who had never met her, had seen her only once, talk about wrinkles she couldn't see herself?

They passed the turnoff to the forest service ranger station and soon could see the twinkling lights of Avery. She glanced at the clock on the dash.

"It's almost ten o'clock," she said.

"Great! That's an hour past my bedtime." Chris beamed. "My dad thinks I oughta go to bed at eight, but we talked about it, and he said we'd split the difference. What does that mean?"

"Subtract eight from ten. That leaves two and dividing two by two leaves one. Add one to eight and you have nine o'clock."

"Huh?"

She laughed. "Sorry, Chris. You know how we're learning to multiply numbers?"

He nodded. "They're hard to remember."

"They'll get easier," she said. "After you learn your multiplication tables and practice a lot, you'll learn how to undo them all by dividing numbers. You might as well learn to like it because the next few years will be full of math."

"Ugh."

She laughed and he grinned. "You're an intelligent boy, Chris. You'll do well if you keep trying."

"Is in-intell…whatever you said…is that the same as smart? My dad says I'm smart." He giggled. "He said I have a memory like an elephant, and I *never* forget his promises.''

The man was definitely a contradiction, she thought. He had managed to spend enough time with his son to develop this strong allegiance, yet had wasted time with a hooker when he could have just as well spent the time with his son. A man might have his physical needs, but still . . . She dismissed such disturbing thoughts from her mind.

She grimaced, thinking of the prostitutes so visible on some Phoenix and Tucson streets. She had assumed that such women stayed in the larger cities where business could be more readily available. Why would there be hookers up here in this logging town with no more than a handful of patrons? She shrugged. One willing patron was all that was necessary. Perhaps this woman was more than a . . . perhaps she had become his girlfriend. But if that were true, why refer to her as his hooker? He was either a redneck logger beyond redemption, or an insensitive male chauvinistic clod.

''There it is! Over there,'' Chris exclaimed as they arrived in town. He pointed to a row of small camping trailers parked across from a café. ''It's the brown-and-white one with the brown pickup. See? Do you see? The one with the hood up. There's my dad! He's working on the truck. See? I knew he woulda come if he could. The truck is really broke down, just like he said. But I know he will be glad to see me. It's been a long, long time.'' He grabbed for the door handle as the car rolled to a stop. His feet hit the gravel on a run; then he ran back to slam the passenger's door.

''Daddy, Daddy, I'm home,'' he shouted.

A tall, dark figure removed his head and shoulders from beneath the hood. His form was silhouetted by the working light hanging behind him. He couldn't be as large as his shadowy figure appeared, Kathryn thought. Why, his height alone was intimidating. Her confidence weakened again as she sat in the dark interior of the car, watching the reunion.

John Brasher held his arms out to his son and swept him up into a massive bear hug, lifting him high off the ground. "God, I'm glad to see you, son. Sorry I missed coming in last week, but Swede's loader broke down in the mud, and I spent the whole weekend up at Skunk Creek getting it out. The ground is thawing fast so I've laid off everyone but Swede and Mugger for a month. If you weren't in school, I would put you to work helping me repair the loader and put some new parts on that old skidder." He tightened his hug for a few seconds before letting his son slide to the ground.

He heard a car door slam and turned to see a woman standing in the darkness. "Is that old Prune Face?" he whispered down to his son.

Chris reached for his hand. "Daddy, you can't call her that anymore. She promised to be nice to you, and I promised that you'd be nice to her."

"Well," John replied, squinting through the darkness, "I guess you're right. We're indebted to her for bringing you up. Have you had supper?"

"No time," Chris said. "We were on the road."

"Tell you what. You take Miss Keith over to the café and get us a table for three. I'll clean up, get this grease off my hands. I might even clean my fingernails for the old... Sorry, son. You take your teacher to the café, and I'll meet you there. Order me a T-bone steak dinner and a cup of coffee, please. I'll buy Miss Keith's dinner and give her some money for gas. That way we won't be indebted to her. I'll be there in about fifteen minutes."

He turned to the trailer as Chris ran back to the woman. He could hear their muted conversation, then footsteps. He glanced over his shoulder as they walked toward the soft lights of the café. Funny, he thought, her hair didn't look as gray as he'd remembered, and she had definitely lost some weight since the parade last fall.

His eyes traveled down the bulk of her coat to her feet. In the dim light he could see a pair of trim ankles. He had expected her to have swollen ankles from being on her feet all day with children. A woman her age would probably have circulatory problems, wouldn't she?

He shrugged. Did it matter whether a crotchety teacher, who wrote terse notes to parents while she waited for retirement, was white-haired or gray? Slim or fat? Not to him. In a few months the school year would end, and he'd be rid of her. He hurried inside the trailer and slammed the door.

He stripped off his stained gray sweatshirt and jeans, then shucked off the rest of his clothing. *Might as well shower for the teacher,* John thought. Standing nude by the kitchen sink, he scrubbed his hands with degreaser. He smiled as he cleaned his fingernails. His sister Natalie had shown him a trick years ago that had saved him from countless potential rejections during the after-hours of his logging career. If he shoved his fingernails into a cake of soap in the morning, the grease and dirt of a hard day's work could be easily removed. Now it was a habit. Over the years several women who had become casual lovers had expressed their delight when he had touched them, saying they liked his touch, that his hands were so clean.

"Some men have such dirty hands," they had complained.

"What about the calluses?" he had asked.

"Oh, they're fine. Touch me again," one woman had murmured and soon the condition of his hands had been forgotten.

Might as well shave, too, he decided, as he dried and dressed in a navy-blue knit pullover. Good Lord, he was sprucing up as though he were meeting a woman on a blind date, he thought as he stroked a day's growth of dark stubble. Well, he didn't know much more about the woman than he would if it actually were a blind date. But blind dates at least indicated a willingness for a relationship on the part of both parties.

Not so here. He had found himself stuck in the mountains fifty miles away from his son while his son was on a week-long vacation from school and old . . . He chided himself for the ease with which he had fallen into the habit of thinking of her as prune face. Now he would find out for sure if her personality matched her face. He snapped his jeans and tugged the navy-blue sweater down over his hips, then ducked his head as he hurried through the trailer doorway, anxious to get the visit over with.

As he entered the café, he scanned the room for his son and was surprised to find him sitting with a much younger-looking woman than he'd expected. Her back was toward the door. Her hair had obviously been dyed since the parade. It was shameful for an older woman to try to cover up the dignity of her age with the contents of a bottle of coloring, John thought derisively. His eyes roamed her torso and down to her hips. This one was definitely well preserved. Almost unbelievably so. His curiosity was piqued.

Chris waved to him, and he strode across the room, sliding into a chair before looking at his dinner guest.

"Good evening, Miss Keith, I—" He stopped in midsentence. He knew he was gaping, but he couldn't do a thing about it. "My God, you're not..." For the first time in years, he felt the heat of embarrassment sweep over his face. "I, ah, I'm sorry. I'm John Brasher, Chris's father. You *are* the same Miss Keith who occasionally writes me notes on my son's progress in the third grade?"

She looked up from her plate directly into his face. She had the most beautiful pair of green eyes he'd ever seen. They were even darker than his own son's. In no way could her skin be compared to a prune's. Perhaps a fine peach or rich cream. Never a prune. He felt like a fool.

Kathryn, too, found herself speechless for several seconds. He was less than two feet from her. The man's sheer size was so overwhelming that for a while she couldn't comprehend his handsomeness. A lock of hair as dark as hers fell over his forehead when he leaned to whisper in his son's ear. Chris grinned, glanced at her and nodded in agreement.

John shook his head, and the hair fell back into place. He needed a haircut, but the shaggy waves brushing the ribbing of his pullover added to his good looks. His eyes were almost as dark as the sweater. As a smile deepened the creases around his mouth, her heart skipped a beat. Chiding herself for reacting to him like a swooning teenager, she frowned and extended her hand.

"I'm Kathryn Keith, and yes, I'm Chris's teacher this year." Her hand was swallowed in his, and when she felt the warmth of his grasp, she wished she had just said hello. His hands were spotlessly clean and his touch was smooth, except for the rigid calluses on his palm. Her eyes flew back to his face.

"What's the matter?" he asked.

She couldn't reply.

Chris giggled. "I'll betcha she thought you would have greasy hands. I told her you might even clean your fingernails.'' He giggled again, sputtering a few drops of milk. Quickly he wiped his mouth and chanced a glance at John.

John smiled again. "It's a private joke, Miss—may I call you Kathryn? I feel silly calling you Miss Keith when you're younger than I am. Frankly, I expected an older woman. I don't suppose Chris blabbed about our nickname for you.''

"Old *Prune* Face?"

He groaned. "Chris, you've got to learn when to keep your mouth shut.''

"Maybe you shouldn't say such derogatory things to him in the first place," she suggested.

"You're probably right," he agreed, then began methodically cutting pieces of steak.

Several minutes passed in silence as they ate. During dessert Chris's chatter carried the conversation. When the waitress presented the bill, Kathryn opened her purse and pulled out her wallet.

"No," John said, holding up his hand, "this is on me."

"Are you sure? I didn't mean to stay so long, but I—I did want to meet you and discuss Chris's..." She glanced at the boy, whose gaze was flying back and forth between his father and her.

Chris yawned and she glanced at her wristwatch. "Goodness, I didn't know it was so late. I must get back to St. Maries." She rose from her chair. Before she could retrieve her coat, John was holding it for her.

After assisting her, John turned to his son. "It's way past your bedtime, Chris. Let's go to the trailer, and we'll bed you down. Kathryn and I can talk over a nightcap."

Chris giggled. "I like hearing you call her Kathryn. When you do that, it's like she's not really my teacher anymore." He wriggled into his jacket.

The darkness enveloped them as they left the café, and Chris slipped one hand into his father's, hesitated, then reached for Kathryn's hand.

Kathryn paused at the trailer door. "I should go," she said, hesitating, but something drew her closer.

"Please come in," John insisted. "Have a cup of coffee...or tea." He grinned.

"Well, all right, then. But just for a few minutes," she conceded, and she accepted his hand up the steps.

In the trailer Chris changed into his pajamas. He stalled in the kitchen. "Can I have a glass of milk?"

"Not just before bed," John said, but willingly accepted a hug from his son.

Kathryn glanced up from the lumber industry magazine she was looking at. Chris ambled closer. Suddenly she found herself hugged fiercely. As quickly as he'd embraced her, he released her, raced to his small bedroom and slammed the door.

She rose from the sofa and moved to a breakfast stool on the living room side of the kitchen. The trailer had more space inside than she had expected.

A sense of uneasiness swept over her as she felt John's eyes swing from his son's closed door to her.

"I didn't expect that," she said.

"I think the student has a crush on the teacher," he said.

"That's not a good idea. How can I discipline him when he..." She smiled. "Well, he certainly is a charmer. We got to know each other in the spring of his second-grade year. He was having trouble with another boy and I helped."

"Fatso Raymond?" John asked, grinning.

She frowned. "You should tell him to not call that other boy fatso. Raymond is a little overweight, but sometimes

Chris starts these brawls by taunting him. And he's jealous of Raymond because Raymond's father lives in town."

John sobered. "There are some things a man can't do anything about. Would you rather have him on welfare and food stamps, or have a father willing to work, even if it's long distance?"

"But he needs your attention, more of your time."

"I give him as much as I can."

"Perhaps it's not enough."

"I try," John said. "Now that I've hired a full-time hooker I can—"

"See?" she cried. "If you have time for a—a—that kind of person, why don't you have time for your own son? Isn't he more important than your own needs and desires?"

"What?" John's face showed his bewilderment.

"When we first met in the café, I thought you were different. I was hoping I had misunderstood. How can you possibly tell everyone about needing a full-time hooker, especially a young boy as impressionable as Chris?"

"How the hell am I going to find one if I don't advertise? I was able to hire one of the best in the business by talking to the fellows at Marble Creek." He glared at her. "Why is my business of so much interest to you?"

"If you really love your son as much as you say you do, you—you'd conduct yourself in a more respectable manner." She slid off the stool and grabbed her purse and coat. "It's late and I'm tired." She thought of the long drive down the winding road and shuddered as she slid into her coat. "You're probably expecting your...hooker back soon, so I'll go now. It was interesting meeting you,

Mr. Brasher. Goodbye.'' She reached for the door handle.

She found herself whirled around, her purse yanked from her hand and tossed to the sofa. He grabbed her shoulders through her coat and tightened his grip.

"What the hell are you talking about?" He towered over her, frightening her. She tried to pull free, but he refused to release his hold. "No one is coming here this late at night, and for your information, I do love my son. Who are you to question the relationship between my son and me? I'm sick of you arrogant teachers who think you know what's right for a family. Just how many children have you had, Miss Keith? How many children have you given birth to and raised in today's world?"

"That is my business," she replied haughtily, "but I've raised fifteen classrooms of other people's children. I've spent more time with them than their own parents have. I've wiped their noses, listened to their fears and hugged them when they needed me."

"If you'd spend more time teaching the basics instead of sticking your nose into social services, we wouldn't have a nation full of high school graduates who can't read an instruction manual or fill out a job application form."

"That's a lie," she challenged, plucking at his rigid fingers pressing into her upper arm.

"I've seen some of them trying to fill out an application for me. It's sickening."

"They aren't all like that."

"Too many are."

She shoved at his chest. "I'll have you know that I've never had a child leave my class at year-end unable to read at grade level, or not knowing how to use the multiplication tables, or any other area of education I'm hired to teach them. They don't all want to learn, but I pride myself in making the material come alive. I can't be responsible for every child who passes through the school system, but I most certainly take responsibility for my students. No school board has enough money to pay me for dealing with overbearing, opinionated parents who don't care one iota about their own children, but who can tell me everything wrong with the system. Now let me go! I don't give a—a—a damn, dammit, if you can condemn the teaching profession and at the same time hire a hooker—a—whore! That's your business, but I don't want any part of it. Now let me go!''

CHAPTER FOUR

KATHRYN STUMBLED as he released her. She retrieved her purse and was almost to the door when he started to chuckle. Soon he was laughing heartily.

"What's so funny?" she asked.

"How long have you been living in St. Maries?"

"Almost two years."

"And before that?"

"Tucson, Arizona," she replied. "Why?"

"My dear lady, and you truly are a lady, I suspect," he said gently as he took her purse and tossed it to the sofa again, "you're upset because I hired a full-time hooker?"

Her mouth remained clamped shut.

"And if I hired a full-time hook tender?" he said.

"I don't know what a hook tender is. All this logging slang confuses me, but I certainly know what a hooker is. Tucson and Phoenix are famous for their snowbird prostitutes."

"Oh, Kathryn," he said, laughing again. "You're unbelievable. You may not be a prune, but you sure are a prude." He took her hand. "Sit down."

She refused to move.

"Sit down and let me explain." Still, she hesitated. "I won't let you leave until I give you a crash course in lumberjack slang." He squinted at her as he unbuttoned her coat and slid it off her shoulders, then reached for her hand again and led her to the sofa. She sat down. When he joined her, the sofa sagged under his weight, and she tilted against him unexpectedly. She tried to move away. He stretched his arm behind her and she flinched.

"Easy," he said, retrieving a large book propped up on the windowsill. "This is one of the best books around for the layman. It's called *Timber Country* and I'll show you a close-up of a hooker or hook tender. They are one and the same." He flipped through the pages. The beautiful photographs caught her eye, but between the shine of the paper and feeling as though she were trapped in a pit, she could see very little of the book.

She tried to straighten, only to find herself sliding closer to him.

"Here's one," his deep voice announced as he pointed to the photograph.

Other than his muscular biceps flexing beneath his sweater each time he moved his arm, she saw nothing.

"I can't see," she murmured.

He twisted around. "You aren't very big, are you?" He grinned. "No wonder you teach third graders. Any older grade and your students would be as tall as you by the end of the school year. How tall are you?"

"Five-foot-three. Is there something wrong with that? How tall are you?" she said, wishing immediately she hadn't asked.

He laughed. "Six-foot-four when I was a marine in Vietnam, but I may have shrunk in my old age."

"You're not much older than I am. If you've shrunk, then perhaps I have, too." She smiled until she tried to move from her lopsided position.

"I was forty in mid-August," he murmured, "and you?"

She tried to thrust herself out of the sinkhole of the sofa, but fell back against his side. "I was thirty-five in

July. What do our ages have to do with the subject?'' she asked with a grunt.

He tilted his head thoughtfully. ''Nothing, actually. I was going to show you a hook tender on the job, wasn't I? Let me help you.'' He laid the book aside. Still sitting, he lifted her bodily off the cushion, over his bent knees and settled her between his legs on the edge of the sofa. Before she could react, he reached for the book. One hand held the open book, the other arm reached around her to point to specific objects in the photograph. ''Comfortable?'' he asked.

''Not really,'' she said, almost stammering.

He adjusted his own position back into the bend of the sofa, then pulled her back with him, fitting her snugly between his legs. ''Is that better? Now you have room to sit.''

She could feel his breath disturbing her hair as he explained the photo. Unconsciously she leaned against him.

''My new hook tender's name is Matthew Blake. He's known as Stompin' Matt in the business. He has a reputation for losing his temper when someone screws up. He tends to curse a lot and throw his hard hat down and stomp on it.''

''Sounds like rather childish behavior,'' she said.

He shrugged. ''He still gets the work done. Matt is the boss of one of my yarding crews. I have crews at four landings. He reports to Swede, who's been my foreman for fifteen years.'' He chuckled and Kathryn felt his chest move against her back. ''It's been said that Stompin' Matt's voice is as big as his temper. He can give orders with several chain saws going and still be heard.''

He answered her questions for several minutes, explaining the controversial aspects of timber falling, reclamation, the effects of current and pending legislation and his own philosophy of multiple-use forestry.

He laid his hand on her bare forearm. "Understand better now?" he asked, his voice reflecting a new huskiness she hadn't noticed earlier.

"Sort of," she replied. She glanced at her watch. "It's past two in the morning. I should start for home." She propelled herself out of his arms and off his lap and stood, nervously smoothing the pleats in her skirt.

He rose from the sofa with a lissomeness that belied his size. "Why don't you sleep here tonight?" he asked.

"No, I . . ." and she stepped away.

"No, no," he said, holding up his hand. "I didn't mean with me. You're jumping to wrong conclusions again. I mean in my bed . . ." He ran his fingers through his dark hair and smoothed it again. "I meant you can use my bedroom and I can sleep on the sofa or in with Chris. There's another bunk beneath his."

"Oh, I couldn't do that," she said.

"Why not?"

"It wouldn't be right."

"Why not?"

"What would people say?"

"Who's going to know? We're two consenting adults. What we do about sleeping arrangements is our business," he said.

"But I'm a teacher," she replied. "People talk about teachers the way they talk about ministers. People expect more from us."

"Sounds like they put you on a pedestal," he said.

"Perhaps, but it's best not to take chances with my reputation."

"People can only be put on a pedestal if they cooperate by climbing up there themselves," he chided.

"That's rather insensitive," she said, bristling. "I try to do what I think is proper. I don't want people talking."

"I'm sorry," he said. "I just don't like others telling me what I can and cannot do. It's one more kind of censorship, and I'm opposed to it on principle. If something's right for me, then it's my business to decide about it. But it's too late in the day to discuss social behavior." He touched her shoulder. "You're tired. Didn't you teach today?"

She nodded.

"Who would take over your class if you fell asleep at the wheel and had an accident? You might even kill yourself. Then people would wonder why you were traveling a logging road at three in the morning. Stay, please. I know Chris would be excited. He talks a lot about you."

"So why did you think I looked like an old prune?"

He shrugged. "He never really described you, and I jumped to conclusions." He chuckled. "He did say you were pretty." He grinned. "He was right."

She gazed up at him.

"You'll get a crick in your neck doing that," he said, grinning down at her. She ducked her head, torn between knowing she should leave regardless of the risk and feeling the exhaustion of a long day. She yawned.

"See?" He took her coat from her and hung it in the small closet near the door. "For your own safety you can sleep in my room. It's at the opposite end of the trailer from Chris's."

She glanced toward the closed door. "I am a little tired." She tried to suppress another yawn.

"Then it's all set. The bedroom is yours. Some sixth sense must have told me you were coming. I changed the sheets just this morning. The room is crowded, but clean.

I don't like a lot of clutter. Hang your clothes in the closet. Make yourself at home. You can have the bathroom first.'' Without another word he disappeared into Chris's tiny bedroom.

JOHN BRASHER HAD BEEN truthful. The room was crowded, but very clean. He apparently used one corner for his business record keeping. A desk was covered with stacks of invoices, a ledger, a checkbook and a pile of unopened mail. On a corkboard behind the desk, she saw two of her letters to him thumbtacked to the lower right-hand corner. He had written the word later across the face of each note with a red pen. Shoved against the desk was a four-drawer, legal-size filing cabinet, the top stacked high with industrial catalogs and magazines.

She considered sleeping in her clothing, but then wondered what she would look like in the morning. She quickly undressed and hung her skirt and sweater on a hanger, then kicked her pumps off and left them where they landed. As she unhooked her bra, she scanned the room again. A photo of Chris stood on his dresser. Another, of two teenage girls hugging each other, was in a frame beside Chris's photo. She moved closer to get a better view of John's daughters. They were each tall and slender, with long, dark hair, and both closely resembled John. She spotted another picture frame lying facedown behind the others.

Cautiously she lifted the photo. A much younger John Brasher stood next to a tall, slender, brown-haired woman. He was holding a little girl who was little more than a toddler. Another girl a few years older was holding the brown-haired woman's hand. Thinking of his past brought a sadness to Kathryn as she carefully laid the photograph down again. Once he had been a happily married husband and father with all the responsibilities of a growing family. What had happened? Chris had hinted that he had been the surprise final child in the family torn apart by broken promises.

She sat on the foot of the bed and removed her panty hose, still thinking about John Brasher. Had he lived alone since his wife had left him for his business partner? How had he reacted to learning he had a son? And what had prompted a mother to give up a boy like Chris and expect a natural father to take him off her hands? True, she had never had a child herself, but she couldn't imagine any woman giving up a child willingly.

John was proving to be very different from what she had expected. She yawned again. *I'd better get to sleep,* she thought and pulled the spread and bed linens down. Shoving her bra and stockings under the pillow, she slid between the sheets and was soon asleep.

"YOU STIR THE PANCAKE batter, Chris, while I get a fresh shirt," John said. "We're having company for breakfast."

"Who?" Chris asked.

"It's a surprise. Now do you remember how to measure one cup of water?"

Chris nodded his head.

"Fine, then measure the water, pour it in and stir. That's all. I'll be back in a few minutes." He left his son alone and carefully turned the knob to his bedroom door. He had been listening for over an hour for signs of movement in the bedroom, but Kathryn was apparently still asleep.

He pushed the door open and stepped inside. She lay on his pillow, her dark hair contrasting sharply with the white pillowcase. Her tossing during the night had pulled one corner of the bed linens loose, and one of her feet protruded a few inches. The blankets had been partially thrown off, revealing one side of her torso clad in a lace-trimmed white slip.

Tearing his eyes from her sleeping form, he searched his closet for a clean flannel shirt. He started when he touched her sweater. It had been a long time since a woman's clothing had hung in his closet, and never in this trailer. Had that been part of the problem in his marriage? His wife had always insisted on living in Lewiston, Idaho, while he stayed at various small logging towns near his work sites. It had been hard to preserve a marriage long-distance, he thought cynically. *You trust a woman until you learn the trust is one-sided. When you discover your own business partner has been consoling your wife in her loneliness instead of drumming up new business, the pill is doubly bitter.* Too late he had learned there were no pieces of his marriage left to be picked up and patched together. No glue could renew the bond of holy matrimony.

He gave up on finding a shirt and reached for the grubby gray sweatshirt he had hung on a hook behind the closet door. He had promised Chris they would go for a hike in the afternoon, but that promise would have to wait until he finished working on the truck carburetor. He didn't want to disappoint the boy. As he turned to leave, he stumbled over a discarded woman's pump.

"Dammit," he groaned, grabbing his injured toe with his free hand, hopping on one foot to keep his balance. He managed to save himself from falling by dropping to the edge of the bed.

Kathryn sat up with a start, blinking several times. Her hair fell over one eye, giving her a sultry, bewitching appearance. One strap of her lacy slip slid off her shoulder.

He was surprised to find her skin delightfully tanned against the white satin of her slip. She inhaled deeply and his eyes were drawn lower. Her breasts were supple, and he knew if he touched them they would be soft, warm, pliant.

"Where am I?" she asked, her voice still husky with sleep. She made no move to cover herself. She ran her fingers through her hair, trying without success to bring some semblance of order to it, but it fell across her eye again. She tossed her head, clearing her face, and looked directly into his eyes.

"My God, you're beautiful," he groaned.

She straightened, revealing more of one breast, and he stifled the desire to reach out to her. She followed his line of vision and realized her state of undress.

"I'm sorry," she cried, grabbing the sheet to cover herself. "I forgot where I was for a minute." She glanced at him. Only the jeans from last night covered his body. The breadth of his shoulders and chest attested to his profession. She had certainly seen bare-chested men before. Yet his nearness as he sat on the edge of the bed staring at her filled her with a longing to touch him. "What are you doing in here?"

Clearing his throat, he rose from the bed. "I'm the one who should apologize, Kathryn. I came in for a shirt and ended up falling in bed with you after all."

She continued to stare at him. When she ran her tongue along her lower lip, he wanted to follow it with his own. He felt an unusual stirring in his loins. He exhaled with a hiss and turned away.

"Breakfast will be ready in a few minutes," he said, his back still turned to her. "Chris doesn't know you're here."

"Thank you. I'll dress. Give me five minutes." He remained stationary, halfway to the door. "If you'll leave, I can get dressed," she said.

"Sorry," he murmured and left the room, closing the door firmly behind him.

A few minutes later she left the bedroom in her bare feet. She had managed to comb her hair, but her purse was still in the living room so her lips were natural and pink.

"Miss Keith!" Chris shouted and hopped down from his perch on the stool. "Great. You're the surprise guest my dad said we were having, aren't you? We're making pancakes for breakfast. Want some?"

She glanced at John, who was smiling at his son's delight.

"Yes, Chris, I slept here rather than drive back last night."

"Wow," Chris exclaimed, "wait till I tell everyone that you spent the night in my dad's bedroom!"

"No, Chris, you can't say that," Kathryn cried, turning pale.

"But why not?" Chris asked. "You did."

"But you just can't." She whirled to John. "I knew I shouldn't have stayed. Now see what you've done? He will tell everyone, and no one will believe me, no matter what I say." Unexpected tears welled up in her eyes. "You can't do this to me, John Brasher." She chewed on her lip to stop its quivering.

The humor of the situation evaporated as an unexpected surge of protectiveness filled John. He stepped close to Kathryn and put his arm around her shoulders.

"This will be our secret, Chris," John said. "Other people will think bad things about Miss Keith if you tell them she spent the night. Do you understand?"

Chris shook his head. "Miss Keith would never do anything bad. I can tell them how she brought me here when..."

John stepped behind her, folding his arms around her and pulling her snugly against him. He stared over her dark head and into his son's face. "No, don't tell them anything. Would you want to hurt Miss Keith?"

Chris's eyes widened. "No."

"Then don't tell anyone anything. No matter what you say, someone could twist it and try to hurt Miss Keith." Her hands clung to his forearms. His arms tightened around her. "I would never hurt her, and I know you would never want to hurt her."

Chris nodded his head in agreement.

"Then promise Miss Keith that you will tell no one, absolutely no one, that she was here," John said.

Chris held up his hand and made his Cub Scout salute. "I promise."

"Good," John said, easing his embrace and finally stepping away. "Then let's eat before the pancakes get cold."

During breakfast John watched Kathryn take a few bites and lay her fork down on the plate. His heart went out to her.

"I'm sorry, Kathryn," he murmured, and she glanced up at him. Her troubled eyes haunted him. "I just wanted to protect you from a possible accident, not start a scandal. I'm sorry."

She nodded, but didn't reply. After a few more bites she laid her napkin on the table. "It's time for me to drive back to St. Maries," she said.

"No!" said Chris as he shot from his stool. He grabbed her arm. "Can't you stay with us just for today?"

"I have things to do in town, Chris. I left Patches extra dry cat food, but she might have eaten it all, and I—"

"But we're going on a hike after lunch. You could come with us, and I can show you what it's like by the creek. It's real pretty and my dad knows all the best spots to see the animals come to drink. Please," he pleaded, dragging out the word.

She shook her head. "I'm sorry, but I can't."

"Please stay," John added. "Make him happy."

Her attention shifted to John, who sat watching them, his face devoid of any discernible expression.

"But . . . I have nothing to wear."

"Sounds just like a woman," John teased.

"I can't go hiking in a skirt and high-heeled shoes," she said.

"Hmm, I see what you mean," he agreed.

"Couldn't you borrow something from my dad?" Chris suggested.

"I don't think we're quite the same size," Kathryn said.

"That's for sure," John said, chuckling.

"You're too big to wear my clothes," Chris said sadly.

"For a few years yet," John said. He rose from his chair. "If lack of clothing is your only reason for not staying, I have a solution. I have to finish working on the truck this morning, but if you're willing to kill time until lunch, we'll eat and go hiking up Skunk Creek. No one's working until the spring breakup dries out so we're in no danger of meeting any logging trucks."

"Won't we get stuck in the mud ourselves?" she asked.

"The truck has a four-wheel drive. I'll be careful," he promised. Then he grabbed his jacket and disappeared through the trailer door. "I'll be back in a few minutes."

While he was gone, Kathryn encouraged Chris to help her wash the breakfast dishes. Several minutes later John returned with a bundle of women's clothing tucked beneath his arm and a pair of hiking shoes dangling from his hand.

"Wow," Chris shouted. "Where'd you get the clothes, Dad?"

"From Sue Tripke," John replied.

"Wow, she's the same size as Miss Keith, and she's pretty, too."

John laughed. "My son only notices the pretty ones. I should have known you couldn't have been old prune face."

"And who's Sue Tripke?" Kathryn asked.

"Her husband teaches the four higher grades at the school," he replied, handing the clothing to her. "I think they'll fit."

She glanced inside the hiking boots. "How did you know my size?"

"I stumbled over your shoe, remember? When I picked it up, I checked your size. Nice small feet—they go with the rest of you." He grinned. "Now, if you'll change and keep this kid of mine busy for a few hours, I'll fix that rattletrap truck and we'll go exploring."

"Let's go to the old depot," Chris suggested excitedly.

"Where's that?" she asked.

"Over the bridge and down by the fishpond," Chris replied, unable to hide his surprise. "Don't you know about the old railroad depot? They have a room with all these old pictures of trains and—and all kinds of neat things."

John chuckled. "The community center has a small museum telling about the old days when the Milwaukee

Railroad still ran. It's rather interesting, if you like history."

"I love it." She excused herself, went to the bathroom and quickly changed.

She reappeared, hitching the jeans up as she picked up her feet. "The boots are a little heavy," she admitted.

"Hey, Dad, look!" Chris cried. "She's still pretty."

Kathryn blushed, looking down at the tan shirt and cream cable-knit pullover sweater that was bagging slightly over the jeans.

"Right on, son," John agreed, chuckling. "Now take Kathryn to the old depot and stay out of my hair for a few hours. Be back by noon so we can eat at the Log Cabin. Now get!"

They spent the morning visiting the community center and anything else in the former timber boomtown that caught Chris's eye. Kathryn read aloud most of the captions to the photographs and occasionally lifted Chris so he could see into the glass-enclosed displays in the museum. Soon he tired of the indoor activity and ran outside. He tarried at the fishpond, complaining that the thick ice covering the top of the pond had yet to thaw.

"I can't tell if the trout are there, dammit," he said.

"Chris, you don't use words like that," she scolded.

"My dad does," he boasted.

"But eight-year-old boys don't."

"Well..."

"They just don't," she insisted.

"Okay," he agreed, "at least not when you're here."

She hid her smile as he ran across the deserted road to a combination tavern and store.

"Not in there," she called, and he stopped after peeking inside the dark interior. A scattering of clouds cluttered the sky. The day was turning into perfect hiking weather, she thought. She couldn't remember when she had gone on a hike or picnic other than those organized for thirty screaming children and three or four home-room mothers who spent more time with their own sons or daughters than keeping an eye on other children. She sighed.

At times she wondered if she had been teaching too long. Other than taking an administrative position, such as a curriculum coordinator in a larger school—which would necessitate relocating to a larger city—what else could she do except change professions completely?

She enjoyed her work, yet occasionally a nagging dis-satisfaction gnawed at her. She usually managed to sup-press the feeling and concentrate on the positive side of teaching: seeing the children leave her grade well versed in the basics of reading and writing proper English and knowing at least half of the multiplication tables. Of course, she usually spent one-quarter of the year remind-ing them of all the rules of addition and subtraction they always seemed to forget during summer vacation.

She thought of the years ahead. *Thirty more years of teaching other women's children... Why had Provi-dence never given her the opportunity to marry and have children of her own? Thirty-five years and all she had ever received was an offer to have an affair with a married man. What had she done wrong?* Kathryn wondered whether she had not been assertive enough. Probably not, she admitted. Once she had overheard two other girls talking about her in the girl's bathroom in the high school in Tucson. "Mousy," they had agreed. "Kathryn doesn't know how to flaunt what she's got," and they had gig-gled as they'd left the room.

She had never forgotten the pain of that experience. Kathryn tried to dress attractively, but knew she wasn't sexy at all. She had become a prim and proper old-maid teacher. Perhaps John Brasher was right in calling her an old prune, only he had tagged her twenty years too soon.

She should have been born a century early. The singles scene was definitely not for her, which was one reason she had chosen to live and work in a small town. At times she wondered if she were hiding from reality, but usually she managed to convince herself she was just adapting to the harsh reality of her own existence. No man found her attractive enough to want her. Yet she had friends who were certainly not pretty, and they had managed to marry and have children. Unable to find an explanation for her long-standing spinsterhood, Kathryn had become more determined than ever to be the best teacher she possibly could be.

She quickened her pace as Chris raced up the road. Following him, she wished she had a camera when Chris went inside a small steel building and peeked out the bars in the door. Someone had painted the word jail above the door. She shuddered, wondering whether the tiny building had ever actually been used for punishment.

They walked around several abandoned buildings.

"I wish we could go inside," Chris said, leaning backward to peer at the boarded-up windows on the second floor of an old hotel.

"Never do that," she warned. "The flooring might have rotted, and you'd fall and hurt yourself. How would your father ever find you if that happened?"

"Okay," he agreed, "but it would sure be a good place to hide."

When they returned to the trailer, John was in the shower. Minutes later he stepped from the bathroom, fastening the top snap on his jeans, moisture still glistening on his bare chest. A sprinkling of dark curly hair covered his chest and ran down his belly. She stared as he pulled on a white T-shirt, then he put on a fresh plaid Pendleton shirt and quickly buttoned it. He unfastened the snap on his jeans and lowered the zipper a few inches, shoved the long tails of his shirt inside, then quickly redid his pants.

Suddenly he glanced up and saw her. His fingers lingered on the metal snap. Caught in the awkward moment, they continued to stare at each other. Finally John cleared his throat. Guiltily she looked away.

"I'm sorry," he said. "I didn't know you had returned. I'm not used to anyone being here. Sorry."

"We should have knocked," she murmured.

"But it's my trailer," Chris said. "I don't have to knock on my own door."

"You're right, son," John replied. "It's my fault. I'll have to relearn some modesty." He filled his jeans pocket with his wallet, knife and other items that men often carry. He slid a pipe and pouch of tobacco into one of the breast pockets of his shirt and dropped in several kitchen matches. A pair of red suspenders completed his attire.

He turned his attention to the waiting people, adjusting the red straps over his shoulders. "Ready to eat?" he asked.

"Yes," Chris shouted, glancing at his father, then said in a more well-mannered tone, "Yes, sir."

John escorted them across the road to the café, and soon they were enjoying hamburgers with all the trimmings. Several of the men in the restaurant glanced at the trio. Finally one ambled over to their table.

"Hello, boss. Have plans during the thaw?" the man asked.

"Sure, get to know my son better," John said.

Chris beamed.

"Just the two of you?" the man asked, glancing at Kathryn. "How about an introduction? Show some courtesy, boss."

"Kathryn, this is Swede Johnson, my foreman," John said. "Swede, meet Chris's friend, Kathryn Keith. We're having lunch so don't let your curiosity run rampant."

Swede tipped his cap. "Nice to meetcha, ma'am," he said, his tobacco-stained teeth showing in a broad smile.

"Thank you, Mr. Johnson," she replied. An awkward silence ensued.

"Anything else, Swede?" John asked casually.

"No, no, boss, just wanted to be neighborly," said Swede, and he tipped his cap again before heading back to his friends.

John grimaced. "If you're through, let's leave. I think we've fed their curiosity enough for today. They'll be talking about you for a week, but they won't have the nerve to ask me more."

CHAPTER FIVE

THEY RETURNED to the trailer. "Bring your coats," John cautioned. "The weather can change in minutes. And bring the plastic water bottles, Chris. We'll each carry one when we're hiking."

"I take it the truck is repaired?" Kathryn asked.

"Yes," John said, taking her elbow and guiding her to the passenger's side of the bronze-and-white crew-cab-style truck.

"You can sit in the middle, Miss Keith," Chris said. "I want to sit by the window. I like to feel the wind."

Gingerly Kathryn accepted a boost into the cab from John, with Chris right behind her. To avoid the gearshift on the floor, she was forced to crowd Chris, but he didn't seem to mind. His attention was on turning his hand into a bobbing imaginary airplane as he hung it out the window. The cold wind touched Kathryn's cheeks with color. She rubbed her arms through her coat.

"Cold?" John asked, glancing at her.

She smiled. "No, it's fine. Rather invigorating."

"Glad you stayed an extra day?" he asked.

"Crazy," she murmured, "but I think so. I usually don't take trips with strangers."

"Now that you've slept in my bed, we're not strangers," John said softly.

"Daddy, you said we shouldn't talk about that," Chris said.

John chuckled. "I forget little boys have big ears."

"What does that mean?" Chris asked.

"That grown-ups should be more careful what they say," Kathryn warned.

"Oh, that," replied Chris. "My mom and Leo used to whisper all the time." He turned his attention back to his bobbing hand, and a comfortable silence filled the truck cab for several miles.

"I'm glad you stayed over," John said, then pulled the pipe and tobacco from his shirt pocket. "Would you hold this?" he asked, handing her the pouch. She held it as he steered over the ruts with one hand and filled his pipe with the other, tamping it a few times. He lit a match with a flick of his fingernail and held it to the bowl, taking several deep draws and exhaling. He blew the cherry smoke out the driver's window.

"Sorry, I didn't think to ask," he said. "Do you mind if I smoke?"

She shrugged. "Your pipe smoke smells nice, not at all like most cigarettes or cigars. But it's not good for you or for Chris."

"I know, and I only smoke when I'm outside on my days off."

"If you can go several days without it, why bother?" she asked.

"I only do it when I'm relaxing and feeling extra good, contented . . . It's hard to explain," he said.

They followed a logging road that wound up the mountainside for several miles, then turned onto a narrower road that was little more than a trail. They parked several yards from a small creek, its banks still covered with a few inches of ice.

Chris was out of the cab in seconds, and Kathryn followed him. John came around to their side and handed them each a flat plastic bottle of drinking water.

"Put it in your hip pocket, like a flask. And here's two granola bars each and a bag of raisins for a snack later," John said. "When, Chris?" he asked, to make sure the boy had heard him.

"Later," Chris mimicked with a grin. "Let's go!"

"Take your jacket, Chris," John scolded.

"But it's warm," Chris complained.

"Tie it around your waist," John insisted. "You may wish you had it before we get back."

Chris groaned, but did as John instructed. "Now can we go? Before it gets dark?"

"Lead the way," John said.

In single file with Chris in the lead, they followed the creek as it wound its way up a narrow mountain valley.

Kathryn hitched up her jeans and tried to ignore the weight of the unfamiliar hiking boots that were a half size too large.

John brought up the rear, enjoying the swinging figure of the small woman in front of him. There was some intangible quality about her he found charming, fresh. She gave no hint of the worldliness of most of the women he knew, yet he sensed a keen intelligence and determination in her, possibly nurtured by years of self-restraint.

He speculated on her personal life. Did she date a lot? Did she have a steady man in her life? He didn't think so. Had she ever married? He had no idea. Children? He couldn't tell; if so, she obviously didn't have custody. With today's changing attitude about custodial care, one couldn't make assumptions.

The path widened and they were able to walk side by side. John pointed out several plants, their stems still naked from the winter. Most were quickly identified by Chris.

"He's very good," Kathryn said.

"We practiced being naturalists last summer and during the winter whenever I found the time," John said. "My time with my son is limited so I try to do my best."

Chris used the heel of his boot to break off a chunk of ice, bit off a piece with his teeth and threw the rest into the creek. They hiked ahead of him for several yards. Suddenly he was between them and taking John's hand. After several strides he reached for Kathryn's hand. They walked silently along the creek for a half mile.

"I wish I had a mom like you, Miss Keith, who would live with my dad and me all the time," Chris said, the words rushing out together.

"Oh, Chris, you mustn't say that," Kathryn said, pulling her hand free.

"My son is playing matchmaker," John said, chuckling.

"Well, explain to him," Kathryn said. "I'm his teacher. I can't be his mother."

"Don't you like me, Miss Keith?" Chris asked, stopping to stare at her accusingly.

"Of course I do, but—"

"I know you didn't like my dad at first, but don't you like him now?"

"Chris, you ask too many questions I just can't answer simply," Kathryn said, reluctant to look at John.

"But if you lived with us, you could cook dinner and I would help wash the dishes, and I wouldn't have to live in St. Maries, and my daddy wouldn't say damn and hell and . . ." He glanced up at Kathryn. "He says them when he does the laundry."

Kathryn looked down at him. "Your father can hire a housekeeper to do all those things."

Chris lowered his voice. "But he likes you. I can tell. He's smoking his pipe." The boy grinned as his gaze shifted from her to John.

"Chris, run ahead and find a place to take a granola break," John suggested.

"But I want to stay with you two."

"Go," John insisted. "Remember the cave just above the spring? Go see if it's dry. Gather some kindling and we'll build a fire in the cave." He glanced toward the sky. "It might rain on us, and a fire will keep us warm and dry if we get caught."

"I hope it snows!" Chris said and raced away.

"I apologize for my son's remarks," John said after Chris had disappeared from sight. "I have no plans for marrying, and I don't think you do, either, so don't take him too seriously." He stopped, reaching for her hand. "But that doesn't mean we can't be friends. I'll talk to Chris and try to explain that just because two adults want to see each other occasionally it doesn't mean an instant family."

"But we may never see each other again," Kathryn said. "You seldom come to St. Maries, and your record of responding to my notes is not very impressive." She tried to free herself and found her other hand captured also.

"That was when I thought you were another person." His hands slid up her arms to her shoulders, drawing her closer.

Her good judgment told her to step away.

He touched a coil of shining hair. "You have lovely hair," he said. She looked up to find his face just inches from hers. "Do you know how beautiful you are?" he asked, easing her closer.

Slowly she shook her head. "Don't tease me."

"Hasn't a man told you that before?"

Again she shook her head.

"Then they've all been blind," he said softly as he drew her against him. "You're like a fragile doll that needs to be handled gently so that no harm comes to her. But you're not a doll. You're a woman and I'm going to kiss you."

She tensed.

"Don't," he said, his voice husky, "don't pull away." His mouth touched hers lightly. "Show me if you want me to continue," he whispered. "I won't force you." His lips moved on hers more firmly, savoring their softness.

Her mouth opened in surprise. The tip of her tongue touched his lips, tasting the salty line of his beard at the edge of his mouth. The texture of his skin awakened a sensual longing too strong to deny. She leaned against him, opening her mouth to his, as her arms slid up and around his neck. The fire of his kiss aroused a flame deep within her.

"John," she moaned, unwilling to believe the voice she heard was her own.

His lips moved across her cheek to her ear, tasting every inch of skin along the way. Her throat was his, warm and inviting, needing to be caressed by his lips. Her hands stroked his hair, tracing the waves, following his hairline around his collar to his throat where her fingers lingered. The warmth of his skin drew her closer.

His mouth returned to hers, savoring the fresh moistness of her tongue for seconds before concentrating on her open lips. Slowly he withdrew, aware that her breathing was as ragged as his. As he gazed into her eyes, she trembled. He drew her tightly against him, shaken by the intensity of the brief moment.

He held her until their breathing calmed.

She slipped from his embrace. With an unsteady hand she tried to smooth her hair. "I don't know what got into me," she murmured. "You shouldn't have...done that."

"I guess we did get carried away for a bit, didn't we?" he replied, his voice warm and low.

As she turned, she gasped. John looked up.

Chris was standing several feet away from them, wide-eyed and very solemn.

"And how long have you been standing there?" John asked.

"I seen you kissing Miss Keith," Chris said.

"Saw," Kathryn corrected.

"Well, I did," Chris said. "I'm not supposed to tell about that, either, am I?"

"No," John growled. Without a word he grabbed Kathryn's hand and led her up the winding pathway. Several minutes later they were in sight of the cave. Its entrance lay several feet up the side of the hill above the spring that fed the creek. An icy rain began to fall, and they quickened their pace.

Chris had performed his chore well. A pile of kindling as high as him was stacked close to the entrance and under the overhang of the mountainside. Another stack of smaller kindling was out of the rain. John broke the bigger pieces of limbs into manageable sizes, using his knee as a brace. He reached into his jeans pocket and withdrew a knife, sharpened the ends of three slender sticks into points and set the sticks aside. Soon he had a small fire burning near the cave opening.

Kathryn tried to ignore John as he knelt and tended the fire. She stared across the mountainside, watching as the rain slowly changed to snow. "How long will this last?" she asked. "Will we be able to get out?"

"I'm sure it's just a quick front," John said. "In an hour or two we can leave. Until then," he said as he reached into a zippered pocket in his jacket, "let's eat." He withdrew a plastic bag containing several wieners and handed it to Chris. "No buns or trimmings," he warned.

"Wow," Chris cried. "Real food and not just granola! Thanks, Daddy." He speared three of the wieners onto the sticks and handed them to John and Kathryn.

After enjoying the roasted wieners, they each ate a granola bar and topped off the meal with a few handfuls of raisins, washing it all down with water from the plastic flasks.

Chris chattered throughout the meal, keeping John and Kathryn laughing at his stories.

John took his large jacket and spread it on the cave floor. "Chris, why don't you lie down and watch the snow? Tell me when it looks like it's going to let up." He took off his watch. "Use this to time it." He found a pencil stub and a few scraps of paper in his shirt pocket. "Check the weather every fifteen minutes," he said. "Mark down if it's heavier or lighter, and let me know in an hour."

Kathryn wondered at John's unusual instructions, but remained silent. Within twenty minutes Chris's head had dropped to the fleece lining of John's jacket and he was asleep.

Kathryn took her own coat and covered him. He stirred, turning over on his side and curling into a ball.

John stirred the fire and added a few pieces of broken limbs. Orange fingers of light danced on the dark walls and ceiling of the cave. Kathryn moved closer to the warmth of the fire.

After checking on his son, John came to her, stopping inches away. Her breathing quickened, and she was confused by the surge of emotion building within her. She wanted him to touch her, but was afraid of her own response.

He touched her shoulders and she turned, finding herself in his embrace. Never had a man's arms felt so natural, so right. His arms tightened around her shoulders, and she settled against his chest, laying her cheek against his shirt.

"Let's sit down," he murmured against her hair and led her to a natural seat carved by erosion in the cave wall not far from the fire.

He sat against the wall and pulled her down to perch between his legs. Settling her comfortably in the circle of his arms, they stared at the flames. He kissed the sensitive skin below her left ear.

"I don't understand what's happening, Kathryn," he whispered. "I just know it feels right, and I'm glad you brought my son to me last night. Was it only last night?"

"It seems ages ago," she murmured.

He nuzzled her ear. "Anyone ever call you Kitty?"

She smiled. "Not since I was a kid in the desert."

"It fits." He kissed her ear. "What desert?"

"Sonora, south of Tucson." She sighed, savoring the silence of the secluded cave.

"Comfortable?" he asked, caressing the smooth bare skin of her forearm where she had pushed the bulky sleeve up.

"Very," she murmured, touching his fingers as they rested on her skin.

"Have you been teaching long?" he asked.

"It seems like forever," she said, then she sighed again.

"Tell me about yourself. What was Kitty like as a little girl?"

"A little desert mouse."

"But a pretty one?" he asked.

"Not really, at least I didn't think so. I was the only child of middle-aged parents. My mother was forty-five when I came along. I was a surprise, to say the least. My father was sixty, and they were making plans for his retirement from the university where he taught classes in general English lit and Chaucer. They were loving parents, very serious and proper and not very assertive. The focus of our daily lives was routine. They were lucky. They gave birth to a little girl who never thought of challenging their authority or questioning their life-style. Some people would call it gutlessness."

He frowned down at her bowed head, wanting to ask questions, but remained silent, holding her loosely in his arms as she continued.

"I was always smaller than everyone else and ungodly skinny. The boys in grade school said my eyes were greener than an alley cat's, and that would make me cry. I was allergic to every plant that bloomed in the Sonora Desert, so my nose was always red from blowing it, until I was fifteen. I spent the next four years taking weekly allergy shots to desensitize myself. My eyes were too big for the rest of my face until I was in my late teens. For a while I wore glasses to correct a muscle problem, and that made me look even more owlish. By the time my face and body matured into their proper proportions, I guess the damage to my self-esteem had been done. I concentrated on being the smartest kid in class." She grimaced. "I learned too late that's not the way to get dates. The girls liked me because I was no threat to them for their boyfriends. Yet what good does it do for a person to be gifted if..." She bit her lips to stop the words.

"If what?" he murmured.

"If no one...but your doting parents..." She stopped again, angry at having exposed such a deep wound. "I'm talking too much. I'm sorry."

He patted her forearm, wanting to console her. "It's okay. Go on, please."

"I graduated from the University of Arizona because it was my parents' choice. Because of my father's career we had always lived a few blocks from the campus. It was silly to live on campus and pay for housing when I could live at home, and...I felt guilty and wanted to save them money. I grew up hearing stories about their retirement plans." She sighed. "But I wanted to live on campus so much. When I look back, I know it was just selfishness on my part."

"Did you ever tell them?"

She shook her head. "I didn't want to hurt them. I knew they would do anything for me, but I never took advantage of their love. I was going to college during the Kent State problem and other campus riots, but I had my nose in my textbooks. Sometimes," she said wistfully as she touched his hand again, "even years later I felt guilty about not getting involved in the social activism all around me. Perhaps I still do."

"Why did you go into teaching?" he asked.

"Because both my parents were teachers. Mother retired after twenty-five years of teaching high school English when she learned I was about to disrupt their orderly lives."

"I'm sure they considered you an unexpected blessing. Don't be so hard on yourself," he said, leaning toward her to caress her cheek. "Doesn't teaching enable you to get involved with the community?"

"Yes, but in a very respectable way and always in a controlled situation. I write self-righteous notes when someone's child misbehaves. I schedule parent-teacher conferences mostly for my own convenience. I get the summer off and complain that my salary isn't large enough."

"You? Complain?" he teased.

"Well, I have a right to. The salary stinks."

He chuckled. "Some of the men who work for me think teachers are glorified baby-sitters."

She stiffened. "That's what I mean. It's one of the lowest paying professions requiring a college degree and comes with little or no respect."

"You can get fired up if a person prods the right nerve, can't you?" he asked, grinning. As if it were an after-thought, he caressed her cheek with the back of his folded hand.

"I don't get fired up half often enough," she said. "I belong to the National Education Association and the Idaho Education Association, but I've never even gone to a convention. Oh, God," she groaned, "I sound like such a chicken, don't I? I teach third grade, which is probably the easiest age to teach. The children know the basics of reading and simple math, and they're not sassy yet. They like to please the teacher and love to play games and share. They seldom start fights and—"

"That doesn't sound much like the eight-year-old I know," he said.

She grinned. "There are exceptions, but actually Chris is pretty normal and very bright. You should be proud of him."

"I am," he agreed. "It's just that we've only been to-gether for a little more than a year. We're still getting to know each other. I want to give him security, but it's dif-ficult when we spend our days apart." He frowned. "Sometimes I catch him looking at me as though he's suspicious. He won't talk about it, but I think he's afraid I might abandon him. I'd never do that, but what a ter-rible burden for a boy so young to bear."

She rose from the stone seat and paced around the cave for a few minutes. When she returned, she sat cross-legged on the cave floor beside him.

"Why isn't Chris still with his mother?" she asked, chancing a glance his way.

John stared at his large fists, then the fire. "Has Chris told you much about his family?"

"No. Only that he has two older sisters. And that his mother had married your... I really know very little. Anyhow, you don't need to tell me about your personal life." She rose again and walked to the cave entrance. "The snow has stopped." She sensed John's presence be-hind her. When he stepped outside the cave, she fol-lowed.

"My wife used the negative aspects of a logger's life to her advantage," he said, resting his hands on his hips. "I paid the bills, worked my ass off and all the while she was having an affair with my business partner. My daughters were ten and twelve when I learned that Helen and Leo had been fooling around behind my back for several years. We had agreed that I would work in the high coun-try and he would do the marketing. I thought he had the hard job because he was on the road a lot. Being the boss of the cutting operations meant I couldn't get home ex-cept on the weekends. He was the salesman, the wheeling dealing hotshot who visited the mills around the area."

He rubbed his hands together. "The timber industry became depressed all over the Northwest. Leo took fewer trips out of town. I had to lay off two yard crews. When I returned to our home in Lewiston one Friday night, I found them together."

"Oh, no," she cried.

He waved his hand. "Not in bed, just . . . together. As soon as I looked at them, I knew. Until that moment I honest-to-God didn't suspect. Little events over the years came back to me, and I pieced them together before they said a word. Oh, hell, maybe I was just too tired to care. Leo tried to explain, but the marriage must have been dead long before that evening because I didn't care. I was sorry for my daughters, but it was as though our marriage was a brain-dead patient on whom Leo had finally pulled the life-sustaining plug."

He shook his head slowly. "I had claimed my conjugal rights up to the end. For the little satisfaction either of us got out of the exercise, I'm not sure why we kept up the charade. She was pregnant when she left me, only neither of us knew it."

"Are you sure . . . you are . . . his father?"

"Leo is redheaded and brown-eyed. Helen has sandy-brown hair and green eyes. One look at that little guy and I knew he was mine. Helen had been sleeping with both of us for years, but I have no doubt that I'm Chris's father."

She smiled. "I agree."

"I first learned of Chris when he was three years old."

"Why so long? Didn't you visit your daughters?" Kathryn asked.

"I made my child support payments through the court. Leo and Helen kept moving, first to Northern California, then Washington, before settling in Oregon. Somehow the time got away from me. What's a man to say to two teenage daughters growing up without him? Each time I'd get their school pictures, I'd be reminded of what I'd lost."

"When did Helen and Leo get married? Right away?" Kathryn asked.

"Leo and Helen never married," he explained. "They've been living together ever since they left Lewiston, but for some reason, they've preferred to keep their arrangement simple. Anyway, I got a subpoena to appear in court in Roseburg and show cause why I shouldn't pay an increased amount of child support for my three children. You can imagine my surprise when she changed the number of children I had sired. I hightailed it to Oregon, and lo and behold there was this cute, dark-haired, green-eyed little boy driving Helen and Leo crazy.

"I was so stunned I agreed to pay. I visited Chris when I could, but it was never more than two or three times a year. No father can get to know his son on a schedule like that."

"Why did it take her three years to contact you?"

He glanced at her. "Chris was born with rather fair hair. I guess Leo thought he might be his, but by the time Chris was two, his hair was quite dark. Leo had a change of heart and began to bug Helen about unloading him. When that didn't work, he talked her into going after more child support."

His smile was more like a grimace. "A few times my girls rode the bus to Plummer, and I'd go get them. They'd tell me stories about Chris and I grew concerned, but didn't know what to do. I know now I should have gotten custody of him long ago."

"What about your girls? Did they enjoy being with you?" she asked.

He nodded, a smile warming his rugged features. "I'd take them to the job sites. They loved it, but some of the men were uncomfortable—they're not used to having women around when they work. Their language is often colorful, to say the least." He chuckled. "Loggers aren't known for their drawing room vocabulary."

A forlorn expression traveled across his face. "But I stayed in touch by mail with the girls. A few years ago my oldest daughter asked me to give her away at her wedding."

He ran his fingers through his thick hair and grinned. "You should have seen Chris in a tux. He had just had his sixth birthday, and he was full of beans. The reception was in Helen's and Leo's backyard and I went. It was the first time I had been in their home for more than a few minutes at a time."

He frowned, thinking back to the experience. "Helen seemed awfully short-tempered with Chris, and Leo was always sending him to his room. Chris and I spent several afternoons together during that visit, and he wanted to come home with me, but Helen would have no part of it. When Sherie moved out and the child support decreased again, Leo convinced her that the money wasn't worth the price of being tied down with a little boy. Chris had started school, and she wanted to travel with Leo. Once she changed her mind about raising him, she couldn't get rid of him fast enough."

"Were you still living in Lewiston?" she asked, coming to stand beside him. He glanced down at her and his face softened.

"No, as part of the divorce settlement the house was sold and we split the proceeds. I bought Leo's share of the business, and by then I had a contract for cutting up here. I had grown up in St. Maries and my sister Natalie and her

family lived there so it was a little like coming home. Helen and Leo had settled in Roseburg, and the girls were
involved in high school activities. I didn't want to upset
them. How the hell could I have taken the three of them?
Provided a home for them when I didn't even have a home
for myself?''

The scowl grew heavier as he recalled the days leading
up to Chris's arrival full-time in his life.

"Natalie got a call on Christmas Eve from Helen saying that she had put Chris on the Greyhound bus with an
older woman who was going to Coeur d'Alene. Chris
would be getting off in Plummer. That was as close as the
bus came to St. Maries. Can you imagine a mother putting her seven-year-old child on a bus and having him get
off in a strange town just because the town happened to
be on the bus route? Coldhearted bitch!''

"What happened?''

"Natalie's husband, Cal, drove the twenty miles to
Plummer and got him. I came down to spend Christmas
with Nat's family, and what a present I had waiting for
me! My life has never been quite the same since. Helen
said she'd send his toys later, but we had to go get them. I
love my son very much. I just wish we could be together
more, but my hours are ungodly long in the summer and
fall so his staying in town with Natalie is the best arrangement we've come up with so far.''

"Chris told me about the fire he started by accident,''
she said.

"It was terrible. I felt so guilty for months,'' he said.
"My God, think what might have happened. I tried so
hard to do what I thought was best but . . .'' He shook his
head mutely.

She touched his forearm. "I'm so sorry.''

He turned to her. "What for?''

"I had so many wrong impressions . . . about you and how you felt about Chris. I'm truly sorry."

He grinned. "I'm just glad he's in your classroom this year. The next time the teacher sends me a note, you'd better believe I'll come running." He reached out and touched her face. "The cold has turned your cheeks rosy. It's very becoming."

Tiny ripples of warmth followed the path of his fingers, drawing Kathryn closer. "I've never met a man quite like you before," she said, "and I've never told anyone about being a desert mouse. Maybe we've both talked too much today." She glanced over her shoulder to the sleeping boy. "Shouldn't we wake him up and get back to town? The sun will be down in an hour or so. It will be dark before I get back to St. Maries."

He blocked her way. "Do you have to go back?" he asked. "Why not stay one more night? We can visit, get to know each other better."

"I don't think that would be wise," Kathryn said, but her voice reflected the longing she felt. "Patches needs caring for."

"Am I in competition with a cat?"

She frowned. "I have things to do. I didn't plan on being away."

"Then let me hold you again, just for a few minutes." John enfolded her in his arms. He kissed her lightly on her upturned mouth, never carrying the kiss into deeper desire.

"Kitty, Kathryn, Miss Keith: are these the three faces of this desert mouse I hold in my arms? The intelligent woman, Kathryn? The prim and proper teacher, Miss Keith? I've enjoyed them, but my favorite is Kit, this woman with me now. I think she's a new discovery for us both. If one personality becomes dominant, I hope it's Kit. She's warm and responsive.''

"No one has ever called me warm and responsive before," she said, awed by his attention.

"Then it's about time."

"You make me feel like a late bloomer."

"Better late than never." His mouth covered hers again, this time claiming it strongly and sensually. She gripped him tightly as she strained upward to be closer to him.

Suddenly John felt a hand slap his buttock, and he quickly withdrew his lips from hers.

"I'm not looking and I won't tell," Chris called as he darted toward the creek, his jacket tails flying. "I'll beat you to the truck. You'll probably just keep doing that kissing stuff anyway," he shouted over his shoulder.

CHAPTER SIX

JOHN BRASHER WOULD BE bringing Chris back to town tomorrow, Kathryn thought, as she dusted the coffee table. He had promised to stop by before returning to Avery.

A week had passed since spending the night and day in Avery and a day had not ended without her thinking of the Brashers. She hadn't asked what they would be doing during their week together. Their personal lives were still very private, as was hers.

She dropped to the sofa, her dusting cloth dangling from her hand. Her mind was filled with tender images of the three of them, but before any memory could come into focus, she would suppress it, refusing to allow such fantasies about what had been and what yet might be to grow. She wondered what John saw in her. Obviously, he found in her some quality that had escaped other men over the years. His eyes had made promises he had not voiced. He evoked an impulsiveness she wanted to explore, a recklessness yearning to be released.

He was a virile, handsome man, who would easily attract the attention of most women. Surely there had been many in his life, women who knew how to please a man, flatter him, satisfy his needs. Pleasing a man was alien to Kathryn. Perhaps he was only playing a game to see how willing she would be to get involved with him. Could she trust his sincerity? Or believe his interest in her was genuine? And what kind of interest was it? Friendship? Or more?

The most frustrating part of this experience was that she had nothing to compare her time with John to, for dates had been few and far between in her life. In high school she had been the class genius, and studying every night had become a habit she had been unable or unwilling to break while attending the university in her hometown. The primary grades in any school system tended to be taught by women. Her parents and their circle of friends had been generations older.

Her best friend in high school, Jill Baker, had remained a close friend at university. Jill had been fortunate enough to live on campus. After classes she and Jill would sit for hours in the dormitory room and discuss their feelings, their hopes for the future, their promising careers. During the spring of their junior year, Jill had fallen passionately in love with a graduate student. Kathryn had listened with half an ear to her obsessive chattering about Forbes Hawthorn, a handsome young man from New York who was working on his master's degree in chemistry.

Sometimes she joined them for dinner, but the couple's mutual infatuation made her feel as though she were invisible, and she began to decline their offers. She wished her best friend the joy and happiness of marriage, but shielded herself from the pain of knowing she would never have a man wanting to marry her.

Occasionally she would stand in front of her mirror and try to decipher the reasons why she was unattractive to the male population. She had finally decided the answer for her single status was fate, pure and simple.

Living alone had become the only life-style available to her. Now, after all the years alone, a man she had been prepared to dislike had awakened a longing in her she wasn't ready or willing to analyze. She had only spent an evening and a day with him. Driving away from his trailer in Avery had left her feeling as though a part of her had been torn out and left behind. The wound was still raw.

She thought back to the principal whose pursuit had driven her out of her birth state. She had initially been flattered by his attention, unaware that he had a wife at home taking care of three preschool children. After several dinner dates he had tried to seduce her as they shared a nightcap in her apartment, but she had resisted.

A week later, while the primary grade teachers waited for him to begin a meeting in the teachers' lounge, another teacher had casually mentioned the principal's wife.

She had been shocked and hurt that he had deceived her. When she had confronted him, he had tried to explain, offering the classic excuse that his wife didn't understand his needs. Kathryn had shunned his overtures for the next few years. Asking for a transfer to another school after the near assault had seemed a perfect solution until fate had enabled him to follow her.

Anger and determination had fired her decision to relocate to live among strangers. She had found peace in the isolation for a while. And now John Brasher and his son had begun to break through her carefully constructed walls of privacy.

Feeling inadequate weakened her confidence. Surely John Brasher would lose interest in her after a few visits. But what if he remained attracted to her? Someday he would want to... Was this unexpected attraction sexual? She had read enough books, seen enough love scenes in movies and television dramas, knew enough about reproduction to know what was involved in sexuality, but she'd never experienced *feeling* sexual.

But what would it really feel like to make love with John? Would he laugh when he learned he was with a middle-aged virgin? Would he be considerate? Gentle? Or would he take her with the eagerness and roughness she had read about in novels? Perhaps he would just walk away. His virility was taken for granted. Single men weren't shackled with the societal restraints placed on women. She closed her eyes, telling herself she was an anachronism, fully knowing most women her age had stopped abiding by the double standard set years ago.

She rested her head against the sofa back, surrendering to the fantasy of being with him. Would he find her body still youthful? Beautiful? She touched one of her breasts, but found nothing sexy about feeling that part of her body through a red sweatshirt and bra.

She dropped her hand to her waist and sighed. This, Kathryn thought, was silly, hopeless, wishful speculation. She would probably die a ninety-year-old woman, still wondering why she had been born female. Life was definitely passing her by. And she was cruelly destined to teach other women's children and never have the opportunity to know what it would be like to experience lovemaking, conception, birth.

An image of John and his son filled her mind. In such a short time he and Chris had become very special to her. Could she be falling in love with a man she barely knew? If this was love, she wasn't sure she was strong enough to survive. She had always assumed love would be a joyful experience, not this painful loneliness that sapped her initiative. Her lesson plans for the coming week had been scattered across her kitchen table for three days.

All she could think about was this gypo logger who wore red suspenders and was savvy enough to survive in an industry famous for its widow making, its migratory living, its expectation that a man should be able to work from before dawn to after dark in order to take advantage of the seasons; an industry caught between progress and conservation, between the insatiable hunger for fine wood in city homes and buildings and the environmentalists who seemed determined to declare every tree a potential wilderness area.

Her heart quickened as she visualized his face. She wished she could go back to the mountains with him and forsake all her responsibilities.

This is crazy, she thought, forcing herself off the sofa. Quickly she finished her household chores, showered and debated on what to wear. She decided on her pajamas and a robe so she wouldn't have to undress for bed a few hours later.

"Shame," she murmured as she searched her closet. Thinking that her standards were slipping, she selected a sage-green cable-knit sweater and matching wool slacks. Tiny pearl buttons ran down one side of the neck opening to the bust line. Normally she would button the opening, but who would see her today? She smiled, noticing the inches of a creamy cleavage peeking through the opening. Risqué but satisfyingly so for a change. She hurried from the bedroom before she gave in to the impulse to rebutton the sweater.

In the kitchen she opened the refrigerator. Nothing there appealed to her. Perhaps she would skip a meal. There was no reason to dirty dishes if she wasn't hungry. Another teacher had asked once how she kept so slim. Kathryn had been tempted to describe the lack of excitement in eating alone, but had stifled the cynical impulse.

Patches mewed and Kathryn fed her. She wandered back to the living room and picked up a paperback novel. After staring at the first paragraph for several minutes, she tossed it down. Obviously, the writer had created no opening hook to catch her attention. She grimaced, knowing it really wasn't the author's fault for her inability to get involved in the story.

The doorbell rang. It was Saturday afternoon, a time when Kathryn expected no one. Resenting the disturbance, she opened the door.

John Brasher filled the doorway.

"Oh," she cried, covering her mouth to hide her surprise and joy, "I thought you were coming tomorrow."

"Chris and I needed to see you today," he said, frowning down at her.

He seemed taller than ever in a pair of navy dress slacks and smoky-blue pullover sweater, its crew neck caressing his throat as he spoke. "May we come in?"

"Of course," she said. "Where's Chris?"

"Back here," Chris said, "behind my dad." He was holding a box with holes cut in the sides. Something inside made a scraping sound.

"May I help you?" Kathryn offered.

"Yeah," Chris groaned. "I didn't know it would get so heavy. But don't peek inside."

Chris's sage-green pullover matched his father's in style, but he wore jeans.

"We've been gone," Chris said. He spotted Patches coming from the kitchen and went off to play with the cat.

She turned to John, who stood a few feet away. "Where did you go?"

"To Oregon to see my family," he said.

"Oh."

"I promised Chris we'd go see his sisters. Debbie lives in Roseburg and Sherie in Winston, just south of there."

"Oh," she said, sighing with relief.

"Helen and Leo live in Roseburg, too," he added.

"It doesn't matter what you do or where you go," she said softly and hurried to the kitchen to collect her lesson plans from the table.

He followed. "You never asked about how we would be spending our time so I skipped over our trip. I didn't want to upset you."

She whirled around. "Upset me? Why would a trip to visit your former wife upset me?"

"I don't know, but it does," he replied.

"It does not," she insisted.

"Then look at me."

"No."

Slowly he turned her toward him. "I saw Helen. I dropped Chris off for a short visit."

Kathryn tried to twist free.

"I wanted you to know," he said, "that other than being the mother of my children, she means nothing to me. Now look at me." He crooked his index finger under her chin and tilted her face upward.

She blinked, trying to hide her tears of frustration.

He brushed one from the corner of her eye. "I missed you, Kit." His lips touched hers lightly. "I thought of you all the time we were in Oregon. Chris's talking about Miss Keith every other minute didn't help matters."

"I missed you, too," she murmured. Capturing his face in her hands, she strained to kiss him again. "I missed you each and every day I was here, wondering where you were and what you were doing. For a man I hardly know, you've caused me a great deal of trouble."

"I'm sorry, Kit. Forgive me," he whispered, and he kissed her deeply. His arms tightened around her, pulling her against his aroused body. Did she feel the same pull between them? He wanted her, more than any woman he had ever met. How on earth did a man bring up the subject of lovemaking to a prim and proper schoolteacher he had spent less than two days with and, worse yet, his own son's teacher? Too many conflicts of interest. Better, he decided, to try to control such thoughts.

He eased his hold on her, allowing her to catch her breath. He looked around the kitchen. Chris was sitting on a chair holding the calico cat in his arms.

"I'll take care of you, Patches," he said. "Daddy and Miss Keith are always kissing. Let's go play," he said softly, and he carried the cat out the kitchen door to the backyard.

Before they could move, he ran back into the room and tossed the tricolor cat to the floor. "We forgot the mouse!" he shouted and ran to the living room. In seconds he returned with the mysterious box.

"What mouse?" Kathryn asked.

"So much for keeping secrets when small boys are involved," John said, chuckling. "You may open your present from the Brasher boys, all the way from Roseburg, Oregon."

"Really? For me?" She looked from father to son. They were both grinning.

Inside the box was a wire-and-plastic cage with tubes and tunnels for a tiny animal to crawl through and explore. Out of the end of one tunnel peeked a gray mouse. Embarrassment swept up her face as she recalled their conversation in the cave.

"It seemed appropriate," John said, laying his hand on her shoulder. "You need company when we're not here. Chris has its mate at Natalie's house. I'm working on convincing him to bring them together in one home."

"In one . . . home?"

John grinned. "Like the idea?"

Kathryn could think of nothing to say. It would be so easy to read too much into all that was taking place. She could end up looking like a fool.

"Maybe you'll bring the mouse to school," Chris added. "I can tell everyone that—"

Kathryn and John frowned at him and he reconsidered. "I won't tell, but you could still bring it to school."

The cat mewed and jumped up on the table, sniffing excitedly at the cage. Kathryn shooed her down. "I'm not sure Patches is trustworthy around a mouse. I hope the cage is sturdy."

"Chris has talked about your cat almost as much as he has about his teacher so we took special pains to find the right cage. The saleswoman assured us it was catproof. Time will tell," John concluded as he moved the cage to the coffee table in the living room. Kathryn, Chris and the cat followed. Within minutes the cat was asleep, her nose pressed against the grillwork of the cage, her tail twitching in her sleep.

"If this continues, we'll have a neurotic cat and a hypertensive mouse," Kathryn said. "Thanks, guys, for thinking of me. Now, are you hungry? I can fix you something to eat."

"No, we're taking you to dinner," John said. "The chef at the Benewah Resort is waiting for us. Grab your coat and let's go eat."

"But . . ."

"No buts," John insisted. "We're taking you out."

The resort, several miles west of town, overlooked a lake skyline. Darkness had fallen and lights twinkled from the other side of the lake.

The dining room was popular. They waited several minutes before being led to a table. Kathryn groaned silently when she saw the prices on the menu. Thrift had been deeply instilled in her so she selected a chicken dish in the middle price range. She glanced up to find John frowning at her.

"Get what you want, Kit, not what you think is easy on my wallet."

The waitress laughed. "Gee, you should be glad your wife is so careful with the budget. And what would you like, young man?" she asked, turning to Chris.

He ordered spaghetti and meatballs, smiling up at the waitress when he returned his menu to her.

"What gorgeous green eyes you have," she said, smiling down at him. "My, my, you look just like your mother, hair and eyes and all. A good-looking family, sir. And what would you like?"

Clearing his throat, John ordered a thick steak, medium rare.

When the talkative waitress had left, John looked at Kathryn. She was rearranging her silverware. He waited for her to speak, but she remained quiet.

"He does resemble you," John said, reaching for her hand. "Perhaps that's why he was drawn to you. I'm sorry if the waitress embarrassed you."

"It's okay," she replied. "Sometimes I get the feeling that meeting you two is like being run over by a steamroller."

"What's a steamroller?" Chris asked, and soon John and Chris were involved in a lengthy discussion of heavy equipment.

Chris fell asleep on the drive back to town, his dark head bobbing against his chest. Although she tried to resist, she gave in to the urge to hold him, drawing his small body onto her lap and cuddling him in her arms. He sighed deeply as he settled against her, and she wondered if he felt so right because he was Chris, her student, or because he was John Brasher's son.

John concentrated on the dark highway, trying not to interfere with the scene being played out in the corner of his truck cab. What made this woman so special, so...lovable? He frowned through the darkness, aware of the erratic beat of his heart. It was silly for a grown man to be reacting this way. But the arousal he felt lower in his body could only be that of a man mature enough to follow his instincts.

He parked in front of his sister's house.

"I'll take him inside, then take you home," he said, coming to Kathryn's side and relieving her of his sleeping son.

She watched his tall form recede in the moonlight, Chris's head resting on his shoulder, his arm dangling down John's back. Trying to rub some of the feeling back into her own arms, she thought of the hours ahead. Would this be the night? No, they had known each other for so little time. It wouldn't be right.

Was she taking a lot for granted to think he desired her enough to want to make love to her? Never had she even considered going to bed with a man. Why now? And why this sense of disappointment that it shouldn't be tonight?

He was whistling slightly off-key when he returned to the truck and climbed in.

"Let's get you home now," he said. "We need to talk."

"I'LL BE GONE FOR A WHILE," John said as she poured two cups of tea from the china pot.

"Gone? How long?" she asked, the hot teapot suspended in midair.

"A month or so."

"A whole month? Why so long?"

"I'm bidding on some timber sales near Bonners Ferry. This contract will be finished by late summer, and I'll be moving."

"Moving...from Avery?"

"And St. Maries," he said, stirring sugar into his tea. "I wanted you to know. I'm lining up some new work for the crews. Swede will cover for me when the thaw is dried out enough and the crews can work again."

"You'll be leaving...for good?"

"A logger doesn't stay in one place for long," he said. "He moves to where the work is."

"But what about Chris? Would you leave him behind?"

"I would rather take him with me, if I can work out the details."

"Oh." She rose from her chair and wandered to the kitchen door. The overhead fixture glared down at her, and she turned the light out, ridding herself of the irritating brightness. She stared into the backyard, studying the shadows cast by the trees and bushes. The darkness enveloped her. Perhaps there was safety in the darkness, the darkness of unexplored emotions, especially the ones provoked by the man sitting behind her. She didn't want to think of him leaving, not when they had just met.

"I have the summer to work out a solution...to lots of things," he said behind her.

"Will I—will we—will you get down to St. Maries during the summer?" she asked.

"Not as much as I would like. The crews have to be at the landings hours before daybreak to be ready for the first logging truck. Time is money for all of us so the drivers try to get as many loads delivered in a day as possible. The season is short. But I try to take at least one day a week off for Chris, and now..."

She thought of the short summer ahead, realizing that she had expected too much. John's time was limited and it belonged to Chris, not to a woman who had allowed her fantasies to gain the upper hand in her orderly life. She had been forewarned the afternoon at the cave. Steeling herself for his speech of rejection, she leaned her forehead against the cool wood of the doorjamb.

She felt his hand on her waist.

"Somehow I'll manage to see you, too, Kitty," he murmured. "I don't know how any of this will work out. It's too new and unexpected, but try to understand."

She stiffened as his hand slid across her abdomen and settled on her hipbone. The heat of his palm spread through the fabric of her slacks. A fire ignited deep within her, fanned by newly unleashed emotions and fueled by anger at the cruel turn of fate that would take him away as quickly as he had come into her life. Fear of losing him twisted her stomach.

Clutching at his fingers, she pulled his arm upward and pressed his hand beneath the fullness of her breasts. She leaned against him. "It's not fair," she cried. "A few more months and you'll leave." She turned in his arms. "Why, why does it have to be this way?"

"I don't know, Kit."

"You're different from any man I've ever met before. I've never wanted to... but now it's all I think about."

"Think about what?" he asked, his fingers exploring her cheek.

Her reply was barely audible. "Wanting you."

He pulled her closer, but said nothing.

"I was always so satisfied," she explained, "so willing to play it safe, but you make me feel as if I'm about to live, for the first time in my life *really* live."

"I know, Kit, I feel the same way," John murmured against her forehead. He ran his fingers through her hair, tilting her face up to his. "I want to love you...tonight."

His mouth touched her cheek, working its way to her lips in agonizing slowness. She turned her face into his path and eagerly sought fulfillment.

"I don't know what the next few months hold for us," he said, kissing her several times, "but tonight can be ours, just ours." His lips sought hers again. Her mouth opened, craving to blend with him, searching for his tongue. When she found it, a tremor ran through her body, and in its wake desire that had lain dormant for too long.

"Yes," she said, "love me tonight." Desperation tore away her restraint. She reached for his hand and led him through the house to her bedroom and turned on a lamp.

He lingered by the doorway, watching her hesitate, her features muted by the soft glow of the lamplight. Instinctively John knew something wasn't right. As she turned to him, her eyes were dark against her pale complexion. Was she frightened? She was petite. Was she afraid he would hurt her? He damned the awkwardness of making love with a woman for the first time. He didn't believe in playing games.

She had made no attempt to undress. Perhaps she was waiting for him to make the first move.

He approached, stopping a few feet from her. He twisted the crewneck sweater over his head and smoothed his hair. The T-shirt beneath was quickly dispensed with, leaving his upper body bare. She stared at his chest.

"Having second thoughts?" he asked.

She mouthed a silent no.

"Then let me help," he said gently as he eased her top from her. A lacy bra shielded her breasts from him. He stepped behind her and unhooked the fastener, sliding the straps from her shoulders and tossing the piece of lingerie aside. He turned her around to face him. Her beauty took his breath away for a moment. Her eyes reflected the passion growing between them. A hint of a rosy flush touched her cheeks, drawing his hand to the delicate bone of her jaw. His fingers trailed down her throat to the valley between her breasts, lingering to enjoy the silky texture of her skin.

He caught a whiff of fragrance, arousing him, making him want to discard the rest of his clothing, but he accepted the discomfort of his own body. This woman before him was still hesitant, almost shy. Yet he sensed she was more than willing to accept his lovemaking. His hand moved to her breast, savoring its creamy fullness. Her nipple hardened as his thumb moved back and forth across it.

She touched his chest lightly, withdrew her hand, then returned it to his body to caress him again. "I'm not sure what to do," she admitted.

"This undressing part of making love is never easy, Kit," he said, dipping to kiss her breast.

She gasped, then sighed as his mouth left her skin.

"Do you like that?" he asked, his voice husky.

"I think so," she sighed.

Her reply puzzled him, but he couldn't stop to analyze her response. The delicate body standing inches from him captivated him. He lifted her, carrying her the few feet to the bed, and put her down. Still partially dressed, he leaned over, feeling her hands begin to move up his body. She was driving him crazy with her hands alone. His mouth touched the pulse point in her throat and slowly began a path to her breasts again. Gingerly he took one nipple in his mouth, bathing it with moist heat. It hardened as she arched against him. He moved to the other breast and satisfied it, but found no satisfaction for his own body.

She moaned and he returned his attention to her face. "You're beautiful, Kit." Her eyes reflected a puzzling innocence that intrigued him.

"Shall we proceed?" he whispered.

She nodded.

"And what do you want to do next?"

"I don't know," she replied.

He frowned. "What about when you've been with a man before? Tell me what you like."

"I—I've never been ... with a man before," she whispered, avoiding his gaze.

"Never?"

She tried to turn away, but he restrained her with his body.

"You're still a ... ?"

"Yes," she murmured. "It's almost a dirty word in today's world, isn't it?"

He squinted down at her. "You're not joking, are you?"

"Sometimes I think my whole life has been a joke," she replied, her voice tinged with bitterness. "I suppose now you're going to tell me you don't fool around with virgins?"

She met his gaze, challenging him with her blunt words.

He grinned. "It's been a few years since such a possibility was relevant," he admitted. She tried to wriggle free, but he stopped her again. "Your sexual experience or lack thereof has no bearing on why I'm lying on your bed with you, Kit."

"Don't make fun of me," she murmured. "I know I'm not a sexy woman, but—"

"I think you're a very sensual woman. I sensed that the very first time you stared at me in the café in Avery. I want to be with you. You're on my mind all the time. Maybe I'm falling in love with you. I don't know. I do know that having you with me and seeing you with my son has changed my view about women..."

Her hand touched his mouth, but he removed it. "... and teachers and life in general. It's too early to tell what will develop so I won't make promises I might not be able to keep." He kissed her. "I do know that tonight I still want to make love to you."

"It's so soon," she replied. "We know so little about each other. Maybe that steamroller has changed into a roller coaster ride. I've never gone to bed with a man and here I am lying in my own with you, and I would be very disappointed if you left me now. I don't know what's happening to me." Suddenly her eyes filled with tears and angrily she brushed them away.

"Maybe you're falling in love, too," he replied, studying her carefully.

"It's too soon. We only met a week ago," she said.

"But we've been corresponding for several months," he replied, grinning. "And I've been hearing wonderful things about the fabulous Miss Keith ever since Chris met you last year."

"But you thought of me as old prune face."

"And never has a man been more wrong."

She sighed. "I was worried that you'd be disappointed to find yourself becoming involved with such a mousy, nonassertive woman."

"Spare me from some of the overly liberated women of today," he replied. "I meet them in the logging bars sometimes. A few times I thought I was going to be attacked on the spot. Maybe I'm old-fashioned, but I like to do the pursuing." He chuckled. "It must be the hunter in our primitive past, carried over the generations in our genes. All I know is that I like a responsive woman, but not one who overpowers me."

"Are you trying to tell me how to behave?" she asked.

"I would never do that." He smiled. "I guess, however, I've lied to you. When I first saw you face-to-face in Avery, you definitely overpowered me. I racked my brains trying to think of excuses for you to spend the night. I even considered disabling your car to keep you there."

"Well, I did stay, right in your own bed, too."

"Yes, and I was awake for hours thinking of you there. I was jealous of the pillow, the blanket covering you, the air you breathed."

She smiled and touched his chest lightly with her fingers. "I was so prepared to dislike you that I couldn't enjoy being there at all. I was determined to reaffirm all my opinions about you, and instead, I found myself drawn to you. It's never happened to me before. Can this be love? I would never have asked if you hadn't mentioned it first."

"We'll have to wait and see," John said, and he rolled onto his back, pulling her with him. When he adjusted the pillows behind his head, she settled in the crook of his arm, her breasts against his stomach, her head on his chest. His hand stroked her back, lingering on her narrow waist.

"You have the figure of a much younger woman," he said.

"Maybe because it's never had a chance to mature...until now," Kathryn said before she kissed the skin next to one of his nipples.

"Do that again, and you'll mature right here within a matter of minutes, and I'll be the teacher."

She laughed and her hand played over his chest.

"Well, aren't you going to test my threat?" he asked.

"You sound as though your pride has been wounded," she teased. "Is this what you mean?" She stroked his nipple with her tongue, lingering until it hardened.

"Oh, God, woman, keep it up, and I'll show you what it's like to be loved by a man." He grabbed her, and they rolled again across the bed.

She giggled at his playfulness until her eyes met his. The blue of his iris had darkened to match the black of his pupil. Never had she seen such handsome eyes, eyes she wanted to drown in. As he began to seduce her again, she felt his arousal pressed against her thigh. If this was love, she wanted to experience it again and again, this warm, intoxicating nearness of a special man, who desired her and told her so, who wasn't turned off by her lack of worldliness.

"Love me," she whispered, "love me now," and she drew his face down until she could touch his lips with hers. "At long last I know why no other man could make love to me. I was waiting for you."

CHAPTER SEVEN

JOHN OPENED THE SNAP on her slacks, his hand dragging the tab slowly down the zipper teeth. His fingers slid inside the elastic of her underpants, caressing her navel.

She moaned when his hand slid lower.

The shrill ring of the phone filled the room, and his hand jerked free.

It rang again. "Who could be calling at this hour?" she asked.

"I don't know, but you'd better get it," he said, releasing her from his arms.

She picked up the receiver from the phone sitting on the nightstand. "Hello," she said, unable to steady her voice.

She covered the receiver and turned to John. "It's Natalie. She wants to speak to you."

"Chris?" he asked, rolling to her side of the bed and swinging his feet to the floor. "Has something happened to Chris?" He took the receiver, and Kathryn listened as he talked.

From the conversation she could tell Chris wasn't involved. Perhaps another family member was, however. Kathryn tried to suppress the embarrassment of them being discovered together by his sister. She slipped into her bra and sweater again and left the room. In the bathroom she ran a brush through her hair, then hurried to the kitchen to perk some fresh coffee.

When he joined her in the kitchen, he was fully dressed. "I'm sorry, Kit."

"It's okay," she said, touching the pearl buttons on the front of her sweater.

"It's not okay at all, sweetheart," he said, his voice still husky and troubled. "I wanted to... Oh, hell, Kit. One of my men has been hurt. I should go to the hospital, see how he is and take care of some of the legalities."

"Do you have time for coffee?"

"Sure," he said, dropping into a chair, his long legs stretched beneath the table. "Thank God it wasn't Chris."

She touched his hand. "Yes. What happened? How did they find you?"

He shook his head. "Damn Swede and Mugger. It wouldn't have happened if I had been there."

"Been where?" she asked. "I thought you had closed down for a month."

"We have, that is everyone but Swede, Mugger and me. Swede and Mugger volunteered to stay up on the ridge to do some cleanup. The forest service guys are overdue for an inspection, and we don't want to be closed down for any reason. They were spreading slash."

"What's that?"

"The cuttings—limbs and brush left from the sawyers and the crews working at the landings," he explained.

"I thought they burned all that."

"We're in an area where the forest service is trying something different. We spread the slash over the area logged, and it helps to stop erosion. The slash decays over the years, and the land is reclaimed, with new trees being planted by the forest service as soon as we're out of there. You don't have the air pollution of the burn."

"How was Mugger hurt?"

He grimaced. "He tripped and fell trying to get out of the way of the loader. Swede was backing up and thought Mugger was in the bushes taking a break. One of the tracks ran over his pelvis. Swede is pretty shook up. He tried to get the air ambulance, but couldn't get through. Apparently, he gave up and put Mugger in the back of the truck and drove into town to the hospital. He stayed with Mugger until they chased him away. Told him to come back when Mugger was out of surgery."

"When did it happen? How long has Swede been in town? Was he looking for you? Did it just happen?" she asked, concerned for John as well as his employees.

"He hit the bars to try to calm down, and when he sobered up enough to remember why he'd gotten drunk, he decided to find me. He couldn't remember Natalie's name, but remembered picking me up there one morning, so a little while ago he woke the household up by pounding on the front door. Of course Chris got into the act when he heard Swede's voice." He nodded his head. "He told everyone I was probably at Miss Keith's, that we've been kissing a lot. So much for secrets."

She smiled and slid into the chair closest to his. "I don't care. Somehow it doesn't seem so important anymore. I guess I would rather be with you than have a spotless reputation."

"We'll work at giving you both," he said, drinking the rest of his coffee. "I had better get to the hospital. Would you come with me?"

"If I could be of any help."

"Just being with me would make it easier," he assured her. "These logging accidents are never easy."

"Does Mugger have a family?" she asked.

"Damned if I know. There must be a next of kin listed on his employee record, but my records are in Avery. He's always been alone. He's a lot younger than Swede. They sort of adopted each other. If it's, well, losing Mugger would be like losing a son for Swede. God, I hope not.''

"Have you ever been hurt?" she asked.

"Twice."

"How?"

He frowned at her. "Once I got caught by a widow-maker."

"What in the world is that? Why don't loggers speak normal English?''

He grinned. "Maybe because we're a peculiar breed. A widow-maker is a limb that hangs in a tree. It's been broken off by a falling tree and then just hangs up there out of sight, waiting to drop on some unsuspecting logger who walks by. They've earned their name. It could have killed me, but instead I was knocked out for a few hours. It was my own fault for not paying attention.''

"I'm afraid to ask about the other time," she said.

"I guess the other was actually worse. Maybe I shouldn't tell you.''

"No. I want to know what kind of life you live," she replied. "I've only seen you in your off-hours when you're...more normal.''

He took her hand. "I was subbing for a driver and misjudged a turn. It was winter and the road was slicker than I thought. I braked and the wheels started to skid, and in a flash we were flying off the road and down a steep grade to the creek. I lost the trailer. The wrappings broke and logs flew through the air like matchsticks. I thought some would slam into the cab for sure, but Lady Luck was on my side that trip. Other than a broken rib, I was un-hurt. I managed to walk back to camp and get taped up. By the weekend I was well enough that Helen never asked what had happened. Actually, I'm one of the lucky ones, having been in the business most of my life. Lumber-jacks aren't known for their longevity, but it's better now. In the old days falling trees got the men. Now it's gasoline-powered chain saws.''

"My God," she said with a gasp. "I never thought much about it. Chain saws mean—"

"Yes," he said, cutting her off. "It can be dangerous work but then those are the risks. The money is good."

"Not that good."

He frowned at her. "The risks, the money and the long hours are three of the big reasons loggers are better off unmarried."

She stared at him, aware of the message he was giving her. "Maybe I should stay here."

"I'm sorry, Kit," he said, rising and pulling her from her chair. "I didn't mean it the way it sounded. Our lives are very different. Yours is represented by stability. I believe you call it tenure. Mine is the typical life of a gypo, an independent logging contractor. If you're going to be a gypo's lady, you'll have to understand what's involved."

He leaned down and kissed her lightly. "I still plan to make love to you, Kit. If not tonight, then soon. My word is good. Just ask my men."

She smiled, sliding her arms around his waist. "What would they say if they knew you were getting involved with a schoolmarm?"

He laughed. "Remind me to tell you all about schoolmarms. They're part of the business. And as for my men, they'd treat you like a lady. I would see to that."

"Sounds threatening," she said, reaching up to kiss him again.

"I keep my threats, too. I've been known to settle scores, but I'm getting too old for that physical stuff now.

I'm ready to settle down in my old age." He kissed her again, this time with passion, his tongue in her mouth. His own physical reaction was evident as she leaned against him.

"I don't think you're as old as you claim," she teased. "I'll remember your promise and try to wait. I've waited so long, I can wait a little longer." She gazed into his eyes, sinking into their dark sapphire depths. "Oh, John," she sighed, sliding her arms around his neck. "I'm too short. I can hardly reach your mouth."

"I'll help you," he said, and he picked her up, holding her against his chest, one hand cupping her buttocks, her feet dangling against his shins.

She smiled, enjoying the eye-level contact.

"Better?" he asked.

She touched his mouth, unable to hide the tremor in her fingers as she traced around his lips. "Yes." She replaced her fingers with her mouth.

The kiss deepened and her arms wound tightly around his neck. Breathless, she withdrew. "I love you, John," she whispered, burying her face against his muscular neck. Slowly he let her slide down his body, making her aware of her continued effect on him.

"I love you, too, Kit. Dammit, I want to stay here with you, but I can't. Please come with me to the hospital. I think I'm going to need you."

OSCAR MICHAELS, known to his fellow workers as Mugger, lay resting in a private room in the small hospital.

"Sorry to bother you, boss, on the weekend and all," he said, his words garbled from the lingering effects of the anesthetic. "My sidekick tried to get a meat wagon, but his radio wasn't working right. Sure hate to bother you like this." His glazed eyes spotted Kathryn lingering by the door. "Hey, the boss brought his lady. Swede said she was a looker." He tried to raise his hand, but succeeded in wriggling a few fingers instead.

"Take it easy, Mugger," John said, stepping closer to the bed and laying his hand on one of Mugger's arms.

"It ain't Swede's fault," Mugger insisted weakly. "He thought I was in the bushes, and I was, only I came back and wanted..." He tried to shift his weight. "It's my own damned fault for... Sorry, ma'am."

"Don't move, Mugger," John warned, motioning to the nurse a few feet away. "Your pelvis is cracked, and you've had some of your large intestine removed. You'll pull your incision open if you try to move." John shook his head, frowning down at him. "You're lucky to be alive."

Mugger gave a weak thumbs-up signal and John grinned. He turned, motioning to Kathryn to join them. She accepted his hand as she came to the bed and gazed at the injured man. She guessed him to be in his late twenties. He seemed, nonetheless, hardly more than a boy. His blond beard was untrimmed and thin.

"Mugger, this is Kathryn Keith," John said, putting his arm around her shoulders.

"Hello, Mugger," Kathryn said, touching his forearm.

Mugger grinned, his pale-blue eyes slightly dilated. "Howdy, ma'am. Glad to meetcha. Always enjoy meeting a gypo's lady. You've snagged one of the best in these here north woods. You take good care of each other now, you hear?" His gaze shifted from Kathryn to John and back to Kathryn. "God, I'm getting sleepy." His eyelids drooped.

The nurse stepped forward. "I have Mr. Michaels's medication for him now."

"Geez, no one ever called me Mr. Michaels before. Hot damn," he said, but then groaned aloud as he tried to laugh.

"You rest now," John said. "I'll check on you before I head to the woods tomorrow, and Swede will be staying in town for a few days just to see if you need anything."

"The bills, I . . ." Mugger's voice faded.

"This one is on me," John said. "I take care of my men. You should know that by now. See you tomorrow morning." John patted Mugger's arm again.

"What if I can't work? My days of being a knot bumper may be over, boss."

John nodded. "You may have to hang up your calk boots, but there's sawdust in your veins. We'll make you into an inkslinger or a flunky."

"Not a flunky. I would go crazy."

"Don't worry. You second-growth lumberjacks have a lot to learn. You'll be settin' in the Pear Tree before you know it. We're no gunnysack outfit and don't you forget it. Now you get some shut-eye. That's an order from the boss."

He took Kathryn's hand and led her from the room. She hurried to keep pace with his long gait. Soon he was helping her into the truck cab and slamming the door. She sensed his composure was badly shaken.

He slid behind the wheel, put the key in the ignition, but didn't start the engine. She reached across and touched his arm. He turned to her.

"These accidents tear me up a little more each time I have to visit someone in the hospital," he admitted. "Are these men's lives worth the timber we cut to satisfy some builder who has an order to build a fancy home for some rich suburbanite who insists on custom kitchen cabinets and inlaid wood floors? Dammit!"

"Mugger is going to be all right," she consoled him. "He will be home in a few weeks."

"Home?" He laughed. "That's the big joke of the logging industry. The logger seldom gets to settle in a home himself for very long. He lives in some shack or cramped trailer and makes do because of the ungodly hours and the remoteness of the woods. And all we get for it is condemnation from some damned environmentalist who never leaves the city and claims we're destroying his precious wilderness. It can drain a man's soul."

"You're upset," she said. "Hospitals can be very depressing. I know. Two years ago I watched my father die in a hospital room in Tucson."

"God, I'm sorry, Kit. I've never asked about your parents. Tell me about them."

She sighed deeply, staring out the windshield. "My father was ninety-three and held on to his dignity until his death. My mother and I saw to that." She turned to John. "My father was a senior adult all my life. My only regret was that I never knew him as a young man like most children do. He was healthy until he suffered a series of strokes the year before his death. They affected his ability to speak. He was always so eloquent, quoting Chaucer and Shakespeare, fretting over the loss of literacy in the college students he taught during the last few years of his teaching career."

She didn't realize she was crying until he took her in his arms and wiped her cheeks.

"When he learned he was going to become a father at such a late age, he canceled his plans to retire and continued teaching until his seventy-fifth birthday. By then I was old enough to be left alone at times, and they began to take cruises, something they had always talked about. They knew they could trust their little mousy daughter to behave during her teen years. What would he think now if he knew I wanted to go to bed with a logger?''

She laughed ironically and then her eyes filled with tears again. Somehow, by talking about her father's death, Kathryn was able to give in to the grief she had suppressed for two years.

''After the first series of strokes, he made us promise that if he became seriously incapacitated, we would never keep him alive on a life-support system. We promised. And we kept that promise. He suffered a massive stroke during the summer two years ago. We insisted they not try to keep him alive. The doctors tried to talk us out of our decision.''

She wiped her nose. ''Finally I lost my temper and accused them of just wanting the fee for the bed. They said I was distraught and I agreed, insisting that they were the major cause. To make a long story short, my father died peacefully in his sleep a few nights later. He's buried in a joint plot in a cemetery on the outskirts of Tucson, near the desert he always loved.''

''How is your mother?'' he asked, massaging her shoulders as he held her.

''She's fine. She just celebrated her eightieth birthday. She owns an apartment in a building for retirees and has lots of friends. Again, I always longed to know her when she was younger. She was brilliant and very musical. She played the piano and gave lessons on Saturday mornings. I can remember climbing up on the bench and sitting beside her while she patiently taught some little boy or girl the scales.''

''Do you play?'' he asked.

She glanced at her outstretched hand. ''Yes, but it's been a while. When I was a junior high student, I had an opportunity to enter a program for young musicians who showed potential for becoming concert pianists. Mother had contacted a man in New York who only took the most promising students. We flew back to audition and he was impressed, but when it came time to actually leave my parents, I just couldn't do it." She shrugged. "So here I am instead, teaching third graders instead of performing around the world. Perhaps I couldn't have made the grade at that. Each year the less promising students were weeded out. It's a demanding career and very harsh on the egos of tender young protégés."

"Someday I'd like to hear you play," he said.

"Pianos are difficult to move around," she said. "I play a little when I visit my mother in Tucson." She stared into the darkness for a few minutes. "I tried to get her to move up here with me, but she declined. She said I needed my own life. She never asks about my personal life. She says it's my business. I plan to see her this summer. We'll have to schedule the summer around our personal commitments, won't we?"

He nodded. "And I always thought life would settle down when I hit the middle years. Now it's worse than ever."

He held her quietly for several minutes.

"Will Mugger be all right?" she asked.

"He won't ever be back to normal. He came damned near to breaking his back. A logger with a bad back isn't much good for the heavier work, but we'll compensate. We'll find a place for him. If he can't make it in the woods, I think I can get him a job scaling for one of the boom companies on the river here at St. Maries. He's methodical and has a knack for numbers. He's not the brightest worker I've ever had, but he's one of the most dedicated, so between Swede and myself, we'll see that he's given work to make him feel useful. It's important."

"What really happened?" she asked.

"The tracks of the heel boom loader backed over his pelvis area on the first pass. When Swede heard the screams, he pulled forward and caught him again. It could have killed him, but he was carrying his chain saw. The casing and engine apparently protected him just enough to let him survive. Sort of like hiding behind a fallen tree. My God, I feel sorry for Swede. It really wasn't his fault, but I'm sure he will take the guilt to his grave."

She eased away from his comforting embrace. "It's past midnight. We'd better get home."

He drove her to the house, but didn't turn the engine off.

"Would you like to come in?" she asked.

"I would love to, but I can't. Tomorrow will be busy. I want to spend the morning with Chris, visit Mugger, then find Swede and tell him to stay in town. I'm sure he's broke and he'll need some money. He tends to drink too much when he's upset so I'll have to threaten him with some dire consequence to make him toe the line. If he stays sober, he will drive the hospital nuts acting like a mother hen, but that's better than being picked up by a town clown and thrown in jail."

She looked puzzled.

"Police."

"Oh." She sighed. "Well, good night," she said weakly, trying to hide her disappointment.

His hand caught her chin. "Remember my promise. I intend to keep it sometime this summer. It will give us each something to think about."

She smiled. "Maybe."

His mouth claimed hers for a long kiss, then reluctantly he withdrew. "I know so. I keep my promises."

THE DOOR OF the third-grade classroom flew open, and Christopher Brasher came racing in, Raymond Crosley in hot pursuit. Chris skidded to a squeaking stop at Kathryn's desk. Raymond lingered near the door.

His green eyes beaming, Chris crossed his denim-covered legs and cocked the toe of his sneakered foot against the floor. He leaned one elbow on Kathryn's desk and peered at her. He was a miniature version of John as he frowned, arching one fine, dark brow.

She glanced at Raymond, then at her wristwatch and back to Chris. "Yes?" she asked, trying to maintain a somber expression. "Can I help you two boys? Class doesn't begin for another twenty minutes. Shouldn't you be out on the playground?"

"Am I still not supposed to know you?" he whispered.

"You know me as Miss Keith," she reminded him.

He tipped his head to one side and grinned. "You know, that's like having you be two different people."

"If you're bright enough to figure that out, Chris, then you're smart enough to follow your father's instructions, aren't you?"

He nodded. "I haven't told anyone about you staying in my dad's bedroom or all the kissing or nothin'," he whispered, cupping his hand around his mouth.

"Chris, you're talking about it now," she murmured. "What if Raymond overhears you? Remember what your father told you?"

"Sure 'nuff, and I won't tell!"

"Good. And why are you and Raymond Crosley in here when you could be playing?"

"I thought you'd like to know."

"Know what?" she asked.

"Well," Chris said conspiratorially, standing tall and snapping one strap of his rainbow-colored suspenders, "Ray and I've been talking it over, and we've decided to be friends."

"Oh?" she said, surprised at this unexpected revelation.

"Yeah," he said, motioning for the husky boy to approach the desk. "This is Miss Keith," he said, and the other boy nodded suspiciously. "She's...pretty nice and...she's my...teacher."

"I know that," Ray whispered audibly.

"Ray and me, we're gonna be sidekicks," Chris continued. "I'm going to let Ray come over to Aunt Nat's and sit in my truck and teach him how to talk logger."

Kathryn suppressed an impulsive chuckle.

"And Chris gets to come home with me every Tuesday so we can go to Cub Scouts together," Ray chimed in. "And if we don't fight for a week, my mom is gonna buy me a pair of suspenders just like Chris's."

"And when did this peace treaty come about?" she asked.

"Last night," Raymond said.

"Yeah," Chris said, "last night when Ray was gonna have his big brother beat me up again. His brother was busy so we talked it over and decided to be friends instead, at least for a while."

She reached for a tissue and covered her mouth. "I think that's great. Now why don't you go out to play again?" she suggested.

"Okay, I just thought you'd like to know," Chris said.

She smiled as the boys left the room, then glanced at her watch again. *Only five minutes left of precious solitude.*

Before today she hadn't seen Chris since their dinner at the lake resort. John had stopped by for a brief goodbye shortly after lunch on Sunday. He had looked haggard.

"How's Mugger?" she had asked.

"Not so good," he had said, leaning against her kitchen table. "Oh, he's going to make it, but he's one hell of a sore guy this morning. I found Swede coping with a massive hangover, and he swears he will never touch alcohol again. I got him a room in a boarding house near the hospital for a few days so he can visit Mugger as often as he wants. He will be back in the woods Wednesday morning. I'll leave for Bonners Ferry on Thursday."

He had pulled her between his legs, resting his chin on the top of her head as her arms slid around his waist. She had buried her face against his shirt, enjoying the strength of his arms around her. How could such a large man be so trim and fit? she had wondered, remembering how he had felt and looked when they had lain together on her bed.

"I wish we had more time," she had said.

"Me, too," he had murmured against her hair.

She had looked up at him. "Will I hear from you while you're gone?"

"When I'm at the motel in Bonners Ferry, I'll call. I promised Chris I would do the same. I don't have reservations so I can't give you a name or number until I get there. Don't stay home waiting. I don't know just when I'll get back to a phone. It might be a while."

"I understand," she had said, trying to hide her disappointment. "I'll be busy with the kids, anyway. They always get a little wilder than usual as the school year winds down. Fortunately, we have two field trips planned."

"Keep an eye on my son?"

"Of course."

"But don't show him any favoritism."

"Of course not," Kathryn had agreed, smiling.

A few more kisses and he had left.

Now, as the buzzer sounded, she tried to concentrate on the afternoon schedule. At times such as these, she longed for the school year to end, almost as much as her students did.

CHAPTER EIGHT

JOHN BRASHER LET himself into the quiet motel room, glad the day had finally ended. He had begged off a side trip to a local bar where loggers tended to congregate in favor of a shower and a catnap before eating dinner.

Exhaustion sapped his usual reserve of energy. Years of conditioning to long hours and hard work had ingrained the work ethic in him. Lately some nameless change had taken its toll.

A week of demanding negotiations, repeated trips to the four sites for sale, calculations and recalculations of contract figures to reaffirm his estimates of profitability. He had learned years before to verify the board feet estimates by doing a few sample scaling estimates himself and to check the quality of the timber. Too many trees with rotting interiors could turn the sale into a losing proposition—a few hours of bending elbows with people who could aid his future in these new tracts opening up to an industry long depressed. John resented such meetings, for in spite of the logger's heavy drinking reputation, he had always limited himself.

He stepped from the shower and grabbed a towel, quickly drying himself off as he paced the room. Wrapping the towel around his hips, he sat down on the bed, then gave in to the impulse to lie down. He could dress later. Perhaps he would just skip eating. Food had lost its appeal in the last few weeks unless he was with . . . his Kit.

A smile softened his rugged features as he thought of her. A petite, dedicated teacher had sailed angrily into his life, only to turn into a loving, responsive woman who had turned his powers of concentration upside down, giving his life a powerful thrust in a new direction.

If only he had more free time, he thought. Time for his son, time to spend with Kathryn. Thinking of her again as he lay on the bed brought an immediate reaction to his body, and he rolled onto his stomach, willing himself to maintain control. Did she have any idea how she affected him? She had become the motivating force in his life lately. Each passing day brought their reunion closer. How would it happen? Where? When? Soon, he vowed.

He considered her inexperience in a sexual relationship and acknowledged to himself that the success or failure of her first experience would be his responsibility.

He had become accustomed to casual relationships since his divorce, with both parties knowing from the on-set the affair would be brief. Such encounters had ended after a few satisfying episodes, with neither partner expecting more than the other had been willing to give.

What was it like for a virgin? He tried to recall those women who had qualified since his puberty and could think of only one during his junior year in high school. She was Jennifer Busbee, who now lived in St. Maries with her teacher husband and five children. How the years changed people. He had been a linebacker on the varsity football team and she, a cheerleader. He still saw her occasionally in town. The encounters always left him curious about whether she remembered that first experimental night in the back seat of his father's Chevy Bel Air sedan. It was just manly pride, he knew. Now he had been divorced for eight, almost nine years, and she was a devoted mother and homemaker, with rounded hips and gray at her temples.

Kathryn Keith's sexual life had been put on hold by her unwillingness to experiment, her dedication to her profession, her shy manner. She was a unique woman and he longed to be with her, teach her what love was all about, satisfy her in so many ways, take her with him wherever his career might go. But her profession didn't allow for mobility. How could they work out their professional differences? There must be a way!

Could he really love her after knowing her for such a short time? Yes, of that he had no doubt. The thought of leaving her behind had brought a physical ache to his chest. The night he had told her of his plans for the future the look on her face had reflected her love for him. She had said the time had been too short, but the calendar days since their first meeting had no bearing on his feelings. If time were the only factor, he could think of several women whom he should be madly in love with, but only Kathryn came to mind when he thought about such deep emotion.

He would not do her the injustice of suggesting an affair. He knew that. So how long would it be before he asked her to make a lifelong commitment?

Life with a logging contractor husband meant one of two possible life-styles: either a marriage with a lot of absences, or one of travel together with little permanence. Marrying him would make her an instant stepmother as well as a bride. It would hardly be fair to her. Thank goodness she and Chris got along well.

As he mulled over his problems, his eyes grew heavy, and he gave in to sleep.

The jarring of the phone ringing in his ear rudely awoke him.

"Hello," he mumbled, throwing his feet to the carpeted floor. "Kit?"

"Sorry, big brother," said Natalie, "it's just your babysitting sister."

Her words grated on him. "Okay, Nat. What's he done now?"

"Nothing," she replied. "He's his usual impulsive self." She chuckled. "What's this Kit business, John? Have I stumbled on your pet name for our prim new teacher in town?"

"None of your business, Nat. Now what's the matter? You wouldn't call me at this hour just to talk."

She laughed and he glanced at his watch. "Oh, so what if it's just seven o'clock? Can't a guy be tired?"

"I assumed you would be going out somewhere," she said. "Like you used to before you became a father again."

"I'm too old for that carousing."

"Thinking about settling down?"

"That's my business."

"If it affects your son, then it's my business," she reminded him. "After all, I've been his surrogate mother for two years."

"Yes, and I appreciate it. I've paid you fairly, but I know it's been an additional burden on you and your family. I'm sorry for that, but I don't know what I would have done without you, sis. I love you."

"I love you, too, John, and I love Chris as much as my own children. Well, if you won't discuss your relationship with Kathryn Keith, I might as well get to the point. Has Helen called you?"

"Helen? Why would she call me? She doesn't know where I am."

"She does now. I told her."

"Oh, great," he groaned. "Why?"

"She called about a half hour ago and said she had to talk to you about Chris."

"I thought this wasn't about my son." He rose from the bed, the phone dangling from his fingers as he paced and talked.

"I meant there was no problem with Chris getting into trouble or being hurt. But, John, I have this funny feeling that maybe Helen has changed her mind about giving up Chris."

He tensed. "The hell she can."

"But you never went to court except to give him a middle name."

"I know and I plan to, but I've been busy and—"

"Then she still has legal rights to her son, and a judge might think you should still be paying child support and visiting your son as per the court decree."

"Dammit."

"I'm sorry, John. Maybe this is all premature," Natalie said. "Anyway, I gave her your number there since you won't be back for two more weeks. I don't know what I would do if she showed up on my doorstep. Would I have to let him go with her?"

"Like hell," he growled. "She has no right . . ."

"Can you come back early if I need you?"

"If it involves Chris's future, of course," John said, "but perhaps you're right. I'll wait and see if she calls. I'll let you know. Now I'd better let you go so I can call Kit— I mean Kathryn."

"I doubt if she's home tonight," said Natalie. "The school is having a spring musical, and every class is involved."

"Damn," he growled. "So why are you home? Aren't the kids in the program?"

"Yes, but Suzanne has a cold, and I'm staying home with her. Ronald, Mark and Chris went with Cal."

"Oh. Maybe I'll call Kathryn later. I'll go eat. If Helen can't reach me . . ."

"Don't count on it," Natalie warned. "If she's set her mind on changing things, avoiding her will only postpone the inevitable."

He said goodbye and put the phone back on the nightstand. Perhaps, John considered, he should phone Helen and call her bluff. What the hell could she be up to? he wondered. *I might as well take the offensive and find out,* he decided, reaching for the phone again. He waited impatiently. On the fourth ring she answered.

"You were trying to get in touch with me?" he asked.

"Oh, John, dear, I'm so glad you called," Helen said.

"Cut the sweet talk, Helen," John warned. "What are you up to now? Natalie said you called."

"I need to discuss our son with you," Helen replied.

"Yes?"

"Leo and I've discussed it many times, and we've reconsidered our decision to send Chris to you. We feel he would be better off here with us, in a home with two loving parents."

"Leo isn't his father."

"Who knows?" she murmured. "There was always some doubt in my mind as to—"

"Not in mine, Helen. He's my son. He will never have a stepfather."

"Perhaps a blood test would be in order to clear the air?" she asked.

"Never," he shouted. The word vibrated in the room, and he forced himself to maintain his control. "Don't waste your money. He's my son. A stranger could tell by looking at him."

"Well, that's immaterial. He needs the stability of a home, not living with an aunt who has enough children of her own. It's no better than being a ward of the courts and being shunted into a foster home. We want him back."

"You can't have him."

"The court gave me legal custody of him. These past months have merely been an extended visitation, and I've been considerate enough to waive child support payments while you were boarding him. Now that school is about to be out for the summer, we want to come and get him and let him spend the summer here in Oregon. That will give him a chance to readjust, and you can resume the support payments...and catch up on some of the deficiencies."

"No deal," John said.

"Do I have to take you to court again?" Helen asked.

"He's where he belongs."

"In a foster home?"

"It's my sister's home, and he's with me on the weekends," John said.

"A weekend father can't provide a child with the love and affection he needs. He needs stability and a mother's love."

"He has my love."

"I think a judge will see it differently, and you'd better start making the payments again, or I'll drag you through the courts until I get every dime that's due me. I was very easy on you in the divorce settlement. Those child support payments make up for only some of the deprivation I've suffered over the years."

Nausea rocked through his stomach as he listened, trying to unravel her motives. "Are you saying you expect me to pay child support when I have custody of my own child?"

"It's a small price to pay if you want to keep him and avoid the embarrassment of washing dirty domestic linen in court," Helen murmured.

"That's nothing less than blackmail!"

"That's your opinion," Helen said. "If you want to keep your son, you'll have to pay for the privilege. Otherwise, I'll go to court and swear his unstable home life and this weekend parenting trip of yours is causing him undue harm. He's always been a hyperactive child. He probably needs medication to make him more manageable."

"He needs a stable home," John insisted.

"He needs his mother," Helen countered.

"He needs two parents who will stay with him and give him love—dependable, unconditional love."

"You can't give him that," Helen chided. "Only a mother can give him that."

Kathryn's face flashed through his mind. "He's going to have a mother," John shouted into the receiver.

"You're lying. You'll have to produce this phantom mother to the judge."

"She's no phantom. She has all the qualities of a mother without ever having given birth to a child. She loves Chris as much as I do," John said. "You're wasting your time trying to get money from me, Helen. You and Leo will have to solve your financial problems somewhere else."

"You're bluffing, dear. You've remained single all this time. Why would you suddenly decide to remarry now? Just to provide your son with a mother?"

"If you try to take my son, I'll see that you—"

"Temper, temper, John. Threatening me won't help you. If you want to stay out of court, be prepared to open that tight wallet of yours. I know it's full. You'll be hearing from my attorney—soon.''

He slammed the receiver down. As he paced the floor, he ran his fingers through his hair. He would find a way to stop her.

KATHRYN COLLECTED HER MAIL and unlocked the front door of her house. Scanning the envelopes, she spotted John Brasher's bold handwriting. Only a week more and he would be home.

''Home,'' she murmured to the empty room. Her house had become a home the few times John and Chris had been there. She missed John terribly, but she had avoided spending time with Chris other than in school. She didn't want to risk hurting him if something came between John and herself. Yet every morning when he breezed into the classroom and grinned at her, her affection for him swelled. Fate had brought them into her life, and in spite of the brief time she had known them, she loved them dearly.

In the three weeks he had been gone, he had called her every few nights, but never had he written. She ripped the envelope open and pulled out a single piece of white stationery showing the logo of the motel where he was staying in Bonners Ferry.

Hesitantly she unfolded the paper, gasping when she saw his words.

''Will you marry me?'' He had signed it, ''Love, John.''

Surely he was teasing. The significance of his question provoked more questions. Why such an impulsive proposal? She touched her flaming cheek with her free hand. What if the proposal were serious and she accepted. Would she remain in St. Maries while he worked in the woods a hundred miles to the north? What kind of a marriage would that be? Had she waited all these years, only to become a weekend bride? But wouldn't weekends with John be better than nothing? And what about Chris?

She glanced at the postmark. The letter had been mailed a few days earlier. She hadn't heard from him since.

A LOUD KNOCK SOUNDED on her door early Saturday morning. When Kathryn opened the door, a weary and solemn John Brasher stared down at her.

"John?"

"Forgotten me already?"

"Of course not," she murmured, admiring the tall form filling her doorway. "Oh, John." She stepped back inside, and he followed her, closing the door behind him.

"I couldn't stay away any longer," he said, sweeping her into his arms. "Oh, Kit, how I've missed you." His mouth sought hers as her arms tightened around his neck.

"Yes, yes, I've missed you, too, my darling." She caressed his face with her palms, reveling in the strong masculine slope of his cheeks, the deep grooves around his mouth as he smiled down at her. Peering into the deep blue pools of his eyes, she felt as though she were drowning. Her heart pounded as she rejoiced at his surprise visit, and stretching to reach his mouth again, she lost herself in his kiss.

Slowly he released her and stepped away, but held on to her hand. "I have to go back tomorrow. Will you come spend the week with me?"

"I wish I could, but..." she shook her head sadly "...I have a class to teach. I couldn't just leave for a whole week."

"Why not? Don't you have sick time or time off for good behavior?"

She laughed. "I do have some days available for personal reasons."

"What could be more personal than spending a week with me in the woods near the Canadian border? It's gorgeous up there, Kit. We could have privacy and get to know each other better."

"But won't you be busy working?"

"Yes, but you could come with me. I can show you what's involved. I—did you get my letter?"

She nodded.

"Have you thought it over?"

"Yes," she whispered.

"And?"

She smiled. "It's crazy, John, but how could I say anything but . . . yes."

Slowly his mouth sought hers again, savoring the warmth and love that she was willing to give him. "Then come with me. Please."

"But . . ." She hadn't asked for a day off since starting her teaching career in this new town. She had accumulated two years' worth of unused credits. She glanced at him, surprised to see uncertainty in his handsome features. "I suppose I could. My lesson plans are all made out for the next few weeks. The class is mostly marking time for school to get out. We have a field trip to a Christmas tree farm on Wednesday."

"Good, then we'll leave today."

"Today?"

"I didn't call because I was afraid you'd talk yourself out of the idea before I came for you. Can't you pack a bag and leave with me before anyone knows I'm back? I didn't tell Chris or Nat or anyone I was coming."

Her hand trembled as she smoothed her dark hair away from her cheek. "I'd have to call the principal."

"Do it, for you and for me."

"What would we do for a whole week?" she asked.

"We'll think of something," John said, grinning.

"This is crazy."

"You're overdue for a little craziness," he replied.

"All right," she said. "I'll call Jason Overstreet before I have second thoughts about the wisdom of all this." Quickly she dialed the home number of the school's principal and explained that a personal problem had arisen and that she would be unable to teach the following week. He started to object, but she stopped him.

"This is unexpected but very important to me, Jason. My lesson plans are already on my desk. The substitute will have no problem understanding them. If it's Maybelle Bosgieter, she knows my style of teaching. We know each other quite well. I'll be gone all week, but will be back the following Monday for sure. Sorry for the short notice." Kathryn hung up before she weakened.

She turned to him. "I don't know how right this is so you had better get me out of here before I change my mind."

Within minutes her suitcase and overnight bag were packed. As he carried them to the front door, Patches strolled into the kitchen, mewing.

Kathryn groaned. "I can't just leave the cat for a week."

"Sure you can." John reached for the phone and dialed a number. "Nat, this is John." He listened. "No, I'm in St. Maries. No, please don't call Chris. Listen, Kathryn needs your help. She's going to Bonners Ferry with me for a week."

He listened for a few minutes, the grin on his face widening every few seconds. "No, she won't be at school. I've convinced her she needs an emergency vacation. I hate to do this to him, but please don't tell Chris until we're out of town. If she leaves the key somewhere, could you come over and check on her damned cat occasionally?'' He listened again. ''Thanks, sis. We'll both be forever grateful to you.'' They agreed on a hiding place for the key, and he said goodbye.

He grinned down at her, his large hands on his trim hips. ''Any more excuses, Miss Keith?''

She sighed deeply before shaking her head. ''I guess I'm ready to run away with you.''

TWO HOURS LATER, as they approached Sand Point, Idaho, Kathryn began to question the wisdom of her impulsiveness. They had spent the time together talking about Chris, his new friendship with Raymond, his progress in school.

''Other than that afternoon he and Ray played hooky and went exploring the hills south of town, he's been very good. Almost too good,'' she said.

''He's probably trying to impress you and still trying to decide how you fit into his life. Do you think he's kept quiet about . . . everything?''

''I hope so, but you know how children are. They love to tell secrets, especially to their best friends,'' she said. ''Perhaps we should have told him that we were going away.''

He shook his head. ''He would have wanted to come with us.''

''We could have brought him, too,'' she said, sending him a sideways glance.

''No, honeymoons should be taken without children,'' he said, reaching for her hand.

She swallowed hard. ''Honeymoon? Now? You want to marry me now? But I thought you meant sometime in the future. You never talked about a date. Oh, John, what are you really doing?''

"I'm asking you to elope with me. We're too old for fancy weddings. I thought something simple out of town would be the best way to handle this."

"But that makes it sound so secretive. Almost on the sly. Until your note you've never mentioned marriage. I thought . . ." She dropped her gaze. "Frankly I was prepared to . . ."

"Have an affair with me?" he said bluntly.

"Yes. Perhaps it's long overdue. Now I feel I've been brought here under false pretenses, as though I'm being kidnapped."

He applied the brake, and the truck rolled to a stop on the shoulder of the highway. "I want you to be my wife, Kit. I know we haven't known each other for long, but the moment I saw you in Avery, I knew." He turned to her. "Didn't you?"

She stared at her hands. "I was afraid to hope . . . Yes, I was attracted to you even while we were arguing, but this is so sudden, so impulsive. Why now?"

He took her hands in his. "I want you to be my wife when I make love to you."

"But I'm willing to—you don't have to marry me just in order to—oh, John, I love you and I don't want you to have regrets in a few months just because you wanted to take me to bed. It sounds, well, terribly old-fashioned."

"Your virginity warrants a traditional approach, and marriage is the only answer." He reached out and took her chin in his hand. "Now will you marry me?" He reached into his jacket pocket and withdrew a gold ring. A modest diamond sparkled in the center, surrounded by a circle of smaller diamonds. He reached for her left hand, holding it lightly to give her the opportunity to pull away.

When she didn't, he slid the ring on her third finger, touching it with his finger as it settled into place.

"We can buy the license on Monday and get married as soon as the law allows. I talked to the lab technician at the clinic in Bonners Ferry, and he's agreed to draw our blood this afternoon and process the tests. We have appointments with a physician Monday morning."

She smiled. "For a logging contractor who has been on a business trip, you surely have been busy with nonbusiness matters, John."

His mouth brushed over hers. "Sometimes my priorities change." His lips parted, capturing her mouth and bringing a burst of desire from her. "Will you marry me? This week?"

"It's still crazy," she said, "but there's a saying about it being better to have loved and lost—"

"I have no plans for losing you, Kit." He grinned. "We can grow old together. There's another saying that ends with the best is yet to come."

She laughed. "From a poem written by Robert Browning to the great love of his life, Elizabeth Barrett. That poem was a favorite of my parents."

"It can be ours, too," John said, looking into her eyes. He touched her smooth cheek with his fingertips. "When the chemistry is right, a man and woman are never too old for romance."

She nodded, gazing into his eyes. "I love you, John, so much I can't believe it. Sometimes it's a joy, but sometimes it hurts, it actually hurts...and I didn't think love would hurt, or make me feel so lonely. I've never been lonely in my life until I met you. Love is such a new experience for me. You've brought many changes into my life."

"Change can be very good for a person," he said. "You'll see. We have our whole lives ahead of us. For me, this is a second chance at building a relationship into a lasting marriage. It takes work by both partners. It won't always be easy. If you're willing to bring two people into your life and love them as much as they'll love you, I know we can make this marriage work."

"Then my answer is yes." She nestled against him. "Won't your son be surprised when he finds his teacher has become his stepmother?"

John drew back. "We can figure out how to break the news to him later. For now, let's get on to Bonners Ferry. We have things to do."

AFTER THE BLOOD SPECIMENS had been drawn, John took Kathryn to his motel. "I'll get you a room," he said.

"We can stay in the same room," she said.

"Too tempting," he replied.

"But why waste your money?"

"I'm not broke."

"Well, neither am I," she said. "If we can't share the same room, then I'll pay for my own."

"You will not," he said. He held out his motel room key. "Go inside, please. It's Room 12. I'll make the arrangements for the other room. No back talk." He left the truck and hurried to the motel office, leaving her to stare at the stubborn set of his broad shoulders, his lean hips swaying slightly as his long stride took him away.

She let herself into the room. Glancing around, she thought of the other time she had been in his room. A few men's toiletries and an electric razor sat on the dresser. Thoughts of actually living with him filled her again with uncertainty. Could she be his wife? She could still refuse. It was her choice, and he had no right to insist she marry

him, not in this liberated age. Did he realize he had selected the least liberated woman in town to be his mate?

Perhaps she didn't know what kind of person she was.
All her adult life she had been alone, making her own decisions, handling her own financial affairs, coming and
going when she chose, free to do as she pleased, when she
pleased. Now there would be a husband and a son to
consider.

A son. Chris had become like a son to her. Of all the
children who had passed through her third-grade classroom over the years, only one had become like her own
child, and never had she become involved with a parent.
She had broken all her self-imposed rules of conduct, after years of convincing herself they were based on professional ethics and were crucial to her career. Was she a
hypocrite now? Or a realist at long last?

John entered, closing the door softly behind him. She
turned as he dropped a key on the dresser. The stillness of
the room drew them nearer. She thought of her responsibilities back at St. Maries, her students, her mother and
friends so far away in Arizona, even the principal who had
driven her to Idaho. Had they all meshed to bring her here
to this motel with this man who was still little more than
a stranger to her?

She ached for his touch. Did he know how much? Her
eyes darted over his torso before settling on his face, only
to find him staring intently at her.

"I couldn't get the other room," he said.

"Why not? Were there no vacancies?"

He shook his head. "The thought of you in another
room, all by yourself..." His arms reached out, coaxing
her closer. "I wanted you here with me," he said, as he
pulled her roughly into his embrace.

"I could spend a lifetime in your arms," she said, sighing deeply. A burst of desire raced through her as she leaned against him. "John," she murmured as his lips caressed her cheek, the corner of her mouth, her chin.

Her head fell back, allowing him room. His mouth caressed the soft skin at the base of her ear before moving to her throat. The thudding in her temples grew stronger when his hand moved to her blouse, and his fingers unfastened a few buttons. His hand slid inside her clothing to linger on the swell of her breasts.

When his warm mouth caressed the valley between her breasts, she trembled. "Yes," she whispered. Sweeping her into his arms, he carried her to the bed. As he gazed at her, she moved slightly, twisting the blouse around her body. He watched as she opened the rest of the buttons. Her dark hair clung to the quilted spread, forming a halo around her face.

"Love me now," she moaned. "I want to know what love is. Don't make me wait," she pleaded, and she held out her hand to him.

CHAPTER NINE

PIECE BY PIECE John removed her clothing, dropping it from the bed. When she lay nude before him, he groaned aloud.

"Kit, you're beautiful, so beautiful."

A surge of confidence filled her as she gazed at him. After years of thinking she was somehow lacking in feminine charm, this man had changed everything, turned her into a sensuous woman able to give him love, accept his lovemaking and experience the ecstasy of fulfillment.

She clutched the quilted spread in one hand as she watched him remove his shirt. His shoulders were broad, muscular, the conditioning from years of hard physical work reflected in his movements. When his hand settled on his belt buckle, her eyes were drawn downward, wondering, curious.

John's fingers slowly lowered the tab, and it grated over the teeth of his zipper. Her heart thudded in her bosom as he removed the rest of his garments.

She restrained her own hand in its desire to touch him. He paused beside the bed. The photos and sketches she had seen in movies and books were no match for this magnificent man who wanted to make love to her. She had expected to be frightened, but seeing him now, aroused because of her, buried any hint of fear beneath the desire unleashed within her own loins.

Now was the time for enlightenment, time to experience the true union of a man and a woman.

His mouth claimed hers, tasting it, and she delighted in his movements, opening her lips to allow his entry. Dazed by his sensual exploration, she arched toward him, anxious to feel him close against her. His mouth moved lower, inch by inch down her body, lingering to kiss her navel and startling her with a tender kiss low on her abdomen. His hand ran over her slender hip and down her thigh, sliding between her knees and upward.

When would this tantalizing movement of his hand ever stop? She had thought they would merely... unite. Instead, he was turning each cell of her body into a tiny flame of desire. She moved her legs apart, and his hand moved closer, sliding over the silky skin of her inner thighs and settling against her, pressing gently and arousing her unbearably.

All the while, he continued tasting her mouth, touching her tongue and sending shards of longing throughout her. His dark head moved down to her throat, testing the pounding pulse before inching toward her breast. He teased the crest by circling it with his moist tongue. She moaned, shifting her torso closer to him, begging for him to take her nipple in his mouth. A tremor raced through her when he satisfied her longing.

She clutched his dark head as he moved to the other breast, bringing it to a heightened peak of arousal. He shifted his large body, suspending himself over her before settling between her legs.

Feeling the heat of his manhood against her, she tensed. He held her face in his hands, kissing her lightly.

"I'll be so gentle, so careful," he whispered, his voice hoarse as he began his entry, pausing to give her time to accept him. As the barrier of her body parted, she cried out, her body stiffening beneath him.

"I'm sorry," he groaned. "Are you all right?" He continued to hold her face, waiting for her to reply.

"I think I might explode," she said with a gasp, her hands tight against his ribs.

"It must hurt." He frowned.

"A little." Her voice wavered. "I want to...please you."

"And I you," he assured her.

She tried to smile, but her body was fighting its own battle of conflicting responses.

"Relax, sweetheart," he whispered, kissing her mouth lightly. "This lovemaking takes getting used to."

They lay together quietly for a few minutes.

"Feeling better?" he asked. "Am I too heavy?"

"No, no, you're fine...I'm fine...oh, John," and she closed her eyes, unwilling to let him see the effect their union was having on her. She moved her hips, marveling at the sensations beginning to build within her. A tiny smile softened her lips.

He kissed her again. Gradually she became aware of the increase in his subtle thrusts. Her body was being turned inside out. Instinctively she knew the rhythm. Her movements matched his, driving herself to a pinnacle of sensual need.

She heard her own disjointed voice cry his name as reality exploded into tiny fragments of ecstasy. Enthralled with the startling experience, she continued to move beneath him, sending him to his own climactic fulfillment.

He buried his face against her hair for an endless moment before shifting his weight to one side and bringing her with him. Settling her in his arms, he continued to catch his breath.

With her fingertips she touched his chest, playing with the coiling hairs scattered down his stomach.

Suddenly he tightened his arms and twisted her head upward. Gazing into her eyes, he murmured, "You're a very passionate woman, Kit."

THE SETTING SUN SHONE across the bed, its dying rays filling the room with a warm pumpkin glow.

John touched her cheek, feeling its soft warm texture beneath his fingers. She stirred. "You were asleep, love. Sorry to wake you," he said.

"I don't know how I could have fallen asleep," she murmured against his chest.

"Lovemaking does that to some people," he replied.

She remained silent for several minutes. "And you?" she asked.

"No," he said, kissing the top of her head. "I rested during your nap. Just holding you was enough." His stomach began to rumble as he chuckled. "I made a shambles of my promise to make you my wife before I made love to you, didn't I?"

"You're forgiven," she said. "I . . ." She tightened her arms around his waist, then suddenly shifted in his arms and turned away from him, burying her face in the quilted spread. A sob escaped her, and Kathryn's body stiffened as he touched her bare shoulder.

"Kit? What's wrong, Kit?" He nuzzled her ear, kissing the tiny lobe lightly.

She shook her head, still hiding her face. The sobs grew louder.

"Kit, honey, are you in pain? Have I done something? Have I hurt you? I tried to be...careful." He rose on one elbow and forced her to turn and face him. "Now tell me why you're so sad."

Her tear-streaked face was flushed. "I'm...not sad," she hiccuped.

"Then why are you crying? I've never seen you cry before. Have I fallen in love with a crying woman?"

She shook her head slowly. "It's just—just that I never thought I would ever...know what it would be like to have...a man make..." She took a deep breath and slowly smiled. "How many thirty-five-year-old virgins have you made love to?"

He laughed. "Just one. And this one is so special that I don't care about any others." He grazed her mouth with his.

"I was probably the only mid-life virgin left on this continent," she said.

"I doubt that. I know a few men my age who have never been with a woman so there must be more women in the same predicament. The whole world doesn't have to be sexually active. People without experience don't flaunt it like those who are active."

"You're joking," she replied. "Loggers have reputations. I've heard people talking, and loggers seem to be..."

He laughed. "I'll admit the two I know aren't loggers, but loggers have been known to stretch the truth a little. Some of their prowess is undoubtedly exaggerated. Part of the myth has grown up over the years, making us into super savage beasts roaming the dark forests of North America." He grimaced. "Did you know there's a myth about Maine loggers that says long ago they vowed to rid Maine of white pine and virgins?"

"Did they succeed?" she asked.

"Almost on the white pines, out the women would never tell. I'm sure it's more myth than truth, probably spread by the city men who didn't understand the logger's life-style and feared the lumberjack when he came to town on annual log drives. Our expectations often get mixed with our fears."

He shrugged. "Sometimes life turns out differently from what we are taught to expect, Kit. Look at us. You thought you would marry as a young woman, and I thought everyone had only one marriage for a lifetime. Now we've found each other, and we have a chance to build a future together. It's never too late. Think of the fun we can have getting you caught up." He grinned. "For a change I'll be the teacher. Ready for lesson two?"

She nodded and her palms worked their way up his chest, surrounding his neck. "Ready," she said, pulling his head down and capturing his lips, surprising them both when she pressed her body against his.

His reaction was immediate. "The student is getting ahead of the teacher," he whispered.

"I was always quick to catch on," she teased. "I used to drive the teachers crazy."

"You drive me crazy, too," he said, sliding his hand down her body. "Now pay attention and I'll show you some new techniques guaranteed to make you want lesson three." His tongue traced a moist pattern around her breasts, teasing their crests into eager points of desire.

As he explored her slender body, her moans grew louder. "Please, John, please, I want to feel you inside me again. Show me, convince me it wasn't a dream." Her hands glided down his body, touching him, guiding him, marveling at the shudder that moved through him.

"How can I refuse you, Kit?" He groaned as he settled against her loins, sinking into her as her legs wrapped around him. "My love. My only love," he whispered, and his mouth claimed hers again as their bodies blended to the harmony of their union.

Later, as they lay resting in each other's arms, he chuckled. "I knew I could never do it again."

"Make love to me?"

He shook his head. "I expect to do that many times. But the first time can never be repeated, can it? This time, was it different?"

"Better," she said, smiling up at him. "This time I knew what to expect. I wasn't frightened. Oh, John, I love you so very, very much." She kissed his smiling lips. "I don't know what lies ahead for us, but you've spoiled me now. I could never give up what we've had today. You've helped me discover a part of myself that I've denied all these years. I still can hardly believe I'm here with you, in this motel room. It's positively scandalous, isn't it?"

"It's our private business," John said. "No one will know. In a few days we'll be husband and wife, so what does it matter? And I meant what I said before you dozed off. You are a very passionate woman."

She glanced away. "I can't believe I'm doing all these wonderful things. It's as though my mind has left my body, freeing me to be the woman I thought I could never be. I thought love had passed me by, that no man would ever find me attractive enough to want me."

"I'll always want you, Kit. That's a promise."

"UNLESS I WANT to get married in jeans or slacks, I had better go shopping this afternoon," Kathryn said, stretching as she lay in bed watching the room fill with early light. She turned to him. "It's been wonderful, John, two unexpected days of..." She glanced at her watch. "The school bell is about to ring, and here I am, lying in bed naked, with you, and I don't want to ever leave. What have you done to me?''

"Are you blaming me for your fall from grace?" he asked, touching her cheek lightly with his fingers.

"No," she said, then kissed the tips of his fingers. "And it wasn't a fall. We've risen to a new plateau...together. But I suppose it can't last forever."

"No, my love, the maid needs to do her work, and I don't know about you, but I'm hungry." He kissed her cheek. "We'll have breakfast. We forgot dinner last night."

"We were too busy," she agreed, arching to kiss him.

"We're living on love, but my stomach says it's time for a meal," he said. "I've got you a key so you can come and go when you choose."

"I'm glad you didn't insist on separate rooms. I would have been very lonely without you," she murmured, sliding her hand over his ribs to his bare hip and enjoying his sharp intake of breath.

"I'm sorry I have to leave you alone this afternoon," John said, "but I'm meeting with the forest service people again. This is the day I find out if anyone else has been bidding against me for the tracts. I'll come back with a few years of work or my certified check."

"Oh, you have to put up money before you get the contract?"

"Of course."

"How much?"

"Just under fifty thousand."

"Fifty thousand dollars?" she exclaimed. "How can you get that much money?"

"I'm not poor," John said, grinning, and he kissed her nose. "Ten years ago I had one job that brought in over a million dollars. But since I sold off some of my equipment, those jobs are out of my league."

"A million dollars?" She frowned as he turned to her, propping himself up on one elbow. "I can't imagine so much money. I thought you were...that old trailer you live in...if you make that kind of money, why don't you..." She felt a wave of heat move up her cheeks. "I'm sorry. I'm prying into your financial affairs."

"Does this mean you aren't marrying me for my money?" he asked.

"How could I be, when I have never given it a thought? Oh, John, when you're around all I can think about is...just you!"

"Then you're marrying me for my body?"

She blushed again. "Yes, your body and your mind and your wonderful personality and your charming smile. Your blue eyes make me shiver when you look at me and you're so big. I've never known a man as tall as you. Money was never a factor. You've always been so overwhelming I never thought about your profession and how much money you have. I don't care. It's none of my business, although I don't mind if you know how much I make as a teacher," and she told him a modest amount.

"For taking care of other people's bratty kids?" he teased, stroking the upper swell of her breast.

"They're not bratty," she replied, slapping playfully at his hand. "A few are, but most of the time I love them all."

"Even my son?" His thumb moved across her nipple.

"Especially your son." Her hand slid up his arm, testing the hardness of his biceps before moving to his shoulder and down his chest. "I fell for your handsome son long before I met his mysterious father. Oh, John, I had so many wrong impressions about you."

He grinned. "And you definitely were not the prune-faced old-maid teacher who had been pestering me with terse notes."

"Were they really so terse?" She tweaked a few dark hairs on his chest.

"Rather." His mouth dipped to her breast, tasting the aroused nipple.

She tried to ignore his mouth. "What made them so..." A tremor raced through her body.

He glanced toward her face. "They were demanding. They made me feel as though I were being reprimanded for my truancy and was being called into the principal's office, as though I were another pupil instead of a responsible parent." His attention returned to her body as his hand slid to her rounded hip. He shoved the blanket aside.

"I'm sorry," she murmured, her hand wandering to his dark head as he moved lower. Excitement overshadowed her alarm as he buried his face against her thighs. His hands moved her legs apart, and he rose above her.

"John?" Her hands clutched at his shoulders. "John." Her eyes clung to his as the heat of his desire found the sensitive core of her need. Her body arched from the bed as a sudden burst of ecstasy scalded her to a new peak, and a shuddering climax moved through her. Her legs entwined his hips, holding him against her until the tremors subsided, leaving her breathless.

"Oh, John," she said, gasping as he began to move again, driven by his own desire to fill her again and again, finally bringing them both to exhaustion at last.

As she lay in his arms, marveling at all that had happened, she sighed deeply. "I never knew..." Her arm tightened around his body.

"Did you think we had done it all these last two days,
my love? Our intimacy has just begun to grow. We can
learn from each other in the days and months and years
ahead."

"But I know so little," she whispered.

"Didn't you tell me you were a gifted child in school?"
He tipped her face up to his.

She nodded.

"Then use some of that latent genius to explore this
new world of ours called marriage."

LATER THAT DAY, with the marriage license in the breast
pocket of his jacket, they celebrated the winning of the
timber sale by driving to Sand Point for dinner and
champagne.

Kathryn dipped a piece of lobster into the crystal dish
of drawn butter, then popped it into her mouth. She
chewed it for several seconds and swallowed. "Sinfully
delicious," she said, smiling across the table at John.

"Almost as good as prime rib," he agreed and reached
for her hand. "Happy?"

She squeezed his hand and sighed. "Exceedingly. I'm
afraid I'll wake up and find this all a dream." She closed
her eyes for a moment, then busied herself with another
bite of lobster. "I found a dress this afternoon. It's not
fancy, but for me it's daring. I didn't want to look like a
grade-school teacher." Her melodious laughter filled the
air, and a couple at the next table glanced toward them.
She covered her mouth with the linen napkin. A giggle
escaped her lips.

"Yes? And what's so funny about buying a wedding
dress?" he asked.

"Every time I saw another woman, I would wonder
what she had done last night or this morning. I couldn't

stop smiling. Is it possible that women who smile the most are in love?"

"It's possible, but you might be overreacting just a little, my love," he cautioned. "Surely you smiled before you came on this trip."

"I was in love with you before this trip."

He nodded. "You make it sound as though you never smiled until you met me. That's flattering, but hardly true."

"Oh, I smiled," she admitted. "But sometimes I had to force myself. It's easier now."

The waiter cleared their plates away. While they waited for dessert, they were content to silently admire each other.

When the waiter set tiny servings of rich cheesecake before them and refilled their coffee cups, they smiled up at him.

He cleared his throat. "Will there be anything else?"

"Not here," John said, his face overly somber.

Kathryn suppressed a giggle as she shook her head.

The waiter mumbled beneath his breath before nodding, then took the tray containing the bill and John's credit card and quickly left.

"You embarrassed him," Kathryn whispered.

"He has too much starch in his collar," John replied. "I wanted to see him bend a little."

She took a small bite of cheesecake. "What happens now that you've won the contract, John?"

"We finish up our work above Avery and move the equipment north."

"How soon?"

"I'm trying for mid-August."

"So soon? That's less than three months away."

"I'll need to get Swede and the others settled. We'll have to hire some new men. I've already scouted for living quarters, but there are always last-minute problems. We'll spend most of the winter cutting for roads to be graded after the spring thaw."

"You log all winter?"

"As much as we can. Some of the best logging is done when the ground freezes. It's the spring that stops us. It depends on the weather, the amount of work we have and the mill orders."

"Don't you get awfully cold during the winter?" she asked.

"That's why loggers wear red long johns. We're tough," he said, tucking a thumb under each armpit and grinning mischievously.

She laughed. "You're teasing. And I'll bet you don't even own a pair of red long johns."

"You're right, but I do wear thermal underwear when the weather calls for it. Loggers learned to layer their clothing long before it became fashionable for you women. Calk boots and wool socks keep our feet warm. The sawyers wear leather pants, which provide a certain amount of warmth. Gloves and knit caps help, too, but when the wind decides to blow on a mountaintop, you have to psych yourself up to endure the elements."

"Doesn't it get dangerous?" she asked. "I'm glad I'm in a classroom with heat and windows."

"If it gets too bad, we stop and drink coffee. Sometimes it's laced with whatever keeps a man's insides warm. But I send them home if it becomes too severe. Time is money, and they hate to stop unless it's completely impossible to work. When hands get numb, accidents can happen. It isn't worth the cost of a man's life or limb to cut a few more trees. I have a good record with the workmen's compensation people here in Idaho. I want to keep it that way.''

''Do you have orders for the lumber you cut?''

''It's timber or logs, Kit. The trees don't become lumber until they're processed through the sawmill.''

''Oh.'' Kathryn frowned. ''I have a lot to learn about your work, don't I?''

''We'll remedy that. This summer, when school is out, I'll take you and Chris, and we'll spend some time up near one of the landings.''

''I'd like that, and I'm sure Chris will be excited. Where do you sell your lum—logs?''

''The ones that are log-house size will go to a log-home company in Western Montana. The larger white pines go to Coeur d'Alene by truck to a plywood mill, and the cedars will go to Washington state. I have verbal commitments for most of the timber, and I'll tie the deals up in writing next week.''

She grew quiet, concentrating on her cheesecake.

''What's wrong, Kit?''

''We'll be back in the real world next week,'' she replied. ''I'll be teaching, and you'll be on the road or in the woods. Our lives will be back to normal, as though none of this had happened.''

''We'll work it out, Kit,'' he promised. ''Our marriage will mean changes, that's all.''

''School breaks for summer in a few weeks,'' she said. ''But summer is your busiest time, isn't it?''

He nodded.

''What happens to me when you move to Bonners Ferry?'' she asked, afraid to hear his reply. ''And what about Chris?''

''You'll both come with me, of course.''

She frowned at him. "But I signed a contract for another year in St. Maries."

"You can break it."

"I don't know."

"Find out," John said, and his voice tightened. "I'm not marrying you to leave you behind."

"But I want to continue teaching," she said. "It's all I've ever done."

"Can't you teach in Bonners Ferry for a few years?"

She shrugged. "Perhaps. I just didn't think about…all this. Moving, changing jobs, having a son to take care of."

"You know Chris already, probably better than I do. Under the circumstances, can't you change jobs easier than I can? Teachers are everywhere. I own my own company. You know that."

She stared at her hands lying on her lap, feeling suddenly stupid and insecure. "I'm sorry, John. I—I just didn't think. Until you wrote me that note, I didn't know you wanted to marry me. I haven't had time to think things through."

"I'm sorry, too," John said more gently, and he took her hand and squeezed it. "I've rushed you. Do you want to wait? I just thought, well, hell, Kit, I love you and see no reason to drag this out, but if you're having second thoughts, we can back off."

"Oh, no!" She met his troubled gaze. "Of course not." She folded her napkin and placed it neatly beside her dessert plate. "Where would we live if Chris and I came with you?" she asked.

"In the trailer," he said simply, and he took a sip of coffee.

"But it's so small. We'd be in each other's way."

He scowled. "That's what Helen always said."

Kathryn's eyes darkened. "I'm sorry. I wasn't complaining. It's just that I have a career. If I lived in the
mountains, I couldn't teach. Chris has to go to school.
We'd have to live in town, and we wouldn't see you very
often and..." Suddenly a choking sensation gripped her
throat.

He studied the silverware still on the table. "I've always had a dream that someday I could provide my
workers and their families with a camp, one that would
have a school and a little store, even if it's just a vehicle
like the old wanigans that used to travel with the logging
camps and river drives."

His fist pounded on the table. "Dammit, it's just not
fair to always tear families apart. Logging is notorious for
doing just that. Do you know the divorce rate in the timber industry is almost as high as it is in police work? Men
stay in the woods, or live in temporary camps where they
spend their time playing cards and drinking too much.
The wives live miles away in a town and get just as lonely.
Sometimes the men are tempted by women who seek them
out and offer them a solution to their loneliness. The
women in town find some man who will give them a little
attention while their husbands are away. The women who
don't fool around and stay home are like widows, raising
the children alone, making the decisions, paying the bills,
often seeing their husbands only on weekends."

"Why don't the men drive home each night?" she
asked.

"If the men did go home each night, they would be so
tired they'd be more like zombies than husbands. So they
camp out in timber towns or near a bar or lodge and spend
an hour of leisure drinking with their co-workers rather
than taking the long trip into town."

"Why don't the wives live in the timber towns with their husbands? I would think they would want to be together," Kathryn said.

"Most women won't tolerate such primitive living conditions."

"It sounds selfish on the wives' parts," she said.

"Avery has some wonderful women who try to keep their families intact, but they are in the minority. And when they get settled in a place and make friends, the sites are logged over and the work moves. When the jobs move, the loggers move with them so the family must decide all over again if they want to stay together and live a transitory life, or if the kids would be better off in a larger town with a school and stability, but dammit, how can you have stability when the family is torn apart?"

Kathryn watched as various emotions played over his rugged features. This was a side of John she had never seen, his compassion for his workers and their personal lives. He seemed raw with frustration.

"Why do they stay with the work if the problems are so great?" she asked.

He shrugged. "Sawdust gets in a man's blood. Why did my great-great-grandfather come over the hump from Maine when the white pines had all been cut? Lumberjacks cleared the land so the farmers could plant their fields and towns could be built, but a logger can't handle civilization for long. Why did my great-grandfather leave Minnesota when the daylight filled the swamp? Why did my grandfather stay in the business when he lost his leg on a log drive? He laughed whenever you asked him. Said his leg was better than his life. He used to laugh and say, 'Holy old mackinaw, I lost some peaveys and lost my leg, but I'll never lose my life in the woods.' He was right. He died in his sleep one night, two weeks before he was to bid on a timber sale in Oregon.''

"What about your father?'' she asked, recalling his sister's words.

He smiled. "My dad had a close call a few years ago. He banged up his shoulder pretty bad. Mom talked him into retiring. Now they live in Yuma, Arizona. Dad says he's crazy to live in the desert, but it's good for Mom's arthritis. He tries to imagine the country before some prehistoric species of loggers cleared the swamp and turned the Southwest into a dry desert. He insists the saguaro cactus, Joshua trees and yucca plants are all mutated trees that need a little rain. He says when he dies they won't need to embalm him because they will find only sawdust in his veins. He's probably right.''

"Isn't it strange that your parents and my mother live in Arizona and we met here in Idaho?'' Kathryn said, trying to lighten the mood.

"Perhaps we'll all get together someday,'' he agreed.

"That would be so nice, but my mother is eighty years old and doesn't travel anymore. We'd have to visit her.''

"Soon,'' he promised.

"I had no idea the work was so demanding. I know the restaurants open at four in the morning, but I'm never up that early.''

"Their early customers are mostly the truck drivers,'' he said. "The yarding crews are already at the landings, getting ready to load.''

She nodded. "The logging trucks rumble past the school at all hours, and most of the students' fathers work in the woods or at the plywood mill in town. I'm still getting used to seeing men wearing red suspenders instead of cowboy belts. Logging has always had a certain mystique about it, but despite the mythology and glamour, there must be many very exhausted men.''

"Sometimes I wonder how a man in this business finds the strength to ever have sex with a woman,'' he said.

She smiled. "I haven't noticed it affecting your libido.''

"You make the difference, sweetheart.''

The waiter returned with John's charge card and slip. When John signed it and laid down a generous tip, the man smiled. "Have a nice evening, folks,'' he said before turning away.

"We will,'' John murmured as he guided Kathryn from the restaurant into the twilight. "We will.''

CHAPTER TEN

"MY WORD, WHO IS this gorgeous woman standing before me?" John exclaimed.

"Do you like it?" she asked, slowly turning around, glancing over her shoulder to see if he approved.

"I love it, and especially the hair. It changes your whole appearance."

She ran her hand through her new short hairstyle. "It was so impulsive. I've always made do with what nature gave me."

He laughed. "No one at school will recognize the former Miss Keith. She's gone forever, replaced by this sensuous woman who's about to become Mrs. John Brasher." He touched one of the curls that graced Kathryn's forehead. "I've always thought women should wear their hair long, but you've made a believer of me. That cut makes you look worldly, sexy, like a woman in love."

She touched the short, tapered back, then ran her fingers through the curly top, pulling a curl down over her forehead in a vampish movement, grinning at him. "Is the style too young for me?"

"You're as young as you feel," John said, smiling, then he pulled her close. "The dress is sexy, too. I thought wedding dresses were supposed to be somber and drab. Plain white or that awful creamy-brown color."

"It's called ecru, and I almost bought one that color so watch your mouth, mister."

"What made you choose this gauzy pastel flower garden?"

She touched the neckline of the dress, stroking her finger across the edge of the yellow, pink and green voile, its subtle shades blending in a delicate swirling pattern.

"Because it's risqué?" she murmured, admiring the rise and fall of a few inches of cleavage. "I've always hidden behind my clothing until now. No more," and she touched her breast again. "I liked the colors and the way wearing this made me feel. It's the new me." She turned her attention to him. "You're very handsome yourself. You must have planned this all along. Otherwise, why did you bring that good-looking gray dress suit and that tie?" She caressed the tiny fleur-de-lis pattern on his maroon tie. "You're very handsome indeed," and her fingers returned to rest on her breast.

"Clever woman," he said, his fingers covering hers as he pulled her close and kissed her. "Well, Miss Keith, let's go change your name. The justice of the peace is waiting."

Within minutes they were waiting to be admitted to the justice's chambers. The secretary kept smiling, making Kathryn feel uncomfortable and on display.

The perceptive secretary offered them coffee. "You're probably nervous," she said. "Just relax. You're the third wedding today. There's nothing to it."

Oh, how wrong the secretary was, Kathryn thought. She flinched when John reached for her hand. The hand on the wall clock jumped a notch, and Kathryn jumped with it.

"Nervous?" John whispered.

"A little," she admitted.

"This isn't very romantic," John murmured. "I'm sorry."

"It's fine," she replied, then concentrated on stilling her pounding heart. Doubts about her impulsive decision raced through her mind, to be immediately replaced with images of their lovemaking, their plans for the future, Chris and his need for a stable family, and John. She hadn't had a chance to tell her mother. What would she think? Clichés of second childhoods, lovers in midlife crises, old-maid teachers being swept off their feet...

The justice's chamber door opened, and a smiling couple hurried out, followed by two giggling friends. "Next," the rotund man said, extending his hand to John.

The secretary and a court stenographer from the office next door were their witnesses. The promises were made, a solid gold band was slipped on her finger and suddenly John was kissing her.

The reality of their marriage hit Kathryn as they stood on the steps of the building. She was Mrs. John Brasher. Kathryn Brasher. Miss Kathryn Keith no longer existed. And this metamorphosis had been brought about by an exchange of trite words she couldn't remember. Images of white gowns and pastel flowers, bridesmaids and flower girls, the mother of the bride crying over the loss of a daughter fleeted through her mind's eye. A tinge of disappointment filled her until John took her hand again.

"You were a thousand miles away," he said, leading her down the stairs.

"More like one thousand five hundred," she admitted. The truck loomed ahead.

"In Tucson?" he asked, opening the cab door and assisting her up.

"It was just a touch of nostalgia," she replied. "I always thought I'd be married in a—"

"Church?" he asked. "I'm sorry, Kit, but does the location make a difference? If it's right, it's right. I couldn't wait any longer. I wanted you, needed you as my wife. I love you."

"I love you, too," she said, accepting his kiss.

WHEN THEY ARRIVED at Natalie's home Friday afternoon, Chris met them at the door.

"Wow, Miss Keith, what happened to you?" Chris said with a gasp. "Did my dad do that to you? Wow, have you changed! Wait till I tell Raymond."

John grabbed his son's sleeve. "Stop. Let's go inside and talk. Kathryn and I have something to tell you."

"But I . . ." Chris's gaze swung from John to Kathryn, and his excited smile changed to apprehension. "Okay, but this had better not be something bad. Did that mean old Mrs. Bosgieter call you? I don't like substitutes. Just because Billy Bates poured glue on my papers and I marked his face with a fat green felt marker, she got all mad and . . ." He sighed deeply. "How was I supposed to know it wouldn't come off?" His wide green eyes sent them both a silent plea for understanding and sympathy. When none came, he added, "So I told her you were on a trip together and she better not—"

"Mrs. Bosgieter never called us, Chris," John said.

Chris's mouth fell open. "She didn't?"

"No, young man, but thanks for warning us." John took his son's arm and marched him into Natalie's house. Chris's enthusiasm waned and his feet dragged until John took his reluctant hand and led him into the kitchen.

Natalie shooed her own three children out the back door. "Should I leave? Do you want to be alone? You both look terribly serious."

"No," John said, "you should stay. We may need your help."

Natalie raised a dark eyebrow to her brother, but he shook his head. "Coffee, anyone?" she asked. No one responded so she poured three cups of coffee and a glass of milk, tossed some oatmeal cookies on a plate and motioned the others to sit down.

John took a long drink of the hot coffee and swallowed. "Chris, when you misbehave in class you'll get disciplined. You can't expect special favors just because I know Miss Keith. And, son, that's what we need to talk about." He glanced at Kathryn and Natalie before returning his attention to his son.

"Your behavior will be more important than ever now," John continued. "Miss Keith and I, we—"

"Are you gonna live together, like on television?" Chris asked excitedly.

John groaned aloud. "No, Chris, well, yes, we are going to live together, but... Chris, Kathryn and I were married yesterday in Bonners Ferry. She's my wife now. She's Mrs. John Brasher."

"Oh my," Natalie said, gasping and spilling her coffee.

John shot her a glance before returning his attention to Chris. Chris continued to stare at them. "Do you understand what that means, Chris?"

"I think so," Chris replied, his mouth pursed. "Not like my mother and that old Leo. If they had gotten married, he woulda been my dad, but I never wanted him for a dad. He—"

"Chris, that's enough," John warned.

"He means like me and your Uncle Cal," Natalie suggested.

"Right," John replied.

"Does that mean we'll be a family, a real family?" Chris asked.

"Yes," John said.

"Wow, that's great, but..." Chris frowned at his father, then Kathryn. "Now what do I call you, Miss Keith?"

Laughter filled the kitchen. Kathryn moved to the empty chair beside Chris and took his hand. "In class you'll continue to call me Miss Keith. At home you can call me Kathryn or Kitty or Kit like your father does, or whatever you feel most comfortable with. We'll work that out," she said reassuringly as she squeezed his hand and smiled.

"Someday..." Chris paused for several seconds as he studied her face, "...someday can I call you...Mom?"

Kathryn swallowed. "If that is the name you really want to use. You don't have to, but..." she paused as she wiped a tear from her cheek "...I would be proud to have you be my son and call me Mom."

"Oh, Miss Keith," Chris cried, plunging into her arms. He buried his face against her cotton knit top, his small arms tight around her neck. "I wanted you for my real mom ever since...ever since I...from the very first time I..." His voice broke. Her arms encircled him, and she pulled him onto her lap.

She held him until his crying stopped and only an occasional sob shook his lean body. She motioned for a tissue, and Natalie gave her a handful. She kissed the top of Chris's wavy dark head. "You can be my son and I'll be your mother." She glanced lovingly at John. "I think that would make your father very happy. Now, why don't you wipe your face and finish your cookies?"

"Okay...Mom," Chris agreed, and he took two tissues. "I'm not really a crybaby."

"I know, Chris, but it's okay to cry, especially at times like these," Kathryn said. She squeezed his shoulders, and he slid off her lap. John's hand appeared with another supply of tissues.

"For you," he murmured.

As she wiped her eyes, she heard Natalie blow her nose, then busy herself refilling the coffee cups.

"Well," Natalie said, sliding back into her chair, "I knew you two were smitten with each other. Cal and I were hoping for wedding bells later in the year."

"And here we were, trying to be so discreet," John said, chuckling.

"Chris doesn't know the meaning of the word," Natalie said.

"Probably not." All three adults looked at Chris.

"Well, I think it's great," Natalie said. "I'm very happy for you both. You make a marvelous couple." She frowned. "But why the sudden marriage?"

"So I could have a real mom, Aunt Nat!" Chris exclaimed.

Natalie's puzzled expression changed to one of concern as she stared at her brother.

John cleared his throat. "Because we love each other and decided not to wait," he said. "We grabbed the brass ring. For some people it only comes around once."

CHRIS BRASHER AND Raymond Crosley ignored the No Trespassing sign nailed to the fence post and scooted beneath the bottom wire of the barbed wire fence.

"Saturday is the bestest day of the week," Chris said, racing up the mountainside ahead of his huskier friend.

"Wait for me," Ray called, and Chris slowed his pace, but managed to stay several yards ahead.

When Chris reached the three boulders that marked the apex of the wooded hill south of town, he crawled up on the highest one and waited. Ray stopped to catch his breath, grabbing onto the lower limb of a pine tree.

"Ouch," he complained. "The needles stick."

"Then get on up here, pardner," Chris called. "We get to eat when you get here. I promised my new mom we wouldn't eat until then." He reached into his knapsack and pulled out two sandwich bags containing bologna on whole wheat bread and dangled them in the air.

Ray licked his lips and scrambled up the last few yards. "Gimme that and stop teasing."

Chris relinquished one of the sandwiches.

The boys sat munching the sandwiches and watching a magpie. When Ray tore a piece of crust from his sandwich and tossed it on the ground, the magpie ventured close enough to snag it. The boys snickered and the startled magpie flew to a branch in a nearby pine tree.

"I'm glad you talked Miss Keith into making bologna instead of roast beef," Ray mumbled with his mouth full. "Roast beef is a pain to chew. Now if this just had white bread, it would be purr-fect."

"She says whole wheat is healthier," Chris replied. "My dad says she's right." He shrugged. "Two against one means they win." He took another bite and flinched.

"What's the matter?" Ray asked.

Chris held his jaw. "I think I have a loose tooth, only it's back a ways." He stuck his finger into his mouth. "Wanna see?"

"Yuck," Raymond said, declining the opportunity. He finished his sandwich. "What's next? I'm still hungry."

"Let's see," said Chris, peering into the red nylon knapsack. "Apples...bananas... Hey, look! A whole bunch of oatmeal cookies. And instead of yucky raisins they have chocolate chips." He shook his head and grinned. "My new mom is the best cook in the whole state of Idaho."

Ray grabbed two cookies and took a big bite out of one. "Right on, man." He took another bite. "But why do you call her your new mom? She's Miss Keith, ain't she?"

"Not anymore." Chris grinned. "Want to hear a secret?"

Ray's brown eyes widened. "Sure."

"Aunt Nat said I shouldn't tell, but I told you about my dad and Miss Keith going away last week and you didn't tell."

"Just my dad," Ray murmured.

"What?" Chris exclaimed. "You weren't supposed to tell *anyone*. You promised."

"I just told my dad. He says fathers and sons are supposed to share, even secrets."

Chris frowned. "What did you tell him?"

"Only that Miss Keith and your dad went away together." He reached for another cookie.

"Did you tell him how come?" Chris asked.

"How could I? You didn't tell me. But my dad said he could guess."

"What did he mean?"

"I don't know, but my dad said it was sin-sinful," Ray replied.

"What does that mean?" Chris asked.

"Brother Bob at church always talks about it," Ray said. "I think it's doing bad stuff."

"Like cussing?"

"Yeah."

"My dad cusses sometimes," Chris admitted.

"My dad *never* cusses," Ray said, proudly.

"Gee." Chris thoughtfully munched another cookie. He mulled over the new secret he wanted to tell Raymond as he reached into the knapsack, pulled out a banana and began to peel it. He broke the fruit in half and handed one piece to Ray, then rubbed his fingers on his denim pant leg. "Maybe I shouldn't tell you."

"I won't tell."

"Like last time?"

"I won't tell if my dad don't ask, but gee, Chris, if he asks, what can I do? I heard him talking to my mom one night and he still thinks we shouldn't be friends."

"Why not?"

"He said loggers are cru-crude, but I don't know for sure what he meant, and that gypos are worse than plain loggers, but he didn't say why. He says you fight too much—"

"No more than you do," Chris challenged.

"My dad doesn't know about our fights."

"How come?"

"My mom didn't tell him," Raymond said. "My dad yells a lot and gets mad. Mom didn't want another fight."

Chris flinched. "I hate it when grown-ups fight. Leo always shouted at my other mom, and if I..." He shuddered. "It hurts when... I'm glad my dad and Miss Keith—my new mom ain't never gonna fight."

"My dad is mean sometimes, but my mom is always nice," Raymond said. "I think I like her the best."

Chris's shoulder stiffened. "Does your mom like me?"

"She says you are a..." Ray paused, then snickered, "...a nice boy." He broke into laughter. "Nice boy, nice boy," he chanted.

"Shut up, Ray, or you can't have any more cookies."

Ray covered his mouth tightly with his hand, sputtering as he tried to stop his giggles.

Chris frowned. "I thought we were best friends."

"We are," said Raymond, who made a Cub Scout salute, snapping his fingers sharply. "So tell me vour secret."

"Okay." Chris glanced over his shoulder at the trees sloping down the hill to make sure they were alone. He cupped his hands around his mouth and leaned close to Raymond's ear. "My dad and Miss Keith got married."

"You mean like a wedding?" Raymond's brown eyes grew round.

Chris nodded. "That's why I call her my new mom. She said I could."

"Gee." Ray considered this new secret. "What's it like to have a teacher for a mom? I'll bet she makes you do your homework whether you want to or not."

"But Miss Keith always makes us do our homework, so that's nothin' new," Chris said. "Since the first day of school she made us do one paper each night and bring it in the next morning. She said it was good practice for later and talked about high school and college. Yuck." He stared thoughtfully at the magpie. "I'm only gonna go through junior high."

"Me, too," Ray agreed. "And then we can join the army and fight somewhere. Maybe there'll be a war."

"Yeah, and we'll shoot machine guns and drive tanks." Chris made rat-a-tat noises, pointing at Raymond. Ray reciprocated and promptly fell off his perch.

Chris broke into laughter as Ray picked himself up and brushed off the seat of his pants. Chris offered Ray an apple.

"No more cookies?" Ray asked.

Chris peeked into the knapsack again and shook his head.

"Okay, an apple is better than nothin'." Ray bit a chunk and wiped the dribble from his chin. "So why did they get married, your dad and Miss Keith?"

"My dad says they're in love," Chris replied, giggling.

"Maybe they were tired of all that kissing you told me about," Ray suggested.

Chris shook his head. "I think my dad is happy. This morning he was sitting on the back porch step smoking his pipe. He only smokes his pipe when he's happy. She said he could do it inside, but he said no. They smile a lot and kiss and stuff like that."

"Where are you guys living now?" Ray asked. "Will you move away?"

Chris shrugged. "I don't know if we'll move or not. And I only spent one night in her house, and that was last night." Chris grinned. "But I really like it, Ray. Now I have a real family, just like you."

"But what if they get a divorce?" Ray asked.

Chris shook his head. "They'd *never* do that," he said confidently. He squinted at Ray. "Does your mom still read to you at night?"

"Yeah, and kisses me," Ray admitted, "but don't tell the other guys."

"I won't," Chris promised. "My new mom sat on the bed last night and read me a story. I coulda read it myself, but I like it when she does it." He sighed. "I like having her for my mom. I know my dad does, too."

"NOW THAT WE'VE TRICKED those boys into leaving, what shall we do?" John asked, drying the last of the breakfast dishes and putting the skillet in the oven.

"We?" Kathryn squeezed the dishcloth and shook it out. "You were the one who began talking about the joys of hiking as soon as Raymond appeared at the door."

"How did I know Chris called him at daybreak and invited him to breakfast?" John replied, taking her hand and leading her into the living room.

Kathryn nodded. "I should have become suspicious when Chris insisted I make scrambled eggs. All during breakfast Raymond stared at me, almost as though he didn't think teachers lived in houses and ate meals like the rest of the townsfolk." She laughed. "He's only seen me in my classroom at school or on playground duty."

"He was too polite to ask why Chris and I spent the night," John said.

Kathryn lingered by the door, watching him as he wandered around the room, familiarizing himself with its decor. His size alone filled the room, making it seem much smaller than before. He reached to the ceiling and swept a slender strand of web from a corner, then turned and dangled it from his finger.

"Oh," she mumbled, "sloppy housekeeping, but I seldom look that high. I hope you didn't marry me for my homemaking ability."

"Of course not."

"Or my parenting skills? I'm used to other people's children. It's going to be different having one in my own home," she said.

"You and Chris hit it off long before I entered the picture, but that's not why I married you, either."

"Then why?"

"Because," he said as he strode across the room, "you were so worldly, so sophisticated, so experienced, and your body was driving me crazy." He loomed over her.

Her breath caught in her chest. "You're teasing me, but I don't care." A wave of color deepened her cheeks. "I've never driven a man crazy with this little body of mine." She grinned. "It's a new experience for me, and I think

I'm going to like it." Kathryn sighed deeply. "But everything is happening so fast. It was only a week ago that you knocked on my door and talked me into running away with you. Oh, John, I've done more living this past week than in my entire lifetime."

"You'll do a lot more in the months to come, Kit." His hand stroked her cheek. "This marriage will be a success. I promise you that. There will be lots of changes, but we'll work them out together. Trust me. This marriage was made in . . ." He stared intently down at her.

"In heaven," she finished, then settled against him. His arms tightened around her. Suddenly she found herself lifted in his arms and carried through the house to the bedroom where they had spent the night.

In minutes their clothing was scattered about the room and his hands were exploring her body, finding new areas of sensitivity. He rolled onto his back and pulled her on top of him. Straddling his hips, she was filled with new excitement at their union. Her eyes widened as she tested the freedom of this new position of lovemaking. His hands wandered up her body, cupping each breast, arousing them to peaks of desire.

Her head fell back as she uttered a moan. She clutched his hands, pressing them closer to her breasts. The heady power of bringing him to his climax filled her with awe as he groaned aloud, "Kit, oh, Kit," his ragged breathing telling her what words need not.

She collapsed against him, her arms around his neck as he rolled her onto her side. He brushed a damp curl from her temple before kissing her lips.

"My passionate wife, how I love you," he murmured against her cheek.

She shuddered, awed at the splendor of their union. "We've only been making love for a week, and I've lost track of the number of times, yet each is more remarkable than the last. Each time you make love to me, I forget all that has gone before." She caressed one of his nipples with her fingertip. "I'm still afraid I'll wake up some morning and find I've been dreaming. Are you real, John Brasher, or just a figment of my imagination?"

He laughed. "I'm not imaginary because I know two eight-year-old boys who are very real. The doors are unlocked."

She flinched and tried to pull away, but he held her against him.

"Let me go, John," she cried. "They can't find us like this."

"You're right," he replied, reluctantly releasing her. "Let's get dressed and lie on the bed again, with the bedroom door open, and talk. We have some loose ends to tie up."

In a few minutes the room was again devoid of scattered clothing, and she was back in his arms as they lay back against several pillows.

"Now for the loose ends," she said. "What's first?"

"Avery and my mail," he said with a chuckle. "My creditors might be looking for me."

She straightened. "Do you have many creditors?"

"Just three banks who share in some of my equipment, and the power company, and the credit card people who financed that honeymoon a few days ago, and the Internal Revenue Service, who suggested I amend my quarterly estimated taxes paid, and the workmen's compensation people, and—"

"Enough, enough," she said, laughing. "What else?"

"The rest of the weekend." He grinned. "Let's go to Avery this afternoon, and I'll bring you and Chris back tomorrow evening." He frowned at her. "That is, if Chris... Can Chris... If it's all right and Chris..." He ran his fingers through his thick hair and tried to smooth it. "Oh, hell, Kit, how can I ask this without you feeling put upon?"

"Ask what?"

"My son has spent the past year with my sister Natalie. Can he stay with you now?" He inhaled deeply and held his breath.

Her brow furrowed as she gazed into his eyes, sensing his uncertainty. "Why would you have to ask?"

"I don't want you to think I'm dumping my son on you."

"Of course he'll stay with me," she said.

"I'll pay," he said.

"Why?"

"It costs money to feed the kid. He has a hollow leg. I'll give you twice what I paid Natalie. That way you can pay the utilities and—"

"John, it's not necessary. I can afford my own home. I managed before I met you so I can manage now."

"No, you can't," he insisted. "What the hell kind of husband do you think I am? Do you think I'd move in with a woman and expect her to—"

"John, you don't understand."

He sat up and crossed his legs, glaring at her, his blue eyes as dark as sapphires. "I do understand, Kit. Normally a woman moves in with a man, takes over his home, his furniture, his possessions, and becomes a part of his life."

She shook her head. "I don't want to take over your possessions, as you phrase it. I married you because I loved you, not because of your material goods."

"But you have this house and all this furniture," he replied. "I haven't owned a home for years. Just that trailer in Avery and you're right, it's hardly large enough for a family. I was wrong to expect you—"

"I don't own a home or furniture, either," she said.

"But this house..."

"I rent it furnished."

"You do?" The puzzled look on his face made her smile.

"Yes." She took his hand. "My mother has an apartment filled with antique furniture that will be mine someday. I sold what furniture I had when I left Tucson. I didn't want to be burdened with such things. I travel light, as the expression goes. You, my darling husband, have more furniture in that wonderfully cramped trailer than I have. I could pack up in a day and have only a few boxes. I've just never been one to accumulate things. My father left me some old and rare books, but they're at Mother's. I'm not a clotheshorse. I do have a set of fine china, crystal and silverware, but that's at Mother's also."

She grinned. "I bought it when I graduated from college and thought some sheik in a flowing black robe would come charging across the desert and take me away to his camp, to ravish me and love me as Ahmed Ben Hassan did to his British captive Diana, but..."

"Who the hell is Ahmed Ben Hassan?" John asked.

"You don't know Ahmed?"

"Should I?"

"He's just one of the most romantic heroes in literature."

"From the classics, I suppose," John said, chuckling. "I've married a literary snob, a gifted child turned into a discriminating reader of fine—"

She tossed her head from side to side, clapping her hands and laughing. "I've read most of the classics, but I read today's writers also. Charles Dickens and William Shakespeare didn't write classics. They wrote commercial contemporary fiction and plays. We, in our snobbery, have put them on pedestals and call their works classic. My father used to always give at least one lecture on literary snobbery because he felt so strongly about it. Commercial fiction is read much more than the so-called 'classics.' The word alone stops many people from reading them. So, my dear man, you're the snob, a reverse snob at that."

He pulled his knees up and rested his elbows on them. "Maybe you're right. So who is this Ahmed fellow?"

"He's the sheik who kidnapped the woman he wanted. He's from the book *The Sheik* by E.M. Hull."

"A man wrote a mushy story like that?"

"No, darling, a woman wrote it but used her initials in order to sell it. Prejudice against women has been around for a long time."

"Good Lord, this new wife of mine is not only beautiful and superintelligent, she's a feminist also."

"Maybe a closet feminist," she said. "There are lots of things about me you don't know, and some I don't know myself."

"They add to your womanly mystique," he replied. "So what did this sheik do to the lovely lady?"

"He sabotaged the caravan and took her to his camp to be his sex slave, only in those days the writing wasn't so explicit. The author left the love scenes to the reader's imagination, but getting the idea was easy enough. In the end she got pregnant, they admitted their love, and after a potentially tragic crisis they lived happily ever after, or at least long enough to have a movie and a sequel produced. Of all the novels I've read, it's the one I liked the best when it comes to love stories.''

"So you read romances and classics," he said. "Anything else?"

"Biographies and autobiographies. I like to learn what makes other people tick." She grew quiet. "My sheik wears red suspenders when he works and takes me to his logging camp in the rugged mountains instead of a settlement in the Arabian desert, and he drives me there in his beat-up truck instead of on the back of a fiery chestnut Arabian stallion."

He held out his arms, and she scooted into his embrace. He pulled her against him and dropped back onto the pillows. The minutes ticked away as she savored the warmth of his arms.

He cleared his throat. "I can't be Ahmed, but I'll be your gypo logger husband and do my best to make you happy, Kit."

"I know you will," she whispered against his chest. "I trust you."

"I would never want to break that trust," he assured her. "Broken promises make trust hard to reestablish. We'll work at prevention."

Her hand stroked his chest, irritated by the material that kept her from touching his bare skin.

"I still insist on giving you money," he said and she smiled. "For the household," he continued. "Do with it what you will."

"I don't need it."

"Then save it," he insisted. "Someday we'll have a normal home: a house and a yard and a dog, a dining room for that fine china of yours, a lawn to mow—the works." His hand moved up and down her arm. "If you have so few material goods, what do you spend your money on, if I may ask?''

"I save it.''

"So my beautiful, intelligent, sexy, feminist wife is thrifty, too! What more could a man ask for?'' He tightened his hold around her. "Unless it was a child.''

"A baby?''

"You aren't using a contraceptive. Why not, Kit?''

"I'm getting too old for the pill. And besides, before you I didn't give a thought to the subject. I didn't need to.'' Kathryn played with the buttons on his shirt. "Sometimes, in just these past few years, I find myself resenting women with babies and small children. I've tried to suppress it.''

"Now you don't need to,'' he said.

Her gaze shifted to his throat. "One Saturday afternoon when I cut through a park in Tucson on my way home, I realized I'd spent most of my adult life taking care of other women's children. I was resentful for a while, then cynical. Now I've accepted my childless fate. But it still seems so unfair. I had become a substitute mother to kids who wanted attention, needed love.''

"You have lots of love to give, Kit,'' he murmured, kissing her hair. "What if you got pregnant? Would you like that?''

"At my age it probably won't happen. If it does, I'll accept it.''

"There can be risks,'' he said.

"I know, but sometimes risks must be taken. I have a friend in Tucson who married when she was forty-two and has two children, and another friend who adopted when she and her husband were in their late forties, after twenty years of a childless marriage. It would be a new experience for me, but what about you, John? You're a father three times over.''

"And about to become a grandfather," he boasted. "My daughter is expecting her first child in late July."

"Your life has been so full."

"But not always happy, Kit."

"Would you want to start all over again?"

"I already have, by marrying you," he said, tilting her chin and kissing her lips lightly. "I'd love to make a baby with you."

CHAPTER ELEVEN

IMAGES OF CHRIS INTRUDED as she lay in John's arms. "We need to talk about something. Perhaps you can help."

"About making babies?"

She patted his chest. "No, silly, about Chris."

"I think he has been pretty good lately," John said, massaging her arm. "No fights and his grades have improved."

"He's almost too good. But sometimes he still antagonizes the other children. Would you talk to him and make him understand something? You could make him realize that his father marrying his teacher doesn't give him extra privileges at school. Sometimes I sense I'm having a honeymoon with your son as well as you, and I'm leery of what might bring it to an end."

"Of course," John replied. "There're only three more weeks of school. You and Chris can come and spend the weekends with me. That will give him something to look forward to and help him stay out of mischief."

"We'll drive up Fridays and come back Sunday evenings. What about this summer?"

"It's flexible. You can stay here in town, or up there with me. My hours will be long, but I'll get back to the trailer whenever I can. June is free, but Chris goes to Roseburg for two weeks in the middle of July. It's part of the agreement Helen and I came to...a few weeks ago."

"You've talked to her recently? Often?"

"Just about Chris," he explained. "I'm going to court to gain legal custody of him in late June."

"I thought you had custody of him since he came to live with you," she said.

"I've been lax at tightening up the legal loose ends," he replied. "She might decide to... Never mind. It's settled now, and I have the terms in writing—signed and witnessed."

"How does Chris get to Oregon?"

"I'm flying with him," he said, reaching for her hand. "Want to come with us?"

"I don't think so," she said. "Meeting Chris's mother after all the things I've heard about her might not be a good idea. Maybe later."

"I understand," John said, searching her eyes as he squeezed her hand.

"I'm going to Tucson in August to visit my mother," she said. "Perhaps you and Chris could come with me?"

He shook his head. "Wrong time of the year, sweetheart. I can't possibly get away, but Chris could go with you. He's a real nut about flying. Definitely a boy of the space age."

"Then everything's settled," she said.

"Not quite. What about our move to Bonners Ferry?" he asked. "Have you thought it over?"

"I'll talk to the principal this coming week," she promised. "But what if I can't find another teaching position?"

"You don't have to work."

"Of course I do. It's my career."

"Then consider an idea I've been mulling over. Until you came into my life I never thought this could really work. It's been cooking on the back burner for years. It may sound corny."

"If it's an idea that's stayed with you for a long time, maybe it has validity. Tell me about it, as we say in the third grade," Kathy said, smiling encouragingly.

"We could start a school in a trailer. Strip it of the furniture and fill it with desks and bookshelves. You'd have a bathroom and a sink for cleanup, and we could serve hot lunches since it would have a stove and..."

"You've really given this some thought, haven't you?"

He stared past her head. "For years. I mentioned it to Helen once, and she thought I was crazy. Helen always thought I preferred to live away from home, but she was wrong. I would have given anything to have spent more time with my girls when they were growing up. You see, Kit, I could do the remodeling, and we could move it wherever the crews go. Damn it, Kit, there are fifteen grade-school-age children among the families of my crews. Just think what it would mean to the men and their wives if you, someone, anyone, but especially you, could run a school. There are one-room schoolhouses all over Idaho and Montana—but this one would be on wheels."

"But I've never taught anything but third grade," she said.

"Couldn't you bone up on the other grades?" John almost pleaded. "Isn't there a special curriculum for one-room schools?"

"Yes, but..."

"Could you check into it? See what's required to make it legal?"

The idea began to catch fire as she speculated on his proposal. "Maybe we could do it." She smiled, her green eyes sparkling. "Imagine the former Miss Keith going from one of the largest school districts in the state of Arizona to teaching in a one-room school on wheels in some remote mountain site. I'll investigate the possibility and let you know. There are financial matters to consider, textbooks and supplies, equipment."

"I'll give a grant to get it started," he promised. "I've been setting aside money in a special savings account at each year-end. Several of the men have told me they'd be willing to have an assessment deducted from their pay if necessary."

"You and your workers all pay taxes," she said. "Perhaps there's a way the state department of education will help with the funding and textbooks."

"We pay plenty of income tax, but not real estate taxes, and that's how most of the school system is financed," he cautioned. "The bureaucrats might hold it against us. Can you find out what our options are?"

"Of course," she promised. "The project sounds challenging, it's new and different. There're many other ways to educate children besides in the traditional classroom setting. We can add a new dimension to the concept of learning."

He pulled her back into his arms and kissed her again. "This time ahead of us is going to be filled with new experiences, experiences of all kinds, some we've never imagined could happen."

The slamming of the back door startled them. Snickers were heard coming from the kitchen.

"Are you through kissing?" Chris shouted. "Ray and I ran out of food so we came home. Can we come in and have a cookie and a glass of lemonade?"

"Mind your mouth, young man," John called back. "Kit and I will never be through kissing."

THE FOLLOWING WEEKS FELL into a routine. Five days of school, followed by a hurried trip to Avery to spend two precious days and nights with John.

Kathryn's period passed, bringing with it a nagging sense of regret. The next Friday night, in the privacy of their bedroom, she told him of her disappointment.

"We didn't make a baby, Mr. Brasher."

"We'll practice some more, Mrs. Brasher," he said, holding out his arms to her. "Practice makes perfect, but if perfection is never reached, think how much enjoyment we'll have trying."

KATHRYN AND CHRIS WALKED home from school together each afternoon except Tuesday. That day Chris, in his blue-and-gold Club Scout uniform, would race off with Raymond and arrive home a few hours later to tell her all about their meeting or field trip. He would show her his completed projects, or let her admire the latest specimen, sometimes dead but more often alive, to be added to his growing collection of insects. They would search through an entomology encyclopedia she had ordered for him from the local bookstore and see who could identify the insect first.

The last Tuesday of the school year began as usual, but within minutes of her arrival at the house, Chris came charging through the front door, throwing his book bag on the floor and racing into his bedroom, slamming the door loudly behind him.

Kathryn hurried to the door, put her ear against it and heard the racking sobs coming from inside. "Chris?"

He didn't answer.

Worried, Kathryn decided nonetheless to leave him alone for several minutes. When she returned and tried the door, she found it unlocked. Hesitantly she turned the knob and entered. Chris lay with his head toward the foot of the bed, one tennis shoe running back and forth across the wall above the head of the twin bed, mouthing threats to some unknown enemy.

She detoured to the bathroom and moistened a washcloth with cold water. When she returned to his room, he was sitting up cross-legged on the bed, throwing darts at a picture of a man he had torn from a magazine and taped to the dart board above his bed. One dart had pièrced the man's right eye. He was still sniffing and trails of dust and tears marred his flushed lean cheeks.

"Here," she said softly, holding out the washcloth. "You'll feel better." She waited while he wiped his face.

"Now can you tell me what's wrong?"

He glared at her. "That stupid ol' fatso Raymond will never be my best friend again."

"Why not?"

"He says his stupid ol' father won't let us be friends anymore." Chris wiped his eyes furiously with the damp cloth again.

"Did he say why not?"

"Yeah!"

"Can you tell me his reason?"

Chris pointed to her left hand. "Doesn't that mean you and Daddy are married, I mean *really* married?"

She held out her hand, studying the two rings. "Of course it does. How could my rings cause a fight between you and Ray?"

"Ray said his stupid ol' father checked the courthouse and couldn't find where you and Daddy had gotten married. He said Ray couldn't play with someone who lives with people who co-cohab-cohab—oh, hell, I don't know the word!"

"Don't use words like hell, Chris."

He mumbled an apology.

"Was the word cohabit?"

"Yeah. What does it mean?"

She sighed. "It's a very outdated word that means a man and woman live together as husband and wife without getting legally married."

His face twisted in confusion. "But don't they do that all the time on television?"

She grimaced. "Sometimes it seems that way. Ray's father is wrong, so very wrong."

"Then prove it! Tell that stupid ol'. . ."

Anger at the cruelty of Ray's father's edict without thought for the two innocent boys mushroomed as she frantically thought of a solution to Chris's problem. "Damn it, I will," she exclaimed.

"You cussed!"

She laughed. "Sometimes it's the only kind of word that fits. We'll solve this right now, and your father won't even need to know about it until we've settled everything."

"Our secret?" he asked.

"Unless he asks."

"What are you going to do?"

"Well." She stared at the marks from his shoes on the wall. "Three things. First, you're going to clean that wall. Second, we'll go visit the pious Mr. Crosley."

"And then?"

"That will be a surprise for you as well as this whole nosy town. Now you get the spray cleaner beneath the kitchen sink and get those footprints off the wall, young man. Then we're taking a trip downtown."

"Yes, ma'am," Chris said, jumping from the bed and scampering out of the room.

She marched into her bedroom and slammed the door. When she found the official copy of their marriage license, she slipped it into her purse, then changed into the sage-green sweater that had become her favorite, leaving the pearl buttons open to reveal several inches of enticing cleavage. She hoped she wouldn't lose her courage before the encounter with Mr. Crosley was played out to its conclusion.

When she returned to the kitchen, Chris had washed his face and sat munching oatmeal cookies.

"Is the wall clean?" she asked.

"Yes, ma'am." He jumped from his chair when he spotted her carrying her purse. "Can I come, too?" he asked excitedly.

She grinned. "Of course. I need you. Doesn't Mr. Crosley run one of the hardware stores on Main Street?"

"Yes. Are we gonna go see him?"

"We surely are," promised Kathryn, and she followed him out the door to her compact car.

"Whatcha gonna do?"

She glanced at him. "You know how that mouse you and your father bought for me acts when he's cornered or angry?"

"He stands up on his hind feet and paws the air, and if I try to touch him, he bites my finger," Chris said.

"Well, my son, Mr. Crosley is going to find his finger bleeding."

"All right, man," Chris murmured. "Hurry."

She parked the car at the curb directly in front of Mr. Crosley's store. Her knees felt rubbery as she stepped across the crumbling sidewalk. "Watch your step, Chris. The sidewalks in this town must be the worst in the West."

"Are you nervous?" Chris asked, grinning up at her.

"I'd rather not say," she replied, praying for strength to follow through with her impulsive decision.

The store was empty except for the owner, who mistook them for customers. "Can I help you, ma'am?" the man asked as he strolled around the counter. When he spotted Chris, he stepped backward, bumping into the corner of the counter. An oath filled the air before his mouth tightened into a narrow strip across his ruddy face.

"Ray says you don't cuss," Chris said, his green eyes piercing Mr. Crosley's fleshy features.

"Mind your manners, boy," Mr. Crosley cautioned.

"You're Raymond's father?" Kathryn asked, approaching the counter.

Mr. Crosley's eyes drifted to Kathryn's sweater. He grinned. "Sure am, and you must be that gypo's woman." He motioned with his thumb toward Chris. "The one living with the kid's old man."

"That *kid* is my son now and his old man is my husband, and I'm no gypo's woman, I'm Mrs. John Brasher. There seems to be a misunderstanding about the legality of our marriage. Frankly, Mr. Crosley, I don't see where it's any of your *damned* business," and here Kathryn paused for emphasis, "but since you've stuck your fat nose into our personal affairs, I want to clear the air."

Mr. Crosley laughed. "I don't care who you shack up with, lady, that's your business. Just don't expect me to allow my son," and he punched his chest with his thumb, "to associate with such goings-on. It's unnatural and immoral carrying on in front of the kid and all."

Kathryn took a deep breath. Mr. Crosley's deep-set, porky eyes were again drawn to Kathryn's cleavage. Her mouth softened enough to give him the impression she enjoyed his attention as she tugged the ribbing down around her hips, causing her sweater to tighten across her breasts. Mr. Crosley swallowed.

God, give me the courage, she prayed silently, as she caught Mr. Crosley's gaze. Her fingers caressed the creamy skin in the V of the sweater opening for an instant. "See this, Mr. Crosley?"

His eyes darted to her fingers, then back to her face.

"This is my body, you hypocrite, and what I do with it is my business. If I want to be with a man, I have every right to do so, and it certainly is no concern of yours. Yes, I'm living with a man."

Mr. Crosley's mouth rolled into a satisfied smirk.

She slapped the folded marriage license hard against his knuckles as they gripped the edge of the counter. "The man is my husband. Open it."

"You're bluffing, lady. I checked at the courthouse, and there's no record of—"

"There is more than one county in this state," she reminded him. "We were married in Bonners Ferry."

"Just a ruse." He pushed the folded paper aside. "Still, I doubt if the school and the other parents want their children taught by a woman—"

"The principal was notified the Monday I returned." She shoved the paper back toward him. "Open it."

"No need to make a fuss." He stepped back. "Like I told you, live with who you want. But a gypo?" He snorted.

"Why the hatred of gypos?" she asked, recalling the fights between Chris and Raymond.

"They're cheats."

"Not John Brasher," she said. "Does he owe you money?"

"No. He doesn't do business in this store."

"Then why the blanket hatred?"

"Most of them are no good, they don't pay their bills," he insisted.

"Who? Name some."

He fidgeted.

"Who?"

"I had two several years back who skipped town owing me—I don't have to tell you my business," he huffed.

"Were those two the only customers who ever skipped town owing you money?"

"No, but—"

"Then why assume all gypos are cheats? My husband is a very honest man. He provides employment for others, he brings business to this town, he sells to the mill and helps keep it going, he pays his taxes just as you do. If a forest service employee didn't pay his account, would you condemn all forest service people?"

Mr. Crosley stared at Kathryn, but didn't speak.

"If the owner of a department store didn't pay his bill with you, would all such business people be forbidden to do business with you?"

"No."

"Would you prevent their children from playing with your precious children?"

His eyes dropped to the folded license still on the counter.

"Open it up," Kathryn said.

He shook his head.

Angrily she grabbed the folded marriage license. "Don't you ever say another thing about the John Brasher family, Mr. Crosley. Absolutely nothing—unless it's good." She felt herself drawn to his bulbous nose. How she longed to whack the marriage license across it and watch his reaction. Her hand inched toward the target.

"Are you gonna hit him?" Chris whispered.

She jerked her hand down to her side and was surprised to see Mr. Crosley's flushed face turn pale. She decided on a change of strategy. "Is Raymond at home?"

"Of course," he said, "my son don't roam the streets."

"Call him," she instructed. "Tell him he can come over and have dinner with Chris tonight."

"But . . ."

"We'll expect him at six sharp."

Mr. Crosley opened his mouth as if to protest.

"No excuses, please," she cautioned, tilting her pretty chin upward. "Six o'clock sharp."

"Yes, ma'am."

She turned sharply and marched from the store, her small, shapely derriere swaying from side to side as she disappeared through the swinging doors.

"YOU GOT GUTS," Chris murmured, staring at her as she tried to fit the key into the ignition. "You were turr-rific. Wait till I tell Raymond what you did."

She steadied her hand and finally slid the key into the slot. "Maybe this should be just between you, me and Mr. Crosley."

"Not even Daddy?"

She smiled. "You can tell him if he asks." She took a deep breath and willed her heart to stop pounding. Never had she spoken to another person quite like that. She had been raised to respect figures in authority. Now she found herself in authority. True, her career in teaching had put her in authority over eight-year-old children, but this was different, truly different. She exhaled slowly. She felt marvelous. The submissive desert mouse had struck back at last.

She turned to Chris.

"My dad would be real proud of you," he murmured. "He likes people with guts."

"How do you know?"

"He told me so," and he twisted as he fastened his seat belt. "That's why I used to fight Raymond. He said I had to learn to fight my own battles."

Kathryn groaned. "Well, don't carry it to the extreme, Chris. You can have guts without fist fights."

"Really?"

"Didn't I do that with Mr. Crosley?" she asked.

"But you almost hit his big fat nose!"

"How did you know?"

He giggled. "Your eyes—they were sort of crazy."

She smiled. "You're right. I came terribly close, and it felt very good."

"Turr-rific?"

"Terrific."

"What's for dinner?" Chris asked. "Ray likes to eat."

"We'll take him to the Cook Shack, and you can order from the menu."

"Great. We'll order the biggest hamburgers they have."

"But first I have one more stop to make," she said.

"Where?"

"The newspaper office. It's time we told the whole town there's a new family in town. Mr. and Mrs. John Brasher and their son Chris."

"All right," he exclaimed, slapping the dash in a staccato beat of excitement.

JOHN CALLED on Thursday evening to say they should stay in town for the weekend. Security problems at one of the landings would necessitate his remaining in the woods all weekend.

"I'm sorry, Kit, but someone has been stealing logs from one of the decks," he said. "We're staking out the area this weekend."

All she could think of was being apart from him for the first weekend during their marriage.

"Next weekend for sure," he promised. "I came down to Avery just to call you."

THE NEXT WEEK'S EDITION of the St. Maries local paper showed a photograph of John, Kathryn and Chris smiling at the reader, with a brief article telling about the marriage, where the new family was living, a few lines about Kathryn's and John's careers and Chris's age. The photograph had been taken from a color print and lacked clarity, but Chris was still delighted.

School adjourned for the summer. Chris was beside himself with excitement, anxious to show the newspaper article to John. When the call came from Avery that all was well, they were packed and on the road in two hours, ready to spend two weeks with John. Natalie had agreed to take care of Patches.

When they arrived in Avery, darkness had fallen, but a welcome light shone from the trailer. Chris was out the car door before the tires stopped rolling. The trailer exploded with activity as Chris began to explain all that had happened.

John knelt before his son, gripping his small shoulders and shaking him lightly. "Stop, Chris. You're making absolutely no sense. She did what?"

He listened attentively as his son gave a breathless account of the argument with Raymond, Kathryn's encounter with Ray's father, the trip to the newspaper office and her insistence they take a black-and-white photo of the color print.

"Even if it turned out no good," Chris said, beaming. "She's got real guts, Daddy. You shoulda seen her."

John glanced up as Kathryn appeared in the doorway of the trailer. Her dark hair was windblown, and she tried to smooth it. Her green eyes caught his, lingering as she slid out of her jacket. His gaze swept over her form, taking in the lavender silk blouse that clung to her breasts and the purple slacks that hid her lower body and legs. He imagined them bare and wrapped around him. How could such an apparently prim woman fill him with so much desire?

He rose to his full height and took a step toward her, but Chris jerked on his shirt. He tore his eyes away from Kathryn and back to his son.

"Later, Chris. First I want to say hello to Kit."

"No, you gotta see it now, Daddy." Chris insisted as he pulled a crumpled piece of newsprint from his jeans pocket. He put it on the counter and began to spread it out, smoothing it with his fingers.

John's attention was drawn to the clipping. He recognized the photo as one taken by Natalie and enlarged for them. He scanned the article, guessing at some of the smudged words. He laughed. "I hope you have another copy, Chris. This one is about finished."

"Oh, we do. Mom bought some extras. Didn't you?" Chris glanced at Kathryn, but she was staring at his father. "Now we're a real family, aren't we? We fight together and everything." He tugged on John's shirt again. "Daddy?"

John touched his son's shoulder. "Later, Chris," he said, moving toward Kathryn. "Did my little desert mouse really cause all this excitement?" he asked, his hand drifting to her cheek. "My son is very impressed. So is his father." His hand settled on her neck, his thumb caressing her jaw as she stepped closer. He saw the pulse at the base of her throat throbbing.

"I missed you," she whispered.

"Not as much as I missed you," he replied, his voice soft and husky. "Never as much as I miss you." His arms surrounded her, drawing her close against him, assuring her of his own arousal. "Don't move," he warned. "I'd be embarrassed for my son to see me like this. Let me hold you, kiss you, give me a chance to calm down. Oh, Kit," John moaned, and his mouth claimed hers, driving all thoughts of his staring son away.

She stretched to meet him, her arms sliding up and around his neck as her mouth opened, her tongue seeking his.

"You're gonna break her back," Chris giggled from his perch on the kitchen bar stool.

John pulled away and took a ragged breath of air. "Go away, son, we're busy."

"You're always busy with that kissing stuff. How can you stand it?" Chris asked.

"Someday you'll understand," John growled. "Until then, why don't you go to the café? We'll be there in a few minutes."

"Great." Chris jumped from the stool and raced out the door.

"Now, where were we?" John asked, gazing down at her. Kathryn's cheeks were flushed, her lips inviting. His hand drifted to one of her breasts, and he felt her nipple grow hard beneath her blouse and bra.

"We were kissing," she murmured. "Like this." Her mouth touched his, nibbling at his lower lip, teasing the slight cleft in his chin and returning it to his mouth again. She stretched to her fullest tiptoe height. "Pick me up," she pleaded. "I can't reach you the way I want to."

He swept her up in his arms and carried her to the sofa. When he dropped to the cushions, he kept her in his arms. Her head fell to his shoulder as his hand unbuttoned two of the gold fasteners on her blouse. Pushing the material aside, he concentrated on the creamy skin above the lacy bra, his tongue tasting the warmth.

She moaned and slid her hand down the back of his shirt.

"We'll never get to the café if we keep this up, sweetheart," he said, drawing her blouse together again. "We'll resume this later."

She sat on his lap and fastened the buttons on her blouse. "I hope so. I didn't drive all this way to hold hands."

"My, my, is this the shy, reserved woman I first met?"

"Miss Prune Face?"

"Mrs. Beautiful." He peered at her. "You look different. Is it the spunkiness or something else? You look . . . softer, more feminine, rounder. Have you gained a few pounds?"

"A few. Does it show?" She slid from his lap and tucked her blouse inside the waistband of her slacks.

"I can't put my finger on it," he said, leaving the sofa and reaching for their jackets. "I'll figure it out. Let's go find out what damage that son of mine—ours has done to my wallet. One of these days he'll discover that steaks are more delicious than hamburgers and shakes. Ready, love?" John asked as he reached for her hand.

As they strolled across to the café, he asked about their luggage. "You planned to stay for more than the weekend, didn't you?"

"Two weeks for sure," she replied.

"Great. I go to court over Chris in three weeks."

"Here or in Roseburg?"

"Here," he said. "Helen signed all the papers, and this is just a formality. Chris doesn't even have to be there. Nor you. Helen and I agreed on all the details."

"Details? What kind of details."

"It's costing me a few dollars."

"To get permanent custody of your own son? How much?"

"The equivalent of child support until he turns eighteen."

"That's almost ten years," she exclaimed. "My God, John, that's blackmail. Why did you agree to so much money?"

"I wanted my son," he said, stopping in the shadows of the building.

Aware of the stiff set of his shoulders, she grasped for something appropriate to say. "It's a shame you have to pay to keep your own son, but now Helen is out of the picture."

"No, she's not," he said, and she heard a profanity mumbled under his breath.

"Does he still have to visit her?" she asked.

"Yes, once a year until he's thirteen. Then he can decide for himself if he wants to continue to visit them. He leaves the week after the July Fourth holiday. When we get back from our float race, I'll fly with him to Portland and drive him to Roseburg."

"Float race?" she asked. "I don't remember your mentioning a float trip. When? Where?"

"On the Lochsa River off US 12." He frowned. "I thought I mentioned it."

"You certainly did not," she said, grimacing in the darkness. "John, I'm your wife. You've got to include me when you make these plans. I feel so left out."

"Sorry, sweetheart," John mumbled, looking sheepish, and his arm went around her shoulders. "It's my one getaway each summer," he replied. "We close for the holiday, and the crews get to spend time with their families. I like to spend mine on the water—white water!"

CHAPTER TWELVE

"ARE YOU SURE, KIT?" John asked. "You can still back out," he said as he and another man lifted the inflated six-man raft from the truck and joined several other groups gathering at the entry point of the race.

"No," Chris said, "we need you. Daddy can't do it alone." He raced to the cab and pulled out an orange child's life preserver and two blue foam vests. "Here, the big blue one is Daddy's, the smaller one is yours and I get the orange one. Now put it on and let's go. We want to win like last year."

John frowned down at his agitated son. "You're getting a little bossy, young man. Kit can decide for herself."

Chris shifted from one foot to the other. "You said you could swim. You have to be better than Uncle Cal. He can't swim, and when he fell out of the boat last year, he—"

Kathryn swallowed. "He fell out?"

"Yeah, but we pulled him back in, and still we won second place. That's why he's driving the truck to the end of the race this year."

"That's enough, Chris," John cautioned. "Each person can decide for himself if he wants to race or be a helper. Everyone is important."

"This year we're gonna be first," Chris said.

The race was a combination of speed and luck, held annually on the Lochsa River east of Kooskia, Idaho, during the Fourth of July weekend. At five checkpoints participants would draw a card from a paper sack in an attempt to complete a winning hand of poker. Points would be given for the completed hands and factored into the finish time of each team.

"We've come all this way," Kathryn said, "and what would you guys think of me if I backed out now?"

Chris grinned. "We might call you a sissy," he teased.

"I wouldn't want that word for a nickname," she said, feigning disdain.

Chris burst into giggles. "Then let's go," he said. "Some of the teams have left already."

"Good," John said. "I'll put in the little ice chest and the thermos and, Chris, you get the waterproof bag with the camera and dry clothes. Kit has the plastic bag of snacks and the chicken. Ready, everyone?"

Chris climbed into the boat, dragging his life vest in one hand.

"Put it on," John insisted.

"But I'm a good swimmer," Chris said.

"Put it on."

"Okay," Chris groaned, and in seconds he had the jacket tightly fastened around his middle with a strap between his legs.

"Can I help?" John asked, coming to assist Kathryn as she struggled with the straps of her life jacket.

"Please," she said. "I'm used to desert swimming pools with stripes on the bottom and sides so you can climb out, and a swimsuit to wear." She glanced down at her worn jeans, sweatshirt and the old pair of tennis shoes on her small feet. "Somehow I suspect I'll get just as wet."

"Maybe," John agreed as he fastened the straps of her lifejacket. As he rechecked all the buckles, he kissed her on the sensitive skin of her neck. "You look sexy even in these rags."

She turned, reaching to touch his waist, longing to feel the warmth of his bare skin. "I feel sexy when you're close."

He cupped her face in his hands. "It's been a good two months, Kit. The best." His mouth hovered over hers.

"Ah, come on, Daddy," Chris called. "You can do that later. We're gonna be the last ones in the water if you start kissing again."

"Smart kid," John said, kissing her once lightly. "We'll take his advice and continue this later." He frowned down at her. "Are you feeling better now?"

"I'm fine," she replied. "I was just a little…sick to my stomach this morning. Probably something I ate last night. I'm fine, really."

"Did you throw up?"

"A little," she admitted.

"Was this the first time?"

"Twice this week. It's probably a summer flu bug going around. Don't worry about me."

"Maybe you shouldn't go. The bouncing and all. Could you be…pregnant?"

"Of course not," she insisted. "I had another period." She didn't tell him how scant it had been. This newly discovered sexuality of hers made Kathryn feel like a teenager, often overwhelmed by her own reactions to John's lovemaking. She wasn't sure she was ready to deal with the complications of pregnancy, even though they had taken no precautions.

"Let's not keep Chris waiting." She slipped from his arms, then ran to the boat. In minutes they were in the raft, bobbing with the current.

"There's the first one," Chris shouted from the front.

"First what?" Kathryn asked.

"White water!"

"Oh," Kathryn said with a gasp, glancing over her shoulder at John as he reached for the oars. The current swept them along as John guided them around several boulders to the inside of the river and allowed the current to shoot them through the rapids in seconds. As the raft settled back to its gentle bouncing, Kathryn breathed a sigh of relief. "That wasn't so bad," she called, slapping Chris's shoulder playfully. "If they don't get any worse than that, I'm tough enough to play this game."

"That's the easy one," John called from behind her.

They executed two more rapids smoothly, with John positioning the raft in midstream. The river leveled out for a mile, and they spotted the first checkpoint. John rowed the raft to the landing and helped Kathryn and Chris out for a break. They drew cards. Kathryn glanced at her card. She knew little about playing poker. Most of her teaching friends played bridge, but she had never become interested in the game, preferring to read a good book. As she slid a ten of hearts into her jeans pocket, she was more concerned with her queasy stomach. It was starting to act up again, and she certainly didn't want to throw up while they were on the river.

She nibbled on several crackers and a slice of cheese.

"Are you doing okay?" John asked, coming close and showing her his king of spades.

"I'm fine," she said. "What did Chris draw?" The boy held up a five of clubs.

Soon they were in the raft again and had maneuvered several more rapids that were relatively easy to navigate. An hour later they arrived at the second checkpoint.

"I got another five," Chris exclaimed. "That makes a pair."

She drew a king of hearts and showed it to John, who groaned. His card had been a king of clubs.

"There goes my chance at four of a kind," he said. "Let's head out."

The river flowed gently for several minutes, but each up-and-down motion of the raft caused her stomach to tighten.

The third checkpoint had picnic tables, and they ate fried chicken and chips from one of the waterproof bags and quenched their thirst with soft drinks. Her card was red with a face on it, but before she could tell John or Chris about it, her stomach began to churn. She shoved the card into her pocket and ran for the bushes.

Chris was in the raft when she returned. "I drew an eight of diamonds," he called and she nodded.

John stopped her from climbing back in. "I can get you a ride to the finish spot, Kit. You're pale. You're sick and you won't admit it."

"I'm fine," she insisted, irritated by his concern. "Don't nag me, John," she said and climbed in without his help.

He scowled and shoved them off into the current. As they floated through a canyon, Chris spotted two mountain goats high on a ledge.

They safely rode several rapids of moderate velocity, with John keeping the raft in midstream. He had grown quiet. Perhaps he was concentrating on the river, she thought. At least now her stomach had settled. She reached into the waterproof bag and retrieved a package of cookies. She offered them to Chris.

His hand paused above the open bag. "Are you mad at my dad?" he asked.

"Of course not."

"He's mad at you," Chris insisted. "I can tell."

"No, he's not," Kathryn replied. "He's just busy tending the oars. Do you want a cookie or not?"

"Are you sure?" he asked again.

"I swear he's not angry," Kathryn replied, smiling reassuringly at him.

Chris took two cookies. She offered the bag to John but he declined with a shake of his head.

Depression settled over her. Maybe he *was* angry at her. Well, he had been nagging her. She thought of their first meeting and the arguments that had ensued. Thinking back to those early days of their relationship brought a smile to her lips.

"I'm sorry, John," she said, twisting in her seat to see him.

He put the oars in the raft and pulled her over the seat and into his arms. "John!" she cried. "Who's steering the boat?" She laughed as he kissed her neck.

"It's not a boat, and the current is pretty steady along here. I'm sorry, too, love. I didn't mean to nag you. I was just worried." He squeezed her against him and helped her back to the middle rib of the inflated raft.

"This river is great for rafting," he called. "Not as dangerous as some in the area. Ever rafted the Salmon?"

"I've never rafted *any* river."

"We'll have to do that one next," he called. "What did you draw?"

"Another red card," she replied over her shoulder, clinging to the ropes as the raft bounced over several riffles. "And you?"

"A four of diamonds," he shouted back.

The next checkpoint came into view. They took nature breaks in the bushes and returned to draw their cards.

"I got a pair of eights now to go with my fives," Chris said proudly. "What did you get?"

"A nine of hearts," she said. "I think I have another heart in my pockets somewhere. None of my numbers match so I don't have a pair of anything."

"Daddy got an ace of diamonds," Chris offered. "That makes two kings, an ace and a four. I'm beating him!"

"We need to get going," John called. "Our time is excellent. Now if among the three of us we have a few hands with good points, we may win first place."

Kathryn shook her head. "Count me out. I have an assortment of numbers, but Chris has two pairs. He can help you win."

She glanced at her watch. They had been on the river for more than five hours. Her shoes were soaked and her feet were cold. The splashing of the oars as well as the waves had drenched her from the waist down. The shadows were getting longer. A wave of exhaustion hit her, and she longed to close her eyes. They had spent the night at her house in town and left before dawn to drive to the poker run starting point. Getting up early had never been a problem before this past week. She had dozed in the truck, resting her head against John's shoulder. And each afternoon at the trailer in Avery, she had taken a nap.

She shook the drowsiness away and rubbed her eyelids. John rowed to shore, and they climbed out to stretch their legs and take another break.

"I'm tired of the front," Chris complained. He stared at Kathryn. "Wanna trade places?"

"Sure," she agreed. Perhaps being in the front would help to keep her awake. "How much longer?" she asked John.

"Less than an hour," John promised, "but we'll have some great white water up ahead. Probably the best of the river."

Looking ahead, she could see the water churning. Boulders were scattered along the banks, making her wonder if a landslide had taken place. She glanced up the mountainsides, but any slide had taken place aeons ago. The timber stand was mature.

The raft drifted to one side of the river, barely missing several boulders.

"John," she shouted, "watch out!"

He pulled on the oars and managed to get them away before any collision. Fear of their plight on the river hit her for the first time since launching into the race.

Ahead she saw more white water, endless thundering rapids ready to suck them under. Terrror swamped her as a wave of icy water deluged the raft, drenching her. She gasped, then turned to see if the others were safe.

Chris was laughing. John was busy rowing toward the middle of the river. When she glanced ahead again, she could see in the distance riffles of quieter water, and her confidence returned.

Suddenly she felt a huge submerged boulder scrape the bottom of the raft, and the raft was lifted out of the water. They perched in midair for an endless second, then plunged into the rapids again.

She was catapulted through the air, and the raft shot past her. John shouted, but she couldn't hear his words. He grabbed at her sleeve, but the material tore free. The undercurrent sucked her into its arms, pulling her along the polished boulders on the riverbed. Her lungs were empty but she fought the desire to inhale. The force of the current tossed her upward again and daylight blinded her, but she had sense enough to breathe. Twice she gasped for air, but on the third try raging water replaced the precious oxygen and she lost her hold on reality.

She was drowning. Chris would grow up without her, John would never know she might be carrying his child. John, oh, John, precious John, who had brought joy to her dormant life, John...

THE RINGING IN KATHRYN'S ears grew louder as she felt her body being rolled over. Water gushed from her mouth and nose, allowing the much needed air to find its way into her starving lungs. She gasped, ignoring the burning in her chest.

She thought of John. "Love you, love you," she mumbled.

"I love you, too, Kitty," replied someone, but the voice came through a tunnel.

Hands pressed on her back, then her chest, pressed again and again. She vomited more water, choking, knowing she was strangling on the river.

"Kit, speak to me," John's voice pleaded, and slowly she opened her eyes. "Oh, my God, Kit, are you all right?" He was leaning over her, fear twisting his handsome features.

"Wha—what happened?"

"You were thrown out of the raft," he said, stroking her hand. "You tried to swim to shore. The current leveled off, and you drifted to the shallow part of the river and onto a sandbar. We got here right behind you, sweetheart. Oh, Kit, I felt so helpless." He smiled down at her.

"When we got to you, you were sputtering and mumbling. You acted very mad about something. I hope it wasn't me."

She struggled to sit up.

"Easy," John said, restraining her. "Sit and rest."

She sat for several minutes with her head resting on her knees. When her heart stopped pounding in her ears, she raised her head and brushed strings of wet hair from her face.

A tiny smile lit up her face. "I was mad about many things, but not you." He helped her to her feet. She leaned against him, willing her legs to held her.

"I'm fine," she mumbled.

"Like hell you are," he replied, putting his arm around her. "You're cold, too. Chris, get the bag with the dry clothing in it."

Chris raced to the raft beached on the sandbar. When he returned, he handed the bag to John. "Is she gonna be all right?"

"Yes."

"Are you sure?"

John nodded again.

Chris sighed deeply. "We've only had her a few months."

"We'll have her with us a lot longer than that, son. You'll see. Now turn your back and I'll help her change into some dry clothing."

Dry jeans over damp underwear made Kathryn aware of how cold she was, and a chill raced through her. John insisted on giving her his flannel shirt to put on over her sweatshirt.

"What about the race?" Kathryn asked, looking at the beads of water beneath the crystal of her wristwatch.

"It's still on and we're beyond the rapids," John said. "The river is the only way to get you to a hospital."

"I don't need a hospital," she insisted. "I'm fine."

"Feel like riding a little farther?" he asked.

"I think so," she said. "Besides, you fellows need that last card to finish your hands."

"You're a good sport, Kit, too good at times," John said, helping her back into the raft.

Twenty minutes later they arrived at the final checkpoint and the end of the race. As John helped her out of the raft, Chris ran to the timer and told him about the accident.

Soon a crowd surrounded them. One woman asked if they needed an ambulance, another offered Kathryn a towel for her hair. A man and his son volunteered to deflate the raft and load it into the truck that had been driven from the starting place by Cal Wright.

"Can you walk, Kit? Maybe I should carry you," John said.

"I'm fine," she said weakly, but she leaned on his arm as they made their way to the woman holding the sack of playing cards.

Chris drew another eight. "Three of a kind," he screamed.

"And you, John," an attractive blond woman said, smiling in a way that was more than friendly.

He smiled in return as he withdraw a card. "Another four," he groaned. "Two pairs. Beaten by my own son. He has a full house."

Chris slapped him on his hip pocket with glee.

"Kit, your turn," John said, and the woman studied Kathryn as she stuck her hand into the sack.

"A queen of hearts," Kathryn announced grimacing. "I have all red cards, but none of them match." She shoved it into the vest of John's flannel shirt.

"What do you mean by not matching?" John asked.

"No pairs or stuff like that," she said. "Just red cards."

"Let me see." The crowd began to gather around them.

She laid the queen of hearts down on the check-in table and then searched her jeans pockets. "They're in my wet pants."

"I'll get them." Chris darted to the truck and returned, shoving the soggy jeans into her hands. "Hurry," he said, hopping from one foot to the other.

She shuddered as she shoved her hand into the wet pocket and withdrew a ten of hearts, then a nine of hearts.

"All hearts," John said. "Maybe you have a flush."

"What's that?" she asked, checking the other front pocket.

"All the same suit, regardless of their order. It beats a straight and three of a kind," he said.

She pulled out a red king, also a heart. "Is that good?"

He grinned, nodding his dark head. "Four out of five. Do you remember what the other card is? Damn it, Kit, find the last card."

She checked one hip pocket, but it was empty. "Maybe I've lost it."

"You can't lose it," Chris cried. "We gotta win!"

She slid her hand into the cold dampness of the other hip pocket and slowly withdrew a folded card. She handed it to him. "You look at it. I don't know what I need to make it good." He started to unfold the card, but she impulsively grabbed it back. "I'll do it." She unfolded it and laid down a jack of hearts.

The crowd roared and clapped.

"Is that good?" she asked, glancing around at all the smiling faces. "They're all mixed up." She began to arrange them in ascending order on the table. "Nine, ten, jack, queen and king, and all hearts. Oh, they do follow a pattern, don't they?"

John hugged her. "Honey, they make up a straight flush. The only hand that beats it is a royal flush. If that nine had been an ace, you'd have had the best hand in poker."

"Oh." Kathryn's puzzled expression changed into a smile. "Do we win?"

"You bet," he said. "Two pairs, a full house and a straight flush, along with the second-best time. We get the trophy and money and a free dinner in Kooskia. And we owe it all to you."

The crowd began to disperse, heading into town for drinks and dinner. "See everyone at Amundson's Café," Cal Wright called, and John waved to him, Natalie and the children.

"Where's Chris?" Kathryn asked.

"He's loading the raft."

"For an only child like me all these Brasher relatives can be quite overwhelming," she said, surveying the crowd.

"You'll get to know them," he assured her. "It takes time."

He pulled her into the crook of his arm and held her. "Thank God you're all right now." He peered into her face. "You're still a little pale."

She touched her lips. "It's probably because I have no lipstick on. I must look a mess," she said, trying to smooth her drying curls.

"You look beautiful and alive." He frowned. "Any more nausea?"

She nodded. "Just a tinge."

KATHRYN LAY ON HER BACK, her hand resting on her lower abdomen. She had seen a physician, and he had confirmed her condition.

"From your description of your scant period, I'd say you conceived in late May." He'd checked over a chart. "Your child should arrive in late February."

"I can't believe it," she had replied. "After all these years?"

"I'm glad you and your husband are happy about it," the physician had said. "Some women your age don't want children. There are risks." She had slowly nodded her head. "We'll want to do an amniocentesis to make sure both the baby and mother are healthy."

"Of course," Kathryn had agreed, and she had left the clinic slightly dazed.

She turned in the bed to John, his deep, steady breathing telling her he was asleep. *So many changes in only a few months*, she thought. A baby in the middle of the spring semester. What would this do to John's plans of a school for the children of the loggers who worked for him? Would he be upset? The pregnancy was her fault for sure. He had suggested birth control, and she had chosen to take her chances. Now a baby was growing in her body, a baby conceived in love and in passion. Part John Brasher and part Kathryn Keith.

What would he or she look like, she wondered. The baby would be definitely dark-haired, probably have blue eyes, but possibly...

John's hand slid across her waist. "Insomnia?"

"Did I wake you?" she asked.

"You've been tossing and turning like a broody hen trying to make a nest," he murmured against her cheek.

"I was thinking."

"About?"

"Everything. Your trip to Roseburg, the baby, moving—everything."

"We'll leave early and drive to Coeur d'Alene. The plane takes off at ten. You can spend the day in the big city. I'll catch the late afternoon flight from Portland, and we'll be back here by nightfall."

"I'll miss him," Kathryn said, sighing.

"Chris will only be gone for two weeks. We'll make this another honeymoon. If you'll stay in Avery, I'll take you to the landings again, and you can learn more about what we loggers do," John promised. "We're running a little behind schedule. We won't get to Bonners Ferry in August. Perhaps late September."

"Have you been taking too much time out for Chris and me?"

He pulled her closer. "A man has to have some time away from business." He rolled onto his side and began to caress one of her breasts, his thumb making circles around her nipple.

"You're going to be a grandfather before you become a father again," she whispered, tracing the line of hair down his body to where it widened. He groaned.

"It's getting impossible to hide my virility." His mouth sought hers in the darkness. "In the old days a man was judged by the number of children he produced, but now times have changed. A man can be sexually active and give no outward proof of his prowess."

"Unless the woman messes up?"

"Having our child is not messing up, sweetheart," he murmured as he kissed her cheek. "I married you because I love you. A baby adds dimension to this new life of ours. It gives us incentive to work out any minor problems we might have."

"What problems?" she asked. "Everything's so perfect."

"Misunderstandings," he said. "Two people don't always think alike. This living together in harmony takes practice."

"As long as we talk, everything will be fine," she assured him. "And did you see Chris when we told him?"

John chuckled. "His eyes lit up like Christmas bulbs. He's already making plans to take him on hikes in the woods and teach him to 'talk logger.' What a boy! And to think I didn't know he existed until he was almost three years old. I don't want that to happen with this child. I want to be with you during the pregnancy, at the birth. Good Lord, I've never seen any of my children born. Helen always wanted to just get it over with."

"Not me," she said. "I want you with me. Parenting today is a joint project."

"I agree, love," John said.

"You can change the diapers," she teased.

His voice sounded a little sheepish. "I refused to get involved in that end of raising my daughters." She felt him shrug in the darkness. "I think I missed out on something."

"Your work kept you away," she whispered, stroking his chest.

"Too much," he agreed. "We'll have to revolutionize the logging industry. I want more than a weekend relationship with my new wife and my son and my... whatever."

"We can find out if it's a boy or a girl when the amniocentesis is done. Do you want to know?"

"I don't know. It would take away the suspense," he said, his hand sliding between her thighs and stroking the satin skin before finding the moist heat he sought. "I'd rather it be a surprise. Just tell me if it's healthy and normal. But even if it weren't, I'd love it because it's us, our very own creation."

She turned in his arms, arching against him, the thrill of her own arousal matching his as she responded to his lovemaking.

Much later, when they lay quietly in each other's arms, she sighed. "It's all too perfect, John. Something will go wrong. I feel it." She shuddered as she tightened her arm around his waist.

"What could possibly go wrong, love?" he asked, kissing her lips again. "Now try to sleep. A pregnant woman needs her rest." He pulled her back against his chest, tucking his legs up under hers and folding his arms across her breasts. He nibbled playfully on her earlobe and squeezed her, then settled into slumber again, his breathing disturbing her short hair as she continued to lie awake.

Gray streaks of dawn filled the room when she finally succumbed to an uneasy sleep.

CHAPTER THIRTEEN

THE HOUSE WAS FULL of Chris's absence. Everything Kathryn straightened remained undisturbed. His baseball mitt and bat were in his room, not lying on the living room floor for John to trip over. The laundry dropped to one load before the weekend.

After two days of getting the house in order, Kathryn packed two suitcases and drove to Avery.

The next morning John took her up to the landings. The men nodded and mumbled a greeting when he introduced her.

"They're quieter this time," she said, sharing a thermos of coffee with John.

He laughed. "They know you're the boss's wife and a lady. Usually they curse a blue streak, especially when trouble occurs. If you stay around, they'll get used to you and return to their usual style of communication." He tossed the dregs of coffee from his cup and screwed the top back on the thermos. "Now let's check out the Donkey Creek landing. That's where Swede and Mugger are working."

"How is Mugger?" she asked, recalling the brief meeting in the hospital months earlier, the night John and she almost... Her eyes flew to John's face.

"Except for Mugger, that night might have moved everything ahead for us," John said softly. He put his arm around her shoulders and led her to the truck.

"Did he recover?" she asked, as they bumped along a narrow dirt road.

"Partially," John said. "He insisted on coming back to work, but that's another reason I want to check everything out this morning. Mugger isn't a complainer, and that might get him into more trouble if he's pushing himself too soon."

The radio crackled to life and John listened, spoke into the mouthpiece, then to her. "A load of logs is coming. We need to pull into the next jail."

Before she could decipher his meaning, they turned into a pullout carved into the side of the mountain seconds before a huge truck barreled past them, its trailer stacked high with cedar logs, pieces of their shaggy bark flying in the wind.

"Good grief, what if this turnout hadn't been here?" she said with a gasp, her hand pressed against her thudding heart. "He would have run right over us."

"Might," John said, shifting back into gear, "but there are jails every quarter mile, and each vehicle is equipped with a radio. Private cars drive these roads at their own risk. Some ignore the warning signs, but they do it only a few times. This is logging country, and the trucks have the right-of-way."

"Considering their size, I can understand why."

He glanced at her. "Want to take a ride in one?"

"I don't know," she replied. "Would I live to tell about it?"

"I wouldn't suggest it if I didn't think you'd stay in one piece."

"Then yes," she said. "I'll put it in my memoirs and tell the children this fall. When they ask me what I did during my summer vacation, I'll say, 'I got pregnant and rode in a logging truck.' Won't they be impressed?"

When they arrived at the steep site of the second landing, they climbed out and John took her hand.

"Hey," a man's deep voice shouted, "the boss brought his lady." A string of expletives filled the air.

John laughed. "Only Swede would give a gypo's lady a greeting like that. He never changes."

Swede jumped down from his loader and strode toward them, his wide grin showing the spaces between his tobacco-stained teeth. He shot a stream of tobacco juice over the side of the graded landing and wiped his mouth with the back of his sleeve.

"Howdy, ma'am," he said, pulling a grease-stained rag from his hip pocket and wiping his hands. "Wouldn't want to dirty those nice clean hands, ma'am," he said as he held up his own grimy palms and declined her handshake.

"Hey, Mugger, get the hell over here and meet the boss's lady again." The air was filled with another string of expletives. "That no-good, lazy lumberjack, he's as worthless as tits on a..." Swede grinned at Kathryn. "Sorry, ma'am."

Mugger took a few limping steps toward them, a gasoline-powered chain saw dangling from his hand. He paused when another man said something to him, then waved and stayed with the crew. Rubbing his back a few times between pulls on the saw, he concentrated on the log pile.

"How's Mugger doing?" John asked, studying the young man.

"Not so good, boss," Swede admitted. "He's not as fast as the other knot bumpers, but they cover for him. I can tell he's still in pain. I reckon when a man breaks his pelvis, his hips get out of whack and that throws his stride off, and when he bends or lifts the saw, well..." Swede took his hard hat off and wiped his forehead. "We may have to find something else for him. But he never complains."

John nodded.

"He's too timid to tell you, boss, but he might be quitting anyhow." Swede glanced fondly at the tall, thin man who had paused to talk with another logger.

"Why is that?" John asked.

Swede grinned. "You know that new little waitress at the café in Avery?"

"The pretty brunette? Isn't she Mrs. Boren's cousin from Los Angeles?"

"That's the one," Swede said, spitting tobacco juice into the dust at their feet. "Well, Mugger fell for her like a load of logs. He spends all his spare time with her, hanging around the café if she's working nights, slipping off to St. Maries or Kellogg on the weekends. Why, the boy's plumb lost his good sense."

"So why would he quit?" Kathryn asked, unable to keep out of the conversation.

Swede squinted down at her. "Well, ma'am, her people have offered him a job in the kitchen. They've known him since he was a sprout and came to visit him in the hospital when he had his accident. Me and the Borens, we're the only family he's had since his folks left the county, excepting the boss here."

"They abandoned him?" she asked.

"Nah." Swede spat again. "He was fifteen and didn't want to go so they gave him a choice. Sawdust was in his blood, and he came to work for the boss here and we been keeping an eye on him ever since. Anyway, the Borens, they say if Mugger and Colleen are serious, then he should have a job that's safer for a family man. I'm afeared he's liable to take it, boss. But he'll level with you all in good time. Probably before we move up north."

John nodded. "Thanks for telling me."

"Sure thing, boss. Well, ma'am, nice to meetcha again. Now I'd best get back to the loader. Here comes the next truck, and you know how cranky them truck drivers can get. They sit around all day, drinking coffee and flirting with purty waitresses, riding in them cushy trucks out of the weather, waiting for the real workers to load their rig, and all they do is complain about the in-ee-fficiency of the crew. 'Time is money, time is money,' they gripe. Well, we know that," and a string of profanity filled the air as he stomped back to the heel-boom loader and climbed into the cab.

Kathryn climbed up the slope, out of the way of the workers, and watched the frantic activity on the right-of-way below her. John moved from man to man, listening to their complaints and opinions, joking with one of the yarding bosses. She smiled as she recalled their first argument over his determination to get a new hook tender.

John stood head and shoulders above most of the other men. He was dressed in a blue flannel shirt, red suspenders, jeans and calk boots like the other workers, but his demeanor as well as his height set him apart. Even a stranger would be able to tell he was in charge. Love for him filled Kathryn with pride as she watched him go to the truck driver.

Were they arguing? Voices were raised, but the words were indistinguishable to Kathryn on the side of the hill. Apparently they had run out of a particular sized log for loading. Three men, including Mugger, were cutting the small limbs from the fallen trees that had been stacked along the side of the road. She followed the line of logs and was surprised to find them running for over a quarter of a mile.

John went to his truck and removed a chain saw from the bed. He went to the men who were delimbing the falling trees, pulled the starter cord and the engine revved to life. He plunged into the work alongside his employees, cutting the small limbs that hindered the loading of the logs. Some of the logs were more than three feet in diameter. She was doubly surprised when the truck driver joined them. She smiled. If they were union men, they were surely loosely organized, she reflected, recalling the disputes and right-to-work laws that complicated her home state's labor history.

John turned his chain saw off and called to Swede. A string of profanity was exchanged between the two men.

"My goodness." Kathryn gasped, covering her mouth in surprise. "Is that you talking, John? No wonder your son knows a few curse words."

When the heel-boom loader was again busy lifting the logs onto the trailer, John spotted her on the hillside. He waved, then motioned for her to come down.

She worked her way around and down the steep hillside. Her boot slipped on some loose dirt, and she fell on her behind, sliding the rest of the way to the road.

John ran to her and helped her to her feet. "Are you okay?" he asked, dusting her pant legs and turning her around. "First I take you on a dangerous raft ride, and now I bring you up here. Maybe you would be safer back in town."

"No! Don't baby me, John. I want to know more about your work. It's all so different. And your language back there! Goodness, I've never heard you talk like that before."

"Sorry, Kit," he said, looking sheepish. 'Loggers aren't noted for their drawing room language. I try to keep it in its place. I suppose I've ruined my romantic image in your eyes, haven't I?"

"Well," she agreed, "your vocabulary was anything but romantic. No wonder your son has a problem at times."

"I've warned him."

"Perhaps it's time to set an example," she chided.

"Playing the teacher again?"

She grinned. "Sorry. I'm used to bossing eight-year-olds. Now," she said, dusting her behind a final time, "you said something about hitching a ride in a logging truck."

"Are you sure?"

"This baby will surely have sawdust in his veins. So he might as well start young." She looked at the loaded truck. "Where will he take them?"

"To the river landing near the bridge in St. Maries," John replied. "They'll be added to the boom they're building and be floated on the St. Joe to Coeur d'Alene."

"Pulled by the tugboats?" she asked. 'We took the children to the bridge one afternoon and watched them. It was fascinating."

"Want to go with him?" John asked.

"By myself?"

"No, we could squeeze in together if you'll sit on my lap," John replied. "Want to cozy up in a logging truck with me?"

"I'd love to."

He took her hand and guided her to the loaded truck, its powerful engine idling noisily.

The driver tightened the wraps on his load, double-checking each one. "Did she accept our offer?" the driver said, turning to him.

"Yes," John said and introduced them. "Kit, this is Steve Davison. We went to school together years ago. He owns this rig, and I know he doesn't want to lose it."

The driver laughed, his brown eyes dancing with delight, adding to his rugged, attractive charm. "The bank and I own this rig," he corrected John, "but I still don't want to lose it. Climb in, folks. I'll be with you as soon as I brand the logs."

"Brand the logs?" Kathryn asked, twisting in the cab to find the driver.

"He stamps the sale number on the ends and sprays them with paint so no one can accuse him of stealing them," John explained.

"How can you steal logs? Aren't they too heavy?" she asked.

"You've heard of cattle rustlers?"

"Of course, I'm from Arizona and we have a history of cattle rustling. Even today rustlers steal them, but they use trucks now."

"Same here," John said. "That weekend I had to stay up here because of security problems, we had lost a load of logs to thieves who came up here at night during the week. They used a self-loader, and made off with a load and sold it in Plummer. We caught the thieves the second night. We convinced the sheriff and a deputy to join our stakeout. The sheriff took them away in cuffs and impounded their truck."

"Oh, John, I didn't know enough to worry. Why didn't you tell me?"

"You've answered your own question, sweetheart." He kissed her cheek. "It doesn't happen often so don't worry."

Steve Davison returned to the cab, and soon they were on their way down the mountain. John positioned her snugly between his legs, his arms around her waist.

They drove to the junction where their road joined another slightly wider dirt road. The driver stopped, climbed from the cab and disappeared.

"He's tightening the wrappers," John said.

Kathryn peered out through the back window of the cab, but the driver was out of sight. She turned to John. "Why?"

"The logs settle," John explained. "Steve wouldn't want them to start to slide."

She shuddered, imagining what could happen to them as well as the other vehicles on the road. Steve climbed back into the cab, turned the key and the powerful engine roared to life again. Soon they were careering down the mountainside.

The wind tore at Kathryn's hair, and the sound of the muffler and exhaust stacks just outside the door pounded in her ears. The driver talked on his CB continually, but the voices were garbled and she wondered how the drivers could understand each other. They passed several empty trucks parked in the turnouts affectionately called jails by the men. Steve waved to each driver as his truck roared by.

As he braked around a curve, Kathryn leaned out the window. No road was visible on her side, nothing but a sheer drop-off to the river below. She clutched John's forearm, suppressing the scream that threatened to explode from her throat.

"It's better not to look," John called against her ear.

The road smoothed out as they approached Avery, and Steve applied the air brakes. He grinned at her. "You know, logging truck drivers tend to be hard of hearing," he shouted.

"What?" she called back. John and Steve broke up laughing. She caught their joke and laughed with them.

At the landing in St. Maries, she stood out of the way and watched as a huge forklift with giant metal claws removed the logs in one load, spreading them out on the ground for scaling.

Within minutes the paperwork was completed, the trailer was lifted onto the back of the tractor and they were on the road again. Without a load the tractor and mounted trailer bounced and vibrated noisily. John tightened his hold on her, trying without much success to ease the jostling.

When they arrived back at the landing, they waved goodbye to the workers and hurried to John's truck. John had two more landings to check, and they had not yet taken a lunch break.

At three in the afternoon, they stopped at the café in Avery and ate. Kathryn breathed a sigh of relief. All she had done was stand around and watch, yet she felt exhausted from the frantic pace of the work.

"Is it always so busy?" she asked, taking a bite of her chicken fried steak.

"The workers have breaks for coffee and the bushes, but they don't linger over their meals," John answered. "Too much work to do and not much time."

HE CAME HOME EACH NIGHT to the trailer, but some nights John fell asleep the minute his handsome head hit the pillow. She worried about the long workdays, the dangers of logging, the inspections of the forest service that could close down an operation, the dry weeks ahead that could bring forest fires, the environmental impact of the work. She knew John was concerned about the wildlife. He had described some of the methods used to prevent pollution of the mountain streams and to maintain the balance of nature in the untamed wilderness where his work took him.

"I love this country as much as a city environmentalist," he had said. "Some of them will visit occasionally, some not at all, but I live here. I want a natural heritage for my children, too, all of them," he had said, his hand sliding to her abdomen.

Once Kathryn had felt a tiny bulge just above her pelvic bone as she lay on her back, but it was too early to feel movement. Her waist was still slim, but she had begun to look at maternity clothing in the department stores. How many changes in her life could she cope with at once? she asked herself as she lay in bed at night, awake with wonder while her husband slept his exhausted slumber.

THEY WERE AWAKENED by loud pounding on the trailer door the morning John was to fly to Portland to get Chris.

Kathryn tried to smooth her hair as she grabbed a robe and ran through the trailer, fumbling with the lock and finally yanking the door open.

Swede stood with his cap in hand. "Sorry, ma'am, but is the boss here?"

"Of course," she said. "Come in and I'll get him." She turned and collided with John as he shoved the tails of his shirt into his jeans.

"What's wrong, Swede?"

"Those damned thieving..." and Swede described the culprits in scathing tones, calling upon deities Kathryn didn't know existed. "They got away with two good loads. Mugger and me, we got there at four, and they had already made off with them. Sorry to bother you, boss, you planning to get the boy and all, but I knew you'd want to know." He lingered on the step.

"Come in, Swede, and have some coffee," Kathryn said, hurrying to the stove.

Over coffee and breakfast she listened as John and Swede discussed the problem.

"Kit, I hate to ask this, but could you go get Chris?" John said tentatively. "I can't leave now."

"Oh, please, don't ask me," Kathryn exclaimed. "I've never been there. I've never met your..."

John rubbed the back of his neck as he paced the cramped quarters. "I can draw you a map. It's either that or he stays another week."

Uncertainty tore at her while she tried to understand John's predicament. "If you'll tell me how to find him, of course I'll go. It's time he came home."

"The flight leaves Coeur d'Alene at ten, so you have plenty of time. Rent a car in Portland and drive to Rose-burg. Here's a map," and he began to draw a crude map of the city on a paper napkin. "Here's the address and phone number, my plane ticket and some money." John peeled several hundred dollar bills from his wallet.

She stared at the map and the money, numb with this unexpected change in their plans.

"Drive carefully, sweetheart," he said, and he kissed her mouth lightly. "I've got to call the sheriff and get to the landing." He hurried to the bedroom and returned with a light jacket, his calk boots and a rifle.

She blanched at the sight of the gun.

"Just in case," he said, lacing up his boots. He kissed her again and was out the door with Swede running to keep up with his long strides.

A few hours later she was getting her boarding pass at the terminal in Coeur d'Alene. The flight to Portland was uneventful, and she had no trouble finding his former wife's residence. But when Kathryn parked in front of the rambling ranch-style house in an affluent part of town, her confidence began to falter.

Grimacing, she opened the car door and approached the house. On the fourth ring of the bell, the door was opened by a tall, slender woman wearing a black satin swimsuit with a red-and-white terry-cloth robe. Her hair was wet, and she looked none too happy at having had her swim interrupted.

Kathryn tried to appear confident. "I'm Kathryn Brasher. John had an emergency so I've come for Chris." The words seemed to rush out.

The woman arched a finely plucked brow, her smile highlighting the sun wrinkles around her mouth and eyes. "If I know my Johnnie boy, the emergency was job related."

Kathryn resisted a retort. "You are Helen... Brasher?" It felt strange calling the woman by Kathryn's own married name.

The woman took a long drag on a filter-tipped cigarette and exhaled, studying Kathryn through the smoke. "So you're the woman Johnnie talked into marrying. Do you know how much you saved his skin?"

Kathryn ignored the innuendo. "Yes, I'm his wife." The woman's manner began to grate. "Is Chris here?" Kathryn asked. "You knew John was to get him this morning?"

"Of course," the woman purred. "How interesting. I knew he was desperate, and I was curious to see you. My son had nothing but... Oh, never mind." She knocked a piece of ash from her cigarette.

Kathryn broke eye contact first. "Please, is Chris here?"

"No."

"Where is he?" Kathryn asked, concern tightening her voice.

"The mouthy little brat is with his oldest sister."

"Why?"

"He kept carrying on about his *new* family, as though the rest of us didn't exist anymore. He's still my son, remember."

"I came for Chris," Kathryn said, unable to hide her irritation. "I don't have time for all this. You should have notified John if you didn't want Chris to stay with you the full two weeks. We would have come for him earlier."

"I'm sure," said Helen dryly as she exhaled smoke through her flaring nostrils.

"Is Chris all right?" Kathryn asked.

"He's worse than ever," Helen declared. "He's like a broken record. Miss Keith this, Miss Keith that, and he's never still. He needs medication to settle him down."

"He needs love and stability, that's all," Kathryn replied, her voice rising. "Are his clothes here?"

"Debbie took them," Helen replied. "After a week of this togetherness, I couldn't take it anymore. Debbie offered to take him off my hands." She laughed. "Thank God I didn't follow through on my threat to take him back."

Kathryn shook her head. "I don't understand. You wanted to have Chris live here with you, yet you couldn't stand him more than a few days?"

"It doesn't matter now," Helen said. "I have what I want and John is agreeable. Didn't John tell you about his little dilemma?"

Some inner voice warned Kathryn to put a halt to the conversation. "Of course, but I didn't come to hear all this. I've come for Chris. May I have Debbie's address?" She grabbed a pen from her purse.

"Don't be hasty, dear," Helen murmured. "It's so very interesting to see you in the flesh. John has remained single all these years. He had trouble accepting the breakup of our marriage, you know. He was heartbroken."

"That's not what he's told me," Kathryn replied, wishing immediately she hadn't taken Helen's bait. "Now, may I have Debbie's address? We have a plane to catch in Portland." She jotted down the address and the hastily given directions.

"I'm sure he's glossed over his feelings to spare you, my dear," Helen said. "I had begun to think he would never take the plunge again. You were Chris's teacher?"

Kathryn nodded.

"Very interesting," said Helen as she turned away. "Well, give John a kiss for me," she said, closing the door in dismissal.

Helen's words haunted Kathryn as she followed the directions to John's daughter's home. The house was in a much more modest part of town and close to the mill.

She dismissed any thought of Helen as she hurried to the door. Before she could ring the bell, the door flew open and Chris was in her arms.

"Oh, Chris, honey, I missed you so much," Kathryn said.

"I missed you, too, Miss Keith," the boy exclaimed, then he began to cry.

She knelt and held him, waiting for his tears to subside. "What is this 'Miss Keith' all about?" she asked gently. "Aren't you my little boy anymore?"

He pulled back and wiped his eyes on his shirt-sleeve. "My other mom said I couldn't call you that anymore. That I had only one mom and mean old...Leo." Here, he spit the word out. "He said I had a big mouth, and I got mad and he spanked me with his belt, and I ran away, but he found me and—and..." Chris's sobs began again in earnest.

She held him until his sobs changed into hiccups, then handed him two tissues to dry his face.

"Hey, you really came for me," he said, grinning through the tears. "Leo said you wouldn't want me back and I told him..." His green eyes glistened. "I cussed him out real good, just like Swede does when he gets mad." He hung his head. "That's when Debbie came and got me. Do you know Deb?" He squinted up at her.

"I know she's your sister."

"You do? How come?"

"John—your father told me all about her and Sherie...and lots of things," Kathryn said.

"And my real mom and Leo?" Chris asked.

"I met her a little while ago, and she told me you were here," she replied.

"You'll like Debbie. She has a brand-new baby. His name is John Christopher after me and my dad. Isn't that great?"

"She had the baby?" Kathryn asked. "When?"

He counted on his fingers. "Four days ago."

"Oh, my goodness, and she had you also?"

He nodded. "I stayed here with Jas. He's Debbie's husband and his name is really Jasper, but he hates it. He and me, we had pizza, and when we went to bring Debbie home, I got to hold Little John." He burst into giggles. "We call him Little John because he sure has to grow tall to be as big as my dad. He's my ne-nephew."

"That's wonderful," she said. "Your father will be very proud."

Chris grew solemn. "Do I really have to call you Miss Keith again?"

"You can call me whatever you want," she said as she kissed his wet cheek. "Frankly, I had become rather fond of being called Mom."

"Great...Mom." He grinned at her. "Wanna meet Debbie and Little John? Jas is at work."

"Sure, lead the way."

Debbie was tall and slender like her mother, but had John's darker coloring. She wore a loose duster but, other than that concession to her figure, she gave no evidence of having given birth a few days earlier. Kathryn liked her from the moment they met.

"Please come in," Debbie said, reaching for her hand. "Chris has been talking about you ever since he arrived." She smiled. "I suspect that might be one of several reasons for my mother's unusual loss of control. My mother is usually super cool, but she can't handle the competition. Chris painted you in glowing colors, talking about your being his teacher and your wonderful oatmeal cookies. Mom always hated to bake."

"John or I would have come sooner if we had known there were problems," Kathryn said.

"I love my little brother. When he was born and Mom and Leo resented him, I took care of him when I wasn't in school. I changed his diapers more than my mother did. Now that I'm older, I can see the situation differently. I think she felt guilty, and he was a constant reminder of my father. To me he was like my very own Cabbage Patch doll, only a lot cuter." She smiled at him and ruffled his hair.

"Ah, cut it out, Deb," Chris said as he jerked away and leaped onto the sofa, sitting with his legs crossed and grinning.

"He can stay here anytime," Debbie said. "Now, want to meet Little John?"

Kathryn nodded and Debbie left.

She returned carrying a tiny bundle wrapped in a blue flannel receiving blanket. She laid the baby on the sofa beside her and opened the blanket.

"We all have the same hair," Chris declared. "Do you think our new baby will have dark hair, too?"

Kathryn looked at Debbie as the new mother smiled fondly at her baby. "Probably."

"Chris told me you were expecting, but he didn't know when," Debbie said.

"Late February," Kathryn replied. "It seems an eternity away."

"I think it's wonderful," Debbie said. "Chris told my mother, too. That just about drove her over the cliff." Debbie laughed softly. "If I know my father, he's very pleased."

"He is," Kathryn replied. "I'm more surprised than he is."

"Dad always was good to us kids," Debbie said. "In spite of the problems he had with my mother and Leo. His only fault was that of working too much. I'm glad Jas works at the mill and not in the woods."

They visited for another hour before Kathryn and Chris started back to Portland. Chris's hand clung to hers as they walked through the terminal and got their boarding passes.

He was quiet on the return flight. "How about dinner at McDonald's in Coeur d'Alene?" Kathryn suggested as the plane descended over the city.

"Okay."

"Are you glad to be going home?" she asked, puzzled by his quiet demeanor.

He shrugged.

"Your dad missed you."

He didn't comment. They claimed their luggage and drove to the restaurant.

His spirits perked up when they slid into a booth. "These are almost as good as the Cook Shack's hamburgers," he said, between mouthfuls.

As they drove through St. Maries and turned onto the road to Avery, Chris turned to her. "I don't want to go there anymore. Helen's not my mom anymore. You are." He stared out the window into the darkness.

"What really happened at your mother's house in Roseburg?" Kathryn asked.

"Nothing," Chris replied as he hunkered down against the car door.

JOHN MET THEM at the trailer door. "Have a good trip?" he asked, first hugging his son.

Chris grunted and wriggled free.

John turned to Kathryn. "What's wrong?"

Kathryn shook her head. "Chris and his mother had some problems. I found him at Debbie's. Helen, well, she . . . said things."

"I thought about you constantly, afraid Helen might give you a bad time."

"She didn't give me a bad time," Kathryn insisted. "She just . . . said things."

"Like what?"

Her chin raised. "Reasons about why you had to—it isn't important."

"God damn it!" John's tone of voice grew harsh. "It's important if you and Chris have clammed up. Now what happened?"

A movement caught her attention. "Not now," she said, motioning toward Chris.

He was crouched in the corner of the sofa, his knees pulled up tightly against his chest. "Are you two gonna fight?" he asked, his voice barely above a whisper.

She jumped when John's arm fell around her shoulder. "No, son, we're not going to fight. If there's a problem, we'll work it out."

Chris slid forward until the tips of his shoes touched the floor. "You promise?"

"We promise," John said, still frowning at his son.

"Okay." Chris darted from the sofa and out the door of the trailer.

"Now," John said, taking her in his arms and pulling her close. "What really happened in Roseburg?"

"Helen made all kinds of insinuations about you and me."

"Based on what."

"That you . . . had to get married."

He grinned. "Sounds like two teenagers in trouble." Smiling, he kissed her mouth lightly. "I hope you told her she was crazy."

"You don't understand," Kathryn said, stiffening in his arms. "She meant you, not me."

He stepped away, reaching for his jacket. "You can tell me all about it later. Whatever she said must be a gross exaggeration. Helen tends to twist the truth to suit her needs."

His arms surrounded her as he pulled her close. "I have to go back to the landing where the logs were stolen, but I wanted to be here when you arrived."

She peered into his blue eyes, wondering if Helen's comments could hold any truth. Could these eyes, reflecting what she had always thought was love, be lying eyes? How could she even ask him? If Helen had been telling the truth, then their marriage was a sham and this baby not conceived in love at all. But if Helen had lied, he would be hurt by her lack of trust.

As his lips covered hers, she forced herself to respond, but couldn't erase Helen's haunting accusations. After a quick meal at the café, John kissed her again and drove off into the night. As she and Chris returned to the trailer, her mind was on her husband and his promise to talk. Hadn't Debbie said that work always came first with John Brasher?

As she lay awake alone in his bed, she lived over and over again the early days of their romance, the sudden proposal, the impulsive marriage. But had it been impulsive? Perhaps calculating would be a better word.

CHAPTER FOURTEEN

THE BED SANK under John's weight. Kathryn glanced at the clock on the nightstand. It was four in the morning with the early promise of daybreak filling the room.

"Where have you been?" she asked, her voice drugged with sleep. "You didn't say a thing. You just rushed off."

"Sorry, sweetheart," he replied. "Sometimes I still act like I'm single. We had a tip that the wood thieves were going to strike again so we staked out all the landings."

She sat up, rubbing her eyes. "Did you catch them?"

"Yes," he replied, stripping out of his flannel shirt and T-shirt. His red suspenders hung down past his hips. In spite of her hurt and anger his undressing aroused her.

"Did everything turn out safely? No gunshots?"

"Just a warning shot," he said. "They hit at two this morning, and we were waiting for them. Damn it, they were the same men we caught before. They were out on bail. The sheriff didn't want to send us any men, but with several thefts in the area, we were able to put enough pressure on his office to convince him his political future might be affected. Elections are coming up and loggers' votes carry clout."

She listened to the sounds of his leather laces as he loosened his boots, unfastened his jeans and sat on the edge of the bed.

"If the logs are branded, why aren't the thieves caught at the mill when they try to sell the logs?" she asked.

"They don't sell them to the mills," he explained. "These guys cut the logs and sell them as firewood, often as far away as Lewiston. The city folks don't know they're not seasoned until they try to burn them. What a shame to have such good logs go up in smoke."

He tossed his jeans over the seat of a nearby chair and stretched, the muscles in his back rippling and twisting. "I should shower," he said and immediately yawned.

"Later," she murmured, sympathizing with his exhaustion.

He groaned as he dropped to the pillow. "God, I'm tired," he said. "Normally I'd be up and out by this time. How do I do it? Day after day, week after week?"

She turned to him, accepting his arm around her shoulders. Her hand rested on his chest, enjoying the warmth of his body against her palm.

Thoughts of Helen's insinuations flooded her, tightening the vice of doubt around her heart. Had he betrayed her in order to keep his son? Her eyes burned and she squeezed her eyelids tight, unaware of the tears falling against his shoulder.

He stretched in the graying dawn, switched the lamp on and turned back to her. "What's wrong, Kit? Worried about me?" he asked, and he kissed her nose, then her mouth.

"Yes," she lied. "I was gone for less than a day and I feel as though I've lost touch with you."

"Maybe it's the pregnancy," he said. "Some women get emotional in their early months."

"You're probably right. Don't mind me. I've been overreacting to every little thing."

"Tell me about your meeting with Helen," he said. "She can be rather...bitchy at times."

"Maybe I'm jealous, but it's hard to believe that you were married to her for so long," Kathryn said. "She made me feel as though I were a pawn and said you had . . . used me to keep Chris."

He laughed. "That's crazy. Don't believe her. She's not happy unless she stirs things up."

"She said you had never remarried because you took the breakup of your first marriage so hard."

"A delusion, Kit," he insisted. "It eases her own guilt about fooling around on me. She's a real bitch. Don't believe what she says."

She studied his features for a few minutes.

His hand on her upper arm tightened. "Believe me." He kissed her mouth lightly and relaxed his hold on her. "How's Debbie?" he asked.

"She's made you a grandfather," Kathryn replied, and she was able to give him a genuine smile at long last.

"When?" he asked, grinning proudly.

"Four days ago," she said. "Debbie is fine and you have a grandson named John Christopher—Little John they call him. She said they tried to call, but of course we were up here without a phone. She promised to send a photo soon."

"Like her?" he asked.

"Very much."

He turned the light out again. "She's a great gal, always was." He yawned and pulled her closer. "I'm sleeping in this morning." In seconds he was asleep.

Perhaps she had overreacted to the problems in Roseburg. Chris was safely back home and the difficulties in Oregon were behind them. John needed his rest.

She needed time to think, to reevaluate her own feelings. The trip to Tucson was only two weeks away, and she found herself glad for an opportunity to be away from him. She couldn't think objectively here with him so near.

JOHN INSISTED on driving them to the airport in Coeur d'Alene.

"There's no need," Kathryn said. "You'll just have to drive back alone," she protested, but he refused to listen.

"I don't know about you two," he said, glancing first at Kathryn, then at Chris in the rear seat, as they approached the outskirts of Coeur d'Alene. "You've both been awfully quiet ever since coming back from Roseburg. Are you sure everything is okay?"

"Everything's fine," Kathryn said.

Chris grunted an unintelligible reply.

At the boarding gate he kissed them both, but frowned as they disappeared through the door to the plane without a backward glance. Whatever was bothering them was serious enough neither wanted to discuss it. Damn Helen for driving a wedge between him and Kathryn. And what could have happened to drive Chris back into his shell?

Chris would be having his ninth birthday in Tucson. John had been toying with the idea of surprising them with his own trip to Kathryn's mother's apartment on his son's birthday.

He detoured to the ticket counter and purchased a ticket to Tucson with an open return. Swede could cover for him if he didn't change his mind and cancel the reservation.

"YOU'RE VERY QUIET," Kathryn said, studying Chris's bowed head.

He stared out the window at the clouds for several minutes. She wondered if he was pretending she was not there. "We used to be able to talk, Chris, but everything has changed since you returned from visiting your mother. What really happened?"

"She's not my mom anymore," he insisted between clenched teeth.

"She'll always be your mother, whether you're mad at her or not," Kathryn reminded him.

Chris looked up at her, his eyes glistening with tears. "Why did my dad marry you?"

"Why do you think he did?"

"Leo said my dad paid them to leave me with him."

"Paid? Yes, he gave them some money, but it was in lieu of child support payment."

"Leo said it was a lot of money." He was quiet for several seconds. "My... mom said Daddy married you only to get to keep me, that if he didn't have a mom for me, the judge woulda took me away from my dad and made me go back to... *her*. I woulda never gone back to them. Never! I woulda run away first. I know lots of hiding places where no one would ever find me." He turned back to the window. "Sometimes I hate everybody," he hissed.

"You mean your mother in Oregon?"

"Yeah, and Raymond's dad."

"Is that everyone?" she asked.

The shake of his dark head was barely discernible.

"Who else?"

"Sometimes... my dad, too." His small chin wavered.

"Me, too?" she asked softly.

"No." He wiped his eyes with the tissue she handed him. "Don't you ever hate other people?" he asked.

"Not actually hate, but sometimes I feel hurt when people have lied to me," she said, trying to suppress her own emotions.

"Are you mad at my dad for marrying you just to keep me?"

"Yes, if it's true," Kathryn admitted, and she sighed deeply, feeling as though she were suffocating in her own hurt.

"It's true," he insisted. "I know. My other mom said she was gonna take my dad to court and the sheriff woulda come for me." He took two quick breaths. "And that he woulda shot my dad if he had tried to keep me." His eyes grew round. "She said my dad coulda been killed, and then I would have to live with her and that mean old Leo forever!"

Concern for the boy's fears overrode her own misery. "Then I'm glad your father and I got married, Chris, no matter what his true reasons."

"I woulda never stayed there," Chris said. A trickle of tears ran down his cheek. "I woulda run away."

Her own eyes grew misty as she kissed his cheek and handed him another tissue. "Do you think about running away a lot?" she asked.

He nodded. "But not so much since you became my new mom. But I still know all the places."

"Tell me about the places you've found," she said.

He shook his head. "They're secret."

"Okay. Perhaps sometime you'll take me to one of them," she replied.

"Cuz you might wanna run away and hide with me?" he asked, grinning through his tears.

"Maybe we already are, Chris," she murmured.

THEY TOOK A TAXI from the airport to her mother's apartment. The discussion on the plane was temporarily forgotten as Kathryn became caught up in Chris's excitement of being in a new city.

"It's big and so hot," he exclaimed, "and those giant cacti. They have arms just like a man. They're even bigger than my...they're great."

"They're called saguaro," Kathryn said, trying not to think of John. "Its blossom is the Arizona state flower and a little bird called the cactus wren is the state bird. It builds its nest in the top of the saguaro."

Chris twisted around in the taxi. "Where are the mountains and the trees?"

The taxi driver laughed. "Where are you folks from?"

"I was born here," Kathryn said, "but my son has always lived in the Northwest."

For the rest of the drive into town, the cab driver gave Chris a snap course in desert flora and fauna that included a roadrunner as it darted across the highway. Gradually Chris regained his usual exuberance. Whenever he turned to her, she forced a smile and joined in the three-way conversation. But John's betrayal was never far from her thoughts. If he had been as desperate as Helen had implied, he would have grasped at any available straw. And she had been the straw in the wind, blown to him by her own vulnerability.

She paid the taxi driver and they thanked him for the enjoyable trip, then hurried into the three-story building on the southern edge of the city.

Kathryn closed her eyes for a moment before ringing the doorbell. A petite white-haired woman, her eyes sparkling with excitement, opened the door on the second ring.

"Kathryn," she cried, holding out her arms.

"Oh, Mother, how wonderful to see you again," Kathryn cried, unable to suppress her tears. She hoped her mother would assume they were tears of joy.

"Come in, come in," Dorothy Keith said. When the door was closed, she turned her attention to Chris. "And this must be Christopher Brasher." She extended her frail hand, and he took it shyly. "Why, he has your green eyes, Kathryn. How unusual."

"Look in the mirror, Mom," Kathryn reminded her. "They're your green eyes, too."

Dorothy Keith laughed. "So they are."

"What do I call you?" Chris asked, peering closer to confirm that in fact the three of them had identical eye color.

"Well, young man, you can call me Mrs. Keith, or you can call me Dorothy, or you can call me Grandma Dottie, or just Grandma, but please don't call me Grandmother. It's much too formal. My goodness, I've waited a long time to see a grandson in this family and what a handsome young man you are."

Chris grinned. "I think I'll call you Grandma Dottie. I have a Grandma Brasher and I call her just plain Grandma, and I have a Grandma Wilson, but I only saw her once."

"Grandma Dottie it is, then. Now come to the dining room table. I have some cookies and iced tea." She served the drinks in crystal goblets and the cookies on fine Haviland china, items familiar to Kathryn since her childhood.

"This stuff breaks," Chris said, reluctant to touch either.

"Just be careful," Dorothy Keith cautioned. "I don't have plastic. Kathryn learned to be careful. I'm sure you will, too."

They went out to dinner. As the sun set, Kathryn took Chris to the swimming pool in the apartment complex. He swam for a few hours while Kathryn lounged nearby and read.

When they returned to the apartment, Mrs. Keith took Kathryn aside.

"Your husband called," she said. "I offered to get you, but he said it wasn't necessary. He wanted to know if you had arrived okay." She peered at Kathryn. "I talked to him for quite a while. He seems like a very nice man."

Kathryn looked away.

"When you called me and told me you had married, I was surprised, Kathryn, but after talking to John, I feel better. Why don't you use the phone in my bedroom and call him?"

"Perhaps later," Kathryn replied.

The hours passed with Chris following Mrs. Keith around the apartment, hanging on to every word she said, and sitting very close to her while she showed him photographs of Kathryn when she was a little girl.

"She's prettier now," he said, after studying a photo of a twelve-year-old girl with owlish glasses and toothpick legs, in shorts and a halter top.

"I agree," Mrs. Keith said, "but to a parent's eyes a child is always beautiful."

"Time for bed, Chris," Kathryn said. "You get the sofa bed."

"Great! Can I watch television?"

"No," Kathryn said. "We're all going to turn in."

The next two days were spent sightseeing, visiting the Arizona Sonora Desert Museum, watching a gunfight at Old Tucson and climbing through the dry caves south of town on the Benson Highway.

John called again on the third day.

"We're fine," Kathryn said, fighting for control at the sound of his husky voice.

"I miss you," he said.

"Chris is having a wonderful time," she said, "but he misses you."

"And you?" he asked.

"I'm having a good time. Have you had any more thefts?" she asked.

"What's the matter, Kit? I thought we had talked everything through, and now you've shut me out."

The hurt of his deception grew tighter, choking the words from her. "You have what you set out to get, John," she replied. "What more can either of us say?"

There was silence between them for a while.

"How have you been feeling?" he asked.

"Fine."

"Kit?"

"Yes?"

"I love you, Kit."

"Do you?" Before he could respond, she hung up the receiver, then grabbed her purse. "I'm going for a walk. I'll be back," she said to her mother by way of explanation, and she was out the door as the phone rang again.

Kathryn walked through the park, trying to sift through her feelings. Her marriage had turned into a ruse. Her body was thickening with a baby conceived out of lust. She had let herself become emotionally dependent on a man who had used her. She loved his son as though he were her own. After a lifetime of reasonable decisions, she had permitted her thwarted sensuality to take control and sweep her into heartbreak. John had defrauded her. Yet as she retraced the steps that had led her to this point in her life, the love she felt for him was overpoweringly strong.

The irony of her predicament was doubly painful as she acknowledged that she still wanted to be with John. Yet she hated the deception, the lies, the pretending. Why had he spoiled everything with his lies? she asked herself over and over again.

As she thought about him, imaginary arms slipped around her, drawing her close. She felt his body press against her, enter her, sending her to a world of ecstasy she had never known before. But it wasn't just the sexual satisfaction she missed: his smiling face, his willingness to share everything he had, except his honesty and his true motivation for marrying her.

If he had been honest with her and shared his problem involving Chris's custody, she might have married him anyway, knowing that her love for him would have provided the bond necessary to build a home life for his son. Perhaps then John would have grown to love her. But instead he had chosen to deceive her, mouthing his affection to seduce her and meaning none of his vows.

She pushed herself from the park bench and slowly worked her way back to her mother's apartment.

Chris was sitting beside her mother on the piano bench, watching her play melodies to songs as he requested them.

"John called again," Mrs. Keith said.

"Yeah, I talked to him," Chris said. "He said he might—"

"Please," Kathryn said, "I don't feel well. I'm going to bed," and she hurried past them to her room.

Alone in the room, she succumbed to the tears that burned her eyes like torches. As she lay in the bed, she made a mental list of her options. If she decided to leave John and dissolve the marriage, she would be too embarrassed to stay in St. Maries alone. But how would she explain her decision to Chris? His emotional stability was fragile, and she loved him as though she had nurtured him with her own body. She could return to Tucson where she had family and friends. She had enough money saved to disappear and resurface in some new location and begin again. Or she could return to John Brasher.

With John she saw two clear choices. She could live the deception, pretending nothing was wrong, but this would eat away at their relationship, and Chris, with all his sensitivity, would somehow know. She could confront John, force him to acknowledge the lie, the hoax, and then what? Would anything be left to start anew?

As she analyzed each eventuality, the list grew and shrank, but when her eyelids refused to stay open anymore, she had narrowed her options down to just two.

The next morning at breakfast she felt her mother's eyes following her every move. However, Chris was the one who confronted her.

"You're mad at my dad again, aren't you?" he asked.

"No."

He put his spoon into his cereal bowl. "You always said I shouldn't lie about things."

"That's right," she replied.

"Then why won't you talk to my dad?"

"He . . . we . . . have a problem."

"Does this mean we won't be a family?"

"Oh, Chris," she groaned, "I don't know."

"Is it about me?" he asked.

She looked at him through tear-filled eyes.

"Don't lie," he warned.

"Then yes, it's about you, but it's not your fault. Try to understand, Chris."

"What did I do?" he asked.

"Nothing. And that's the truth, Chris." She had to change the subject before her self-control was shattered. "Let's talk about something else."

He ate two more spoonfuls of cereal before looking at her. His face was expressionless. "Can we go swimming this morning?"

She glanced at her mother. "After lunch. I need to shop for a few pieces of clothing this morning. I seem to have gained weight since I got here. Nothing fits."

Her mother nodded. "Chris and I'll keep busy while you go out, Kathryn. I remember when I was carrying you. Clothing should be loose enough not to bind."

Chris giggled. "You're getting fat with our baby, aren't you? Will it be here soon?"

Kathryn shook her head. "Not for several months."

"That long?"

"After Christmas."

"How big is he now?" Chris asked.

Kathryn had read a book to him about fetal development before the trip to Oregon. Now she held up her hand and measured the appropriate distance between her thumb and index finger.

Chris laughed. "He would really be a Tom Thumb, wouldn't he?"

The morning passed quickly as she searched several shopping centers to find tops and pairs of slacks that pleased her. She felt silly when she saw other women much further along in their pregnancies. Nonetheless, her thickening body could not be ignored any longer, especially when she tried to button or snap her regular jeans and slacks.

On her way back to the apartment, she stopped at a specialty shop and bought some pool toys for Chris. Chris had established a rapport with the senior adults who frequented the pool. They treated him like their own grandson, plying him with baked goods, playing water polo with him until he had worked his way through several dozen opponents. At night he slept soundly, never giving her or her mother any problems when they suggested he retire for the night.

When she watched him sleep, her heart would tighten. Some trick of fate had brought him into her life, she, who looked as though she was his natural mother. Was he like his father? Had he plotted to bring John into her life also, or had their meeting been merely a coincidence? A shuddering sigh passed through her as John's image came vividly alive. How could she possibly live without them?

She loved them both. If only John had been honest, if only he'd loved her for herself alone, without the strings of his past life complicating their relationship, knotting their love into this tangle of doubt.

The days in Tucson fell into a routine of swimming and exploration. The heat of the August sun had no effect on Chris as he soaked up every experience of the "Old West." They took a drive to Tombstone and the Patagonia range country. An afternoon in Nogales resulted in a photograph with Chris sitting on a placid gray donkey, an oversized sombrero on his head, with only his beaming smile showing. Often the three of them would have dinner beside the pool. Afterward Kathryn and her mother would chat while Chris enjoyed one last swim before bedtime.

TWO DAYS BEFORE THEY WERE to leave, Dorothy Keith watched her daughter toss the wrappings from fast-food hamburgers into the trash can.

"Kathryn, stop fussing," Dorothy said. "Please sit down."

Kathryn's surprised expression brought a smile to her mother's face.

"You've been here for almost two weeks, dear. I've loved having you and Chris visit. I'm so glad you came," she said softly, and she took a sip of her iced tea.

"I hope Chris wasn't too noisy or too—"

"He has been a delight," Dorothy Keith assured her. "Even my neighbors have commented on how much they've enjoyed his company. He's a charmer. Is he like his father?"

"I..." Kathryn's mouth tightened. As the final days of the vacation had drawn near, her anxiety had grown increasingly strong. She knew she couldn't live with John and pretend that all was well.

"John called again this afternoon," Dorothy said. "While you and Chris were visiting Jill Hawthorn and her family."

"Why didn't you tell me?" Kathryn asked.

"It wasn't necessary. We had a long chat."

"What about?"

"His plans for his family." Dorothy straightened her frail body in the wrought-iron chair. "He's very concerned, Kathryn. He wants to come and talk about whatever has come between you."

"He's had months to do that," Kathryn replied. "He lied to me. There's an expression in Idaho, Mom, about being treated like a mushroom."

Dorothy frowned. "I don't understand."

"It refers to being kept in the dark and having a certain animal by-product fed to you. I always thought it was an obscene saying until—now I understand completely."

"Oh, Kathryn, you must be wrong about John," Dorothy exclaimed. "He sounds so sincere, so...caring."

"You're wrong, Mom. He doesn't love me. This baby ,." Kathryn's hand slid to her rounding abdomen beneath the lightweight lounging robe she wore over her maternity swimsuit. She squeezed her eyes shut, trying unsuccessfully to suppress the tears that burned there.

"He loves you very much, Kathryn. You've misjudged him."

Their conversation was interrupted by splashing and laughter from the pool. Two white-haired men were giving Chris a run for his money in an impromptu race across the pool. Dorothy and Kathryn turned their attention to the swimmers and joined in the applause as Chris finished second.

When he came to their table, his eyes were red from the chlorine in the pool, but the dark spikes of his wet lashes again reminded her of John.

"Guess what?" Chris exclaimed. "Everyone is having a party for us tomorrow night. Right here! Because they like us. At six o'clock sharp, Mrs. Larson says. We're having hot dogs and cake and ice cream."

Kathryn smiled. "Sounds like you selected the menu."

Chris beamed. "How'dya know?" His voice lowered to a whisper. "It's really for my birthday, but that part is supposed to be a secret."

"Then how do you know it's a surprise birthday party?" she asked.

"Dutch told me."

"That's wonderful, Chris," Kathryn said, "and how did everyone know it was your birthday?"

He glanced away. "I told Dutch and he told..." He looked back to Kathryn. "Secrets are hard to keep, aren't they?"

She smiled. "Usually. Tomorrow we'll stay in out of the heat and relax until the party begins."

"Will you play the piano with me again?" he asked. "I like to watch your hands. Someday will you learn me how to play?"

"Teach," she said.

"Yeah, teach, too."

"You'd have to practice every day."

"Every day?" Chris scowled at her.

"If you want to be good."

He frowned. "We don't have space for a piano anyway so how could I practice? Do you think we'll ever have a house, a real house that's just ours?" His mouth drooped.

"I don't know," she replied.

"How come you don't have a piano in St. Maries?"

"This piano is mine. Someday, when we...when I..." Tears threatened again. She sprang from the lawn chair and ran to the apartment building, unwilling for Chris to see her cry.

CHAPTER FIFTEEN

JOHN BRASHER WAS WORRIED as he returned to the landing. Impulsively he had driven to Avery in midafternoon, hoping to reach Kathryn by phone at her mother's in Tucson. He had missed her more times than not, and she had returned only one of his calls.

They had never met, but Kathryn's mother had been warm and friendly on the phone, telling him of the delightful visit, expressing genuine affection for Chris.

"He can be a little hyperactive sometimes," John had admitted. "Nothing broken? I'll pay for the damages."

"He's been fine."

"He can be quite changeable."

"I've noticed," Dorothy had said. "When he's happy, he bubbles with life. When he's anxious, he gets very quiet."

"He's been very quiet since he returned from visiting his mother. I'm worried about him, frankly," John had said. "Thanks for taking him into your home and treating him like a—"

"A grandson? That part was easy. He looks just like I always imagined a son of Kathryn's might look," she had said. "I'm so glad for Kathryn. I've been concerned for her over the years. Her father and I have always wanted happiness for her, but she's always been so alone."

"Chris brought us together," he had said, and then he'd related their initial encounter to Dorothy Keith.

"But now everything has changed," John had admitted.

"Yes, she's withdrawn. She cries easily," Dorothy agreed.

"Maybe it's the pregnancy," John had said, hoping to hear his mother-in-law confirm his hopes.

"No," she had said. "She won't talk about it, but, well, John, we've never met, but you are my son-in-law. I want to see my daughter happy before I die. She doubts your love."

"She said that?"

"She has said very little, but she's convinced you married her under false pretenses. She's hurting very much. She feels trapped."

They had talked for a few minutes longer, then said their goodbyes.

"Don't tell her I'll be there tomorrow," he had cautioned.

"Yes, it's best she not know."

Now, as he twisted the steering wheel to maneuver around a sharp curve in the rut-filled dirt road, he recounted every word of the conversation. Ever since Kathryn's trip to Roseburg to bring Chris home. Helen. More had happened between Kathryn and his former wife than Kathryn had admitted. Now John intended to find out just what.

JOHN GAVE THE TAXI DRIVER the address of Dorothy Keith's apartment building. The heat was unbearable. It was one hundred and ten degrees at two in the afternoon.

"This isn't so hot," the driver said and gave several recent readings that made John cringe.

John's short-sleeved polo shirt was sticking to his back. No wonder he had seen so many people, even men, wearing shorts and tank tops, he reflected. He had never worn a pair of shorts in his life, except for swim trunks.

He paid the driver and stood on the sidewalk, staring up at the three-story building, its adobe-colored stucco walls a symbolic barrier to his future. Somewhere inside was the woman who had made his life worth living, the only woman he had ever truly loved. Helen and he had had marriage thrust upon them, with their oldest daughter born seven months after the wedding. But that had been over twenty years earlier.

A woman no longer had to be married to have and keep a baby. Was Kathryn upset enough to want her freedom again? He had been deprived of the right to Chris's affection for too long. Was it about to happen again? Not if he had a say in the matter, John decided.

He found the apartment number, rang the doorbell and waited impatiently. Tilting his head, he heard the faint sounds of footsteps. The door was drawn inward by a white-haired woman, petite and lovely in spite of her frail appearance.

"John?" she murmured, smiling softly.

"Yes," he whispered, finding himself caught up in their conspiracy. "Does she know?"

"No, nor Chris."

"Chris can't keep a secret worth a damn—darn. Sorry, Mrs. Keith." He warmed to her smile. "What do I call you? I'm not used to having a mother-in-law again."

"Try Dottie," she suggested.

"Thank you, Dottie." He followed her inside.

"They're in the living room," she said, motioning down the entryway to where he could hear the notes of a sad piano piece.

"She's playing Chopin," Dorothy Keith murmured. "It's been years since she's played, but a talent such as hers is never lost. Perhaps set aside. She decided against becoming a concert pianist."

He nodded. "She told me."

"Then I hope some day she can be a music teacher. She's wonderful with children. Her caring is just what your son needs." She smiled and took his arm, her head reaching inches above his elbow. She patted his forearm reassuringly as she guided him toward the living room.

As he listened to the melancholy melody, a fleeting image of what Kathryn might have become raced through his mind. He knew her only as a public schoolteacher, a woman who had charged angrily into his busy life, accusing him of neglecting his son. Her virginal condition at such a late age reminded him of her sheltered existence in spite of her independence.

Each night, as he tried to sleep alone, thoughts of her would consume him. God, how he missed her. And now this chasm had widened between them, caused by his own doing. He had called Helen from the airport and had learned more of her brutality, how she'd twisted the motivation for his impulsive marriage to Kathryn with her wicked tongue. He should have been there to protect his vulnerable Kathryn.

Now he was here to surprise them, to celebrate Chris's ninth birthday, to make amends to Kathryn, to convince her he had married her for only one reason, love.

He paused in the entryway to the living room, slightly uncomfortable in its formal setting. His eyes were drawn to the two people sitting side by side on the piano bench. All he could see of Chris was his bowed head and his bare feet dangling from the bench. Kathryn blocked the rest of his young form.

Kathryn's profile filled his vision. Her short dark hair formed a cap around her delicate face. He frowned as his eyes stroked her upper torso. They must have spent many hours here swimming. Her skin glowed with a golden desert tan. But it was her body that held him captive. She was wearing a blousy top, its straps little more than threads over her tanned shoulders, its pattern of white-and-gold tiny abstract flowers scattered across a field of sage green that he knew would match her eyes.

Those eyes. How he longed to have them look at him again, filled with love, with passion, with caring for both him and his son. He shook his head, brutally honest in his thoughts. To hell with his son's needs. They could wait. He wanted her for himself alone. Didn't a man have a right to security, too? To love, to the loyalty of a woman who loved him enough to understand what he needed in his own life?

He frowned as he studied the style of the outfit. The slacks were white, matching the white leather thongs on her small feet. But the top—he didn't remember ever seeing the outfit before. The style was full, billowing around her midsection, emphasizing her condition. She was carrying their child, conceived only a few weeks after their hasty marriage. He mentally counted the time. It was only a little more than three months. Lord, he had only known her a few months longer.

There had been too little time to discover the inner feelings of another person. But wasn't she in the same predicament as he was? No wonder she had accepted Helen's explanation of his motives.

Damn his business. Damn the summer work schedule of logging. Damn the long days and short nights, nights when he should have been home with her to begin laying the foundation of their future. Damn himself for being so shortsighted. He groaned aloud.

Kathryn's hand stopped in midair over the ivory keyboard. Slowly she turned. The expression on her face would haunt him forever. Her mouth opened in surprise seconds before tightening. Her eyes were filled with pain, pain caused by what she thought were his broken vows. Her hand went to her breast as the color drained from her face, giving her complexion a sickly paleness beneath her tan.

She rose from the bench, and her heel caught the claw foot of the piano bench leg. As she stumbled, he ran across the room and caught her, steadying her for an instant before sweeping her into his arms and carrying her to the sofa. She tried to leave his lap but he held her tight.

He pressed her head against his chest. "I love you, Kit, so very much. I couldn't stay away. The timber be damned, I wanted to be here with you."

He felt the wetness of her tears on his shirt front, but she made no sound as he held her.

He saw his son and Dottie Keith moving cautiously toward them, Dottie's hand on Chris's shoulder, holding the boy back.

"Daddy, when did you get here? Why didn't you tell me you were coming for sure? Did you come special for my birthday? Do I look taller?" Chris stretched as tall as his tanned thin legs would lift him.

John glanced over Kathryn's dark head to stare at his son. Chris was dressed in a tank top and cutoff jeans. "Must be all this warm sunshine, Chris. I think you *have* grown since I saw you last. Have you been behaving for your new grandmother?"

"She's not Grandmother," Chris replied. "She's my Grandma Dottie and I like her, and I haven't broken a single thing. She trusts me," he said, beaming.

"We get along fine," Dottie Keith confirmed, "just fine," and she pulled him closer.

"Everyone's having a birthday party for me tonight around the pool," Chris said.

"Yes," Dottie Keith added, "and why don't we go down and check on its progress? We'll be back in an hour or so," she said cheerfully as she waved her hand.

As Chris and Dottie went out the door, John closed his eyes, dropping his chin onto Kathryn's head. Still she didn't move.

"Kit?" he whispered. "Please talk to me. I had to come. You wouldn't speak to me when I telephoned or return my calls. Why, Kit?"

She pulled away and reached for a tissue, then slid off his lap. "I'm sorry," she murmured. "Crying never solves a thing."

"And what will solve this division between us?" he asked. "Give me a chance, Kit. You ran away from me. That's not fair. I know it's not been easy for you, being single for so many years and then finding yourself involved with us Brashers, but we love you. Chris needs you. I need you. Have I asked you to give up too much by becoming my wife? Are you having second thoughts? I was afraid you might not come back, Kit. Were you thinking about staying here in Tucson?"

She wiped her nose. "The thought has crossed my mind." After a thoughtful silence, she looked into his eyes. "No," she said, sighing deeply, "I was coming back. What else could I do, considering all that has happened?" Unconsciously she touched her loose top. "I don't really need this, but everything else is so uncomfortable. I've never had a weight problem before."

"You look beautiful," he said, rising from the sofa. "Can we have a talk?" he asked, reaching for her hand.

She shook her head. "Not now, please. I'll just cry. I don't want to spoil Chris's birthday party." She went to the window and looked down at the poolside crowd. His presence was palpable behind her as he glanced over her bare shoulder.

"We'll talk when we get back to St. Maries," she promised. "Now, why don't we join everyone outside? Can you help me carry some presents? Your son has quickly become everyone's favorite grandson. I'm not sure how we'll get all of his gifts in the suitcases for the flight home." She laughed nervously.

"We'll manage," he replied, sliding his hand around her waist.

Slowly the tension left Kathryn's body, and she settled against him, savoring his strength and confidence. If only she could discuss her feelings with him, without the embarrassing outburst of tears that came each time she thought about Helen's cutting declaration, his own refusal to... The burning moisture began to sting her eyes again.

"Of course," she said, but when she stepped away, he captured her again, easing her against him. His hand cupped her chin, and he tilted her face up to his. Her mouth trembled beneath his as he kissed her, and her lips were cold, but for an instant he felt a softening and a hint of response.

THE PARTY LASTED until ten. Chris thrived on being the center of attention and grew progressively more excited as he opened each present. The elderly women kissed his cheeks while the men shook his hand as he thanked them all. When he challenged two of his favorite men friends, Clyde Bender and Dutch Swenson, to a last race in the pool, the three of them were off and diving into the wa-

ter, wetting the bystanders who didn't react quickly
enough to avoid being splashed.

"He's made a lot of friends, hasn't he?" John remarked as he sat beside Dottie Keith. Kathryn was on her
mother's other side.

"Yes," Dottie replied. "He needs a lot of love and security, and he's found it here for these two weeks." She
reached for Kathryn's hand, then John's. "Please try to
give those things to him back home as well. He's a very
sensitive little boy, almost fragile in his vulnerability.
From what Kathryn has told me about his life, he's had
precious little stability."

"But I've tried to give him that," John insisted.

"That doesn't undo those first several years when he
must have felt very unloved," Dottie explained. "Protect
him from the pain and rejection he's experienced in the
past. He's too young to be so..." She paused. "I've
worked with troubled children before, years ago, both in
school and in a program with the courts where I taught
them the basics of piano." She squeezed both Kathryn's
and John's hands. "He's emotionally battered."

John pulled free and straightened. "I've never..."

Dottie took his hand again. "Not intentionally, John,
but count the hours or days when he's actually had your
undivided attention. I know your job takes you away. But
view it from Chris's perspective. First a mother who didn't
want him, a stepfather who resented him, then a father
who placed him with his aunt when what he really needed
was you. Poor, poor darling Chris. In his few years of life,
he's lived with constant rejection. He desperately wants to
find security with you two. Please don't disappoint him.
He might not survive."

DOROTHY KEITH'S WORDS haunted him later that night as John carried a drowsing Chris to Dorothy's apartment. Kathryn and her mother followed, carrying some left-over cake and punch while Clyde and Dutch found two boxes to hold the presents and insisted on carrying up Chris's gifts.

John took his son to the bathroom while Kathryn fixed his sofa bed. Chris never stirred when they left him there in his cutoffs and tank top and pulled a sheet over him.

Dorothy disappeared quietly into her bedroom, leaving John and Kathryn alone in the dark living room.

"Want a nightcap?" Kathryn asked. "Brandy? Wine?"

"No, thanks," he replied. "I'm tired from the flight and party." He frowned down at her. "Do I get to share your bedroom, Kit?"

She stared back at him.

"I could bed down on the floor out here," he said, clearing his throat. "I don't want to press you."

"Come," she said, guiding him to the room where she had stayed for the past two weeks, a room that had become a prison, its isolation giving her no chance to avoid thinking of how much she missed him. In spite of the pain in her heart, she wanted him, desired him, needed to feel him become a part of her, to restore in her the confidence that perhaps they could work out their problems, if not for themselves, then for Christopher.

While John disappeared into the bathroom, Kathryn undressed. She felt overwhelmed by shyness as she frantically searched through her lingerie for something to wear. When she heard the bathroom door open, she grabbed a pale-yellow gown and slid it over her head. The lace-trimmed hem brushed against her tanned thighs a few inches above her knees. Matching lace shoulder straps ran down the front of the gown to form a tiny yoke across her bosom. The shimmering nylon tricot sent shivers through her body as she scrambled into bed.

The only light was from the small lamp on his side of the bed. He paused by the door, closed it quietly and turned the lock.

Her heart thudded erratically when her gaze scanned his body. He wore only the bottoms of a pair of blue pajamas. The drawstring hung low on his hips. Her eyes moved lower, wondering if he were reacting to her. A subtle movement beneath the fabric confirmed his arousal. Her eyes flew to his face.

Was he trying to fight his own desires? No sign of emotion disturbed his rugged features as he walked toward the bed. She slid down between the sheets as he dropped to the bed, but the gown failed to move with her. As her eyes centered on the dark, curling hair scattered across his broad chest, she realized the gown was now above her hips. She moaned aloud in frustration as her hand disappeared beneath the sheet. She tried to tug the garment down past her hips again.

He turned to her. "What did you say?"

"Nothing, I just—"

"But I heard you," he insisted. He propped himself up on one elbow and gazed down into her face.

"It was only...my nightgown."

His mouth softened. "Your gown said something?"

"No," she whispered, "but it's giving me problems."

"Where?"

"It's nothing."

"Let me help," he said slyly, and his hand disappeared beneath the sheet. Her hand fell to the mattress as she held her breath, torn between pleading with him to leave her alone and screaming for him to touch her.

Through the twisted material she felt the heat of his palm as it settled first on her waist, then on her bare abdomen. She sensed his curiosity when his fingers explored the slight rounding of her body.

"Our baby," he murmured.

"Yes." She held her breath as his fingers began to move downward, caressing her thighs, her knees, then up to her hips before sliding between her legs to press against her moistness for several seconds.

Suddenly his hand was on her breasts, teasing her nipples into hard buttons of desire. He hadn't spoken a word. His dark head blocked out the lamplight as his mouth touched hers, his teeth nibbling at her lower lip until she wanted to cry out her need.

Her hands loosened the string of his pajamas and pushed them away from his body. She encircled him, exploring him, urging him to fill her body.

"Please," she breathed, "make love to me, John." Her legs opened as he came to her, his body still hesitant and poised above her. "You've made me dependent on you, addicted to your lovemaking. I don't just need you, I want you. My body—I don't understand my own body anymore. All I think about is you. Make love to me, John," she pleaded, and her hands slid over his hips as he lifted her to him.

Joined to her in his own passion, he gazed into her eyes, wanting to sink into their green depths. Her breathing quickened as he settled into her, withdrew and settled again. When his thrusts began to intensify, he knew, in spite of their differences, he would do everything in his power to make her believe in him again.

She moaned aloud, his name on her lips as she arched against him, clinging to his body as his own convulsive climax took control, sending them into their own private world of passion, to settle moments later in each other's arms.

He reached for the lamp and the room was plunged into darkness. "Don't move, sweetheart," John said, and he rolled onto his side, taking her with him. "Don't pull away. This is only the beginning," he promised.

As they lay together, their breathing had barely returned to normal when she felt him begin to respond again. Still inside her, his subtle rhythm increased, bringing her to the edge of fulfillment. His mouth sought her breasts, bathing them with moist flicks of his tongue.

Her nails dug into his shoulders while he explored her body, his mouth searing her with its heat, bringing her close to release again and again. But close was not enough, and she pleaded with him to come with her, to share her ecstasy, to explore new worlds of desire and satisfaction.

Hours later they lay asleep, her head nestled against the curve of his arm, her back pressed against his warm body, his arm protectively around her waist.

WHEN MORNING CAME, Dottie Keith insisted that Chris play quietly until breakfast could be postponed no longer.

"Why are they still asleep?" Chris asked. "Don't we have to catch our plane for home this afternoon? They're gonna miss the plane," he said, wriggling restlessly on his chair.

Dottie slid several more dollar-sized pancakes onto his plate. "Your father and your mother are learning to love again, I hope," she explained, smiling and winking at Chris.

"You mean they're kissing and hugging and all that stuff again?"

"You're a wise young man," she said, kissing his cheek.

He tilted his head. "You're probably right, Grandma Dottie. They used to do that all the time. That was when my dad smoked his pipe."

"Well," she said, "perhaps he'll start to smoke it again. Now, if you'll go knock on their door very gently, we'll see if they'll come join us for breakfast."

On the flight back to Coeur d'Alene, Chris sat beside another young boy, leaving John and Kathryn alone. A tenuous peace had lingered between them from the night of lovemaking. Each hesitated to take its permanence for granted.

"We'll start over," he had promised as they had dressed that morning. "We'll go slow and correct the mistakes we made the first time around."

THE PHONE WAS RINGING when Kathryn unlocked the door to the house in St. Maries.

"I'll get it," Kathryn called back to John, who was busy unloading the boxes from the back of the truck. They had had to drive both vehicles from the airport. Chris had insisted on riding with his father to keep an eye on the birthday gifts. As Kathryn had followed the truck over the winding hills to home, she had watched John's and Chris's animated head movements through the rear window of the cab, wondering what they were discussing. She fervently hoped they could work out their difficulties.

Their lovemaking the night before had laid a partial foundation to their vows of renewal, but they had promised each other an open discussion of everything that had become a stumbling block in their brief marriage. She hoped the time to talk would be later this very night.

The phone rang again. Kathryn tossed her purse down on the sofa and ran to the phone. "Hello?"

"Is Johnnie there?" a woman's voice asked.

"He's outside. Who is this?"

The woman laughed coyly. "Why, his first wife, of course, the mother of his children." Recognition shook Kathryn.

"I'll call him," Kathryn offered, wanting to bring the intrusive call to a quick conclusion.

"That's all right," Helen said. "Just give him my message."

"Yes?"

"It's time for John's payment, past time actually."

"Payment? What payment?"

"Why, my dear. Hasn't John explained our little agreement?" Helen said.

"Yes," Kathryn replied, hedging for an instant, "but I don't remember all the details."

"If I know John, he's twisted it to fit his needs," Helen said. "It's quite simple. If he can provide our son with a mother, a permanent home and sends me three payments of seven thousand two hundred each, then Chris can live with John permanently." She paused. "When the final payment is made, I'll agree to give up all legal rights to Chris. You can adopt him if you want."

"That's like selling your own son," Kathryn cried.

"Not really," Helen replied. "We both get what we want. I need the money and John wants his son. But you're part of the settlement, my dear." She laughed. "You're the mother factor in his solution. Didn't he explain his problem when he proposed marriage?"

"Not...fully." Kathryn fought to keep her mind clear. "And if he doesn't keep his part of the bargain?"

"I get Christopher and the child support payments are doubled," Helen explained. "I can't put up with him on what John is willing to pay. John always was tight with his money. He refuses to acknowledge inflation. I wanted to take Chris to a child psychologist, but John refused to pay for that, too. There's obviously something wrong with the boy. His temper is positively explosive. He has no control and spanking does no good at all. Leo used to—" She paused. "Frankly, John is getting off pretty easy. He gets the benefits of having a wife as well as giving Chris a mother. Simple. Love doesn't even enter the picture. He told me he was very lucky to have found you." She laughed cynically.

"I'm sure," Kathryn murmured. "I'll give him your message."

It was as if a steel plate pressed against her chest as she watched John and Chris lugging the boxes and suitcases into the house.

"Who was on the phone?" John asked as he shoved the final box into Chris's room.

"Helen."

He straightened. "What did she want?"

"The rest of the money you promised her."

"The . . . money?" He frowned at her.

"Yes, she said you weren't living up to your agreement."

"And what else did she say?" he asked.

Kathryn's eyes searched his features for the truth. "How can you continue to lie?"

"Lie? About what?"

The last hope of their future washed away with the renewed hurt of his deception. "Why you had to marry me."

"I didn't have to marry you. What are you talking about?"

"Then just why did you bother?"

"Because I love you."

"You're lying! You married me for only one reason. Why can't you be honest with me?"

"What the hell did Helen say to you, Kit? We had patched up our difficulties and now—"

"And now the truth comes out," she said, her voice laced with sarcasm. "You married me for only one reason—to keep your son."

"Chris has nothing to do with it," John replied, his voice rising with each word.

"Chris has everything to do with it," she shouted. "If Chris were not here, there would be no need for me...for us!"

CHAPTER SIXTEEN

"YOU'RE CRAZY," John shouted back, reaching for her shoulders.

She jerked away. "No, John. For the first time I really understand what you've done. You've used me, and I can never forgive you for that. You used me," she shouted.

Suddenly the room was filled with a piercing scream. Chris stood near the front door, his face ashen as he clung to Patches, who was nestled in his arms.

"Why are you fighting?" he sobbed.

"Chris, go to your room," John ordered.

"No!" Chris tightened his hold on the squirming cat.

"Chris!" John stepped toward him.

"No, and you can't make me. You lied to me. You both lied to me. You said Miss Keith would be my mother and that we could be a family just like Raymond's and Aunt Nat's. You promised!" He turned to Kathryn. "You said I was just like your own little boy, but you lied, too. You don't want me. You lied, both of you." He stepped back to the doorway. "You're gonna get a divorce, aren't you? Just like everybody else, and you won't be my mom anymore, will you?"

"No, Chris," Kathryn said, holding out her hand. "You don't understand. I can't stay with you if your father keeps—"

"You promised," Chris screamed. "You both promised, and you broke your promises. I hate you, I hate you both. And I don't want to live with you, either." Sobs racked his body as he stepped back into the darkness, slamming the door behind him.

John charged the door, yanking it open. "Chris, get back in here," he demanded. He stepped onto the porch. "Chris?"

Kathryn joined him on the porch.

"He's gone," John said, moving down the steps to the sidewalk.

"We'll look for him. He's angry," she said. "He'll be back in a few minutes. He can't go far with no jacket and carrying Patches."

They searched the neighborhood street by street and through each alley, but found no trace of Chris. Finally they returned to the house. The minutes ticked away as they busied themselves with unpacking. The clock on the mantel chimed nine o'clock, and still there was no sign of Chris.

When they called the police station to report him missing, they were rebuffed.

"He'll be back," the dispatcher assured them. "We've had three runaways just this week, and they all showed up when they got hungry. Boys do that. If he's not back tomorrow, call us again. Don't worry about him. He's probably at a friend's house."

"Raymond," Kathryn cried. "He must be at Raymond's house."

But when they called the Crosley residence, there was no one home.

Midnight passed.

"Where could he be?" John asked.

She touched his arm tentatively, and he embraced her. As she nestled against him, images of Chris filled her thoughts. "He must be cold," she murmured. Suddenly she pulled away. "We have no right to be warm and comfortable when he's so cold." She jumped from the sofa and began to pace the room. "Let's call Raymond again."

This time Mrs. Crosley answered and said they had been to a neighboring town to visit relatives and no, they had no idea where Chris might be. She suggested telephoning some of the boys' mutual friends. Calls to the families proved fruitless.

The hours dragged as the night wore on.

"The radio! Call the station and have them issue a bulletin," John said.

"The radio is off the air until 6:00 AM," Kathryn reminded him.

He sank to the sofa, his shoulders slumped in defeat. She touched his arm. "We'll find him, John."

He turned to her. "This is all my fault," he said, his features twisted with guilt. "You're right. I took advantage of you. I fell in love with you, but I refused to wait to marry you. I needed an instant mother for my son. Helen was putting the pressure on me. She wanted the money, not her son." He rubbed his hands over his eyes. "I grabbed for the only solution I could think of. I wanted you from the start, Kit. That's no lie. But I rushed you, I didn't give you a chance or our marriage. Perhaps you're right. I don't deserve you or my son or a family. I've screwed up all our lives."

He rubbed the tense muscles in his neck. "But we did have a family for a while, didn't we, Kit? We gave Chris two parents who loved him. Why couldn't it have continued?"

Her heart went out to him. She began to massage the muscles of his back through his shirt. "It can," she murmured, kissing his cheek. "I love you, John."

"And I love you," he vowed. "I've never lied to you. But I needed you so much for my son that I couldn't bring myself to level with you about my problem. Do you believe that? What if you had said no? I would have lost my son, and I've had him for only a few years."

He twisted around and pulled her hands away from his shoulders. "Can you ever trust me again?" he asked, squeezing her hands.

She grasped his large hands in hers, turned them over and examined their palms. "These hands have made love to me," she murmured, "they've held me when I needed comfort. They've worked hard in the woods to provide for your family. They've played with your son. They're strong, but I've seen how gentle they can be. They're you, John." She kissed one palm. "I want them to hold me again. I love you, John, so very much. And yes, I want to trust you again. Perhaps I just needed to hear you admit that there was some truth to what Helen said. All the facts pointed to the validity of her accusation, but I wanted to hear the truth from your own lips."

She dropped to the floor and clung to his knees. "I want to build the family Chris needs. I want our child to have an older brother who can love him and show him how to do things as they grow up together. I don't care where we live, only that we're together."

She looked at John, her eyes filled with concern. "Oh, John, I'm so frightened for Chris. What if he's injured somewhere? What if he's lost? What if he—God forbid—never comes back? Children can disappear."

He pulled her from the floor and into his arms again, holding her while the night drifted into a cold gray dawn. "We'll call the radio station at six and then the police," John said.

After giving a description to the disc jockey at the station, they called the police. "Wait a few more hours, folks, then let us know."

A mewing came from the kitchen.

Kathryn jumped from the sofa. "They've come home," She ran to the kitchen as Patches crawled through the pet entrance in the kitchen door. The soiled calico cat mewed again, rubbing against Kathryn's bare leg. She bent and picked up the cat. "Where have you been?" she asked softly. "And where is Christopher?"

The cat mewed forlornly, and Kathryn put her down on the floor.

John yanked the kitchen door open and called into the breaking dawn, but a chilly silence was all that greeted him.

Over coffee they made a strategy list.

"We should call Natalie."

"Perhaps he went to Avery instead, to the trailer where he's always felt so at home," she suggested.

He shook his head. "How could he get there? It's almost fifty miles. He couldn't walk it."

"You're right," Kathryn agreed. Then she recalled the conversation on the plane to Tucson. "John, let's call Raymond again. Chris told me once he had lots of hiding places where no one could ever find him, but he and Ray always shared secrets. Maybe they shared hiding places, too."

She called Ray's house and asked to speak to him.

"Sure," he boasted. "We made forts on the hill, and we found three caves on the other side."

"Could you take us to them?" Kathryn asked. "Chris was very angry when he ran away, and we want to help him. He's been gone all night, and he must be cold and hungry. Can you help us?"

"Sure."

Within the hour Raymond had led them to the caves. At the first cave Kathryn held her breath as John and Raymond shone their flashlights into the dark interior.

They reappeared a few minutes later. John shook his head. "Not a sign of him."

The search through the other two caves was also fruitless. Afterward they dropped Ray off at his home. "Thanks, Ray for helping," John said.

"Gee, Mr. Brasher, I hope Chris is okay," Ray said as he closed the door and waved to them.

"We had better get back to the house in case someone calls," Kathryn said, taking John's hand.

He grimaced and nodded.

Several people called to express their condolences. The search-and-rescue unit director, who had once worked for John, called and offered to launch a search.

"Thanks, but let's give the radio announcement a little more time," John said. "Surely someone has seen him."

Shortly after ten the phone rang.

"You the folks looking for a lost boy?" a man's voice asked.

"Yes," Kathryn cried. "Have you seen him?"

"Think so." The man cleared his throat. "I'm Roger Owens. Live up on Badger Ridge."

"Please, talk to my husband, Mr. Owens." Kathryn handed the phone to John.

"I'm Chris's father," John said. "Have you seen my son?"

"I 'spect I gave him a ride."

"To where? When?"

"Late last night," the man explained. "The boy told a believable story. Said he had been riding in the back of his father's pickup, said that his cat had run away. The boy said he'd jumped from the truck when his father had stopped at the turnoff north of St. Maries. Said his father didn't know he had jumped out. Said he would be real worried when he got home and discovered his son missing. Hell, I believed the boy so I gave him a ride into Avery. Dropped him off at the café about midnight."

"Oh, thank God," John said.

"Didn't know he was a runaway until I turned on the radio this morning, but I was on my way to the woods. Just got back to a phone. I saw him go into the café. Hope you connect up real soon. He seemed sort of depressed for a kid so young."

"Thanks," John said, hanging up the receiver. Quickly he dialed the number of the Log Cabin Café in Avery.

"Sure I saw him, John," Mrs. Boren said. "Chris came dragging in here about midnight. Said you had given him permission to get a hamburger, that you were out of food. I put it on your account. I watched him walk toward your place. Say, where are you calling from?"

When John explained what had happened, Mrs. Boren groaned. "Poor kid," she said.

"Could you go check the trailer and see if he's there, please?" John asked.

"Sure."

Several minutes later Mrs. Boren returned.

"No sign of him, John, but the window screen above the sink is gone, and the door is unlocked," she said. "He's been there, but it doesn't look as though he spent the night. The beds are all made. The place is as neat as a pin except for some camping gear pulled from a closet. Do you own a red sleeping bag?"

"Yes, and a blue one. It's Chris's bag."

"There was no blue one, only the red one. Good Lordy, what if he's run away into the woods? Does he know his way around, John?"

"To a certain extent. Thanks, Mrs. Boren," John said. "We're coming up. Be on the lookout for him, would you? He's very upset. He must be hiding up there somewhere."

When John explained what Mrs. Boren had said, an alarm went off deep in Kathryn's mind.

"Wait," she murmured. "I remember something he said once...months ago. If only I could remember exactly. Chris told me once he's afraid of the dark and likes the streetlights. He would never run away into the woods. There's no moon." A mental image flashed through her thoughts. "I know! I know where he is. Hurry, John, I know where to find him!"

"WHERE?" JOHN PLEADED as they raced through town and onto the highway to Avery. The road followed the river grade of the shadowy St. Joe River for miles.

"The old hotel near the Milwaukee Railroad depot," Kathryn said. "I know he's there. I can feel it."

"You mean that ramshackle building that's all boarded up? How do you know for sure?" John asked, his knuckles white as he gripped the steering wheel.

"Remember that very first morning I was there?" she reminded him. "Chris and I took a walk, and he was so fascinated by that old, abandoned building. He wanted to go inside, but I warned him that it might be dangerous. He said it would be a perfect hiding place. He kept going back to it, almost as though he were analyzing it and storing away information about it in his mind for future reference. There was a light pole not far away, but I'm sure the bulb had been shot out. Oh, John, I'm sure he's there. He must be so frightened. Poor darling.''

"God, I hope you're right, Kit.''

Within the hour they braked to a stop at the café. Mrs. Boren and most of the patrons from the bar and café came to the door.

"No sign of him, John,'' Mrs. Boren said.

A tall, sandy-haired young man worked his way through the crowd.

"Mugger, how are you?'' John asked.

"Fine, boss,'' Mugger replied, extending his hand. "Sorry to hear about Chris.''

A slender, dark-haired woman came with him.

"Can we help, boss?'' Mugger asked, motioning the young woman closer. "This is Colleen.'' He put his arm around Colleen's shoulders. "Honey, this is John Brasher and his woman, Ki—Kath—Mrs. Brasher.''

Colleen smiled and Kathryn nodded.

"Boss, we plan to get married and stay here in Avery. I meant to tell you later, but now's as good a time as any. You've been great to me, boss, and we want to help you any damned way possible. We hope to have a family ourselves real soon so Colleen and me, we want to do what we can to find that boy.''

"Thanks, Mugger,'' John said. "Kathryn thinks he might be hiding in the old hotel near the depot.''

"Damn, that place is a death trap,'' Mugger replied, shaking his head and frowning.

"We know,'' John said, "and we don't want to frighten him. He might be hurt, or he might try to run away again. So give us a little time to get there first. Meet us by the tavern in thirty minutes. If he's not at the hotel, we'll form some search parties and comb the whole town. Got to go now, Mugger, but tell everyone thanks. We may need them yet so have them on standby just in case.''

Mugger and Colleen stepped aside. John shifted the truck into gear and quickly drove across the bridge into the older section of Avery. The abandoned hotel loomed on the horizon, looking ugly and neglected. The exterior had long since given up its color to the harsh elements of nature. Only the plywood barricading the windows showed any signs of recent attention.

John applied the brake and allowed the truck to coast quietly to within a few yards of the building. ''Get the flashlight from the jockey box,'' he said. Kathryn opened the glove compartment and took out two lights. One wouldn't work and she tossed it back inside. John put his finger to his mouth as he opened his door and motioned for Kathryn to follow.

They walked around the building, searching for signs of entry. Near the back entrance several boards had been pulled loose and were dangling on rusty nails. ''In here,'' he beckoned, holding the boards aside.

She crawled inside and waited for him to join her.

''Keep the light off until we know if he's here,'' John whispered. Taking her hand, he worked their way through the trash and debris that littered the floor of the lobby. Suddenly John stooped and snatched something from the dusty floor.

He turned on the flashlight, holding it a few inches above his cupped palm. A crumpled shiny yellow wrapper with blue letters that read Butterfinger was visible. ''It's fresh. I can still smell the chocolate. He's here,'' John hissed. He flipped off the flashlight. ''Let's check the rooms on this level.''

They found nothing except a pack rat's nest. They returned to the lobby, and John looked up the staircase.

"Look," he said, pointing to small footprints in the dust on the stairs. He took three steps up. Suddenly the shattering sound of breaking timbers filled the air, and John jumped to the floor. "Dammit, the planks are rotten," he exclaimed, frowning at the splintered step and its riser. "I'm sure he's up there."

"Let's look through the rooms on this floor again," Kathryn suggested. "Turn on the light so we can see better."

Several rooms were examined. "What are you looking for?" John asked.

"I'm not sure," Kathryn admitted, "but let's keep going."

There were still three rooms to search when a sound caught Kathryn's ear. "Listen," she said softly, and she touched John's arm.

The muffled sounds of sobbing came to them as they opened the last door on one side of the hallway.

"I don't remember this room," John murmured. "How could we have skipped it? Chris?" he called. "Can you hear me?"

They stepped inside and were assailed with the dusty smell of broken timber. Rotted cheesecloth-like material hung from the ceiling.

"Daddy?" a trembling voice called. "Miss Keith? Is that you?" The voice broke again.

John shone the flashlight toward the ceiling. A gaping hole caught the beam, sending shards of light to break through the darkness of the upper floor.

"My God," John groaned. "What happened, Chris?"

"I tripped," Chris called between sobs, "and I fell and the floor caved in and I almost fell through and...I'm sorry, Daddy."

"It's okay, son," John said. "We'll get you down. Can you scoot to the opening?"

"No!"

"Please, Chris, just crawl toward—"

"I'll fall." Chris's panic-filled voice rose frantically.

"We've got to see where he is," John said, searching the room for something to stand on.

"Use me," Kathryn said, coming close to him. "Lift me up and I'll see what it's like up there. Let me have the light."

"Good idea." John squatted. "Climb onto my shoulders, Kit. You'll be higher, closer."

Cautiously she did as he suggested. As he began to stand, she felt her balance slip and clutched his hair. "Easy, Kit," he cautioned, and he tightened his grip on her knees.

The old building had unusually high ceilings, and as John straightened, Kathryn's head brushed against the ceiling.

"Duck," John ordered as he began to inch his way to the gaping hole. She straightened and slowly stretched through the opening.

"I see him," she said. "He's way back in the corner. Oh, John, he's so frightened," she whispered. "Chris, wave to me."

The boy crouched in the dark corner saluted them weakly.

"Can you work your way over here?" Kathryn called.

Chris shook his head, violently opposed to any suggestion that he move. "I'll fall."

"No, you won't," Kathryn said calmly. "I'll be right here, and we'll catch you if you—"

"No!" Chris backed away deeper into the shadows.

"I'm putting you down, Kit," John said. He knelt and dipped his dark head, enabling her to climb off his shoulders.

"What did you find?" he asked. "How is he? Where is he?"

"He's crouched in the corner," Kathryn replied. "He's terrified. He has the sleeping bag and a bag of potato chips and a flashlight, but the batteries are weak. The boarded windows allow no light in. Oh, John, he won't move. Someone has to go get him."

"Dammit, I'm too heavy to go up those rotten stairs," John exclaimed.

"But I'm not," Kathryn said. "I'll go up there and coax him to the opening. If I can get his legs over the edge, you can reach him and pull him out."

"You might get hurt yourself," John said.

"But it's the only way, don't you see?" Kathryn said. "He's too frightened to stay up there until we get a rescue squad. This building should have been condemned long ago."

"It was, and it's scheduled for demolition in a few weeks," John said. "All right, go, but for God's sake be careful."

"You wait here," Kathryn said, kissing his cheek quickly. "I'll hurry." She raced for the lobby.

Cautiously she worked her way up the rickety stairs, testing each board before putting her weight on it. Several boards had already broken from some earlier climber. She wondered how many of the area children had explored this building and somehow managed to escape unharmed.

As she approached the second-floor landing, the entire staircase groaned and creaked. She jumped two steps and gained her footing on the second floor seconds before the stairway groaned a last sickening time and collapsed from its own rotten weight.

She pressed her hand to her chest, trying to catch her breath. "Oh, dear," she moaned softly, realizing she was now as trapped as Chris. "I'm coming, Chris," she whispered, and she hurried down the darkened, dusty hallway to the room where she thought he was trapped. She jerked the door open and searched the room, but the floor was intact. It was the wrong room. "Chris, where are you?" she called.

"Here," a faint voice answered.

She opened another door, but the room was undamaged. Frantic, she jerked open the next door and almost stepped through the hole in the floor.

"Kit, is that you?" John called from below.

"Yes, yes, I've found him," Kathryn cried, scanning the dark room through tears of frustration.

"Mom?" Chris called weakly from across the room.

"Yes, Chris, I'm here. You're safe now. We'll have you out of here in no time. Stay right there. I'm coming to you." Gingerly she worked around the hole, feeling her way along the walls and trusting none of the flooring beneath her. What seemed to Kathryn an eternity was actually only seconds before she'd reached the little boy huddled in the corner of the dark room. His eyes were wide with panic as he clutched the flashlight with its fading orange beam. She crouched over him.

"Chris?" she whispered.

He scooted into her arms, sobbing hysterically as she tightened her hold on him. "Oh, baby, you're fine now. Everything's going to be fine, just fine." She continued to soothe him and hold him until his crying gave way to occasional sobs.

"There's no light," he said. "I thought there was a light, but—but the boards...they made it so dark in here...and my flashlight...it worked for a while, but..." His thin body shook as a tremor moved through him.

"The light outside has been shot out, Chris, but it's daylight now."

Slowly he raised his head. "Really? I thought it was still nighttime."

"No, sweetheart, it's almost noon." She tightened her arms around him. "I bet I know a hungry boy."

"I ate a candy bar and some potato chips, then I got sick and thought I was gonna...and I need to go to the bathroom, but..." His arms clung tightly around her waist.

"I have a solution to all your problems," she said. "Let's get you out of here and go to the trailer, then we'll get you the biggest hamburger the Log Cabin Café can make on that grill of theirs. Did you know Mugger is learning to cook there?"

"Mugger?" He looked up at her. "You mean Swede's friend Mugger? He's not gonna be a logger anymore?"

She nodded. "He's decided to try something new."

"Gee, I'll bet Mugger is a good cook," he said.

"Why don't we find out for ourselves?" she suggested. "Now then," Kathryn said, extricating herself from his tight grip. "First we'll toss the sleeping bag down to your dad. We'll need it when we go camping, won't we?" She pushed the blue bag over the edge.

"We? All of us?" Chris asked, hiccuping twice.

"Yes, darling, all of us. We're a family, aren't we?"

His dark head nodded and a tiny smile lightened his peaked face. "Don't forget my potato chips," he said.

"Of course not." She tossed the bag of chips through the opening.

"Got them," John called. "Is Chris ready to come now?"

Chris frowned at the hole. "What if it starts to break, what if—"

"Your father is ready to catch you," Kathryn said. "Now turn onto your stomach, and I'll help you crawl backward to the hole."

Skepticism was plainly visible on his young face as Chris began to work his way closer to the opening.

"Lie on your stomach," Kathryn suggested, "and I'll help push you." She took his hands. "Fine, your feet are over the hole." He scooted backward again.

Chris's eyes widened. "Daddy has my ankles! I can feel his hands."

Pieces of the ceiling broke away from the opening and bounced to the floor below. The boy shrieked in alarm.

"It's okay," Kathryn said. "Scoot some more, just a little bit, and you'll be down and safe."

Suddenly he disappeared from sight, and she heard John's excited voice.

"I've got you, Chris! Are you okay, son? Really okay?"

"Sure," Chris giggled between hiccups. "Not a scratch." Kathryn sensed the hug she was sure John was giving him.

"Hey, fellows, don't forget me," she called, her concern growing when another piece of ceiling broke away and fell to the floor below.

"Find a support beam," John suggested. "It'll bear your weight."

"I can't tell where they are," she replied.

"Then put your legs over, and I'll grab your ankles and help you down."

"Okay," she said, realizing just how scary a maneuver she had coaxed Chris into. Slowly she inched her bottom across the floor and dropped her feet through the ragged opening. The warmth of John's large hands surrounded her ankles, filling her with the confidence to scoot closer to the opening. His hands slid up to her calves.

"Come on, Kit, I've got you," he called.

As his hands found her knees, the floor began to crumble, and she felt herself begin to fall.

"Jump, Kit, jump!" John shouted.

She jumped as the floor disintegrated beneath her. Her scream filled the room, and she came flying down. Her knees caught John in his midsection, knocking the air from his lungs as he cushioned her fall.

Cautiously she crawled up from him and stood up, dusting herself off. John lay on the floor, gasping for air. She dropped to her knees and touched his cheek. "John? Are you all right?"

He groaned. "For a little woman, you sure pack a wallop," he said between gasps.

"I'm sorry, darling, did I hurt you?"

"Daddy, are you hurt bad?" Chris asked, tugging at John's shirtsleeve.

John clutched his side as he sat up, resting his head against his knees. "I'm . . . fine," he said, gasping. "I just . . . need to . . . get my breath."

John continued to sit on the floor, his arms crossed on his jeans-covered knees, his head resting on his forearms.

"Hey, boss," Mugger Michaels called from the lobby, "are you folks okay? Did you find the boy? We heard all this banging and crashing and figured we'd better join the rescue." Mugger peered down at John. "Boss, are you okay?"

Slowly John rose to his feet, flexed his shoulders, touched his side lightly with his fingers and grinned.

"We're fine, Mugger, just fine." He smiled at Kathryn and held out his hand. When she came close, he pulled her against his side. "Son," he beckoned, his other hand gesturing to Chris.

Chris inched toward his father, finally stopping a few feet away. "I'm sorry, Daddy, for running away, for making you worry. Are you still mad at me?"

John shook his head and smiled.

"What about her?" Chris nodded toward Kathryn. "Are you still mad at her?"

"Not at all, son. We talked it out. We love each other very much, and we both love you—too much to let a misunderstanding break us apart."

Chris's dark head hung down. "I lost Patches. She wanted to go home, and I tried to keep her inside my shirt, but she scratched and I let go and—and—"

"And like all smart cats, she found her way home," John said. "She's fine. I'm sure she's waiting to see you."

"Really?" Chris beamed as he sidled closer.

"Dirty but safe," John said. "Kit fed her just before we drove up here."

"Are we still moving up north?" Chris asked.

"Yes, in a few months," John confirmed.

"And does Patches get to go with us?" Chris asked.

"Yes."

"And does that mean . . ." Chris squinted up at Kathryn, continuing, "does that mean Mom wants to come with us after all?"

John reached for his son and pulled him against his other side. He glanced at Mugger and noticed Colleen had joined him, shyly taking his hand.

John sighed deeply. For the first time he felt the confidence to answer his son's question. "Of course, Chris, we're a family now. We might not always agree on everything, but we'll be a family forever. And in a few months when you have a little brother or sister, he or she will be part of our family, too. Because families stick together, no matter what."

"Promise?" Chris asked.

John pulled Kathryn and Chris closer and hugged them tightly.

"No matter what happens to us in the future, Chris, that's a promise I'll always keep."

EPILOGUE

Two Years Later

"WE HAVE THE BEST SCHOOL in the whole world, Mrs. Brasher," Jessica Holbrook said, tossing her blond head of long beautiful curls.

Kathryn Brasher glanced up from the papers she had been grading and smiled. "I agree, Jessie. We're very fortunate." Jessie was the only fifth-grade pupil in the school and at times the little girl tried to lord her budding maturity over the younger students.

Kathryn surveyed her pupils. The July air was warm and dry, and early in the day she had moved everyone outside to the play area John and some of his workers had built for them.

She thought back to the time shortly after Chris's failed runaway attempt. Kathryn had convinced John to accept family counseling for all of them, but especially for Chris. The three months of therapy with the local mental health psychologist had been invaluable to them all.

Kathryn had taught in St. Maries until Christmas and was pleased that Maybelle Bosgieter had agreed to take over her class permanently. Kathryn had left her classroom in capable hands.

They had moved to Bonners Ferry in early January after spending the Christmas holidays with Natalie and Cal and their family. Preliminary road building began, only to be halted in early February when an unusually heavy storm left the equipment snowbound. John had called a halt until after the spring thaw.

They had found a house in town, and when Kathryn had gone into labor in mid-February, John was home. In spite of his doubts, he had helped her through labor, assisted in delivery and been the first one to hold his newest offspring, a robust, seven-pound, dark-haired boy.

The memory of the smile on John's face when he'd placed their son on her breast in the birthing room would stay with her forever. They had agreed to name him Marcus Keith Brasher after her father.

She had returned to the hospital a few weeks after delivery. Complications had caused hemorrhaging. A blood transfusion was required to build her strength back up, and then she'd had to deal with an unexpected crisis. A second doctor agreed with her gynecologist's recommendation of a hysterectomy.

She had cried gallons of tears. "But I wanted more babies."

John had wiped her tears away. "We'll just have to count our blessings with this one, love," he'd comforted her. "Marcus is very special. I'm sure he and Chris will keep us busy enough to prevent us from getting old and settled."

Now, as she watched Marc toddle across the playground, she felt blessed several times over with this precious baby. He was seventeen months old, had dark, curly hair and John's blue eyes. His favorite word was no.

Although she had decided to stay home for the first year after Marc's birth, John's dream of a school for logging families had haunted her. Two spring thaws brought home a much bigger problem than the physical location of the school. The work schedule of the loggers just didn't coincide with the traditional school schedule of the logger's child.

When the seed of a solution began to grow, she gathered the wives and explained her idea. The other women were ecstatic. Up until now the men were home during the spring while their children were free during the summer, the very time when the men were working long, intensive hours. There must, they'd all decided, be another way.

A change from the traditional school seemed to be the answer. Kathryn had written to the state department of education and detailed her proposal for a loggers' school, presented her credentials, described the classroom and its mobile advantage, told of her husband's willingness to cofinance the program and asked for the department's approval of the nonstandard schedule and to supply the books and a grant to help remodel the mobile classroom.

Much to her surprise, officials had approved her request, even offering a rural education consultant's services when needed. The woman had paid them a visit earlier in the month and had been so intrigued with the school that she had stayed two days, taking copious notes as well as giving suggestions for the different ages of the students.

Now the children attended school from May through January, with short breaks for the usual summer and fall holidays. The families were able to take vacations during the spring, avoiding the hordes of summer tourists. Best of all, the fathers were able to be closer to their children, to get to know them, love them and understand them as they grew, and the wives were relieved of the pressure of being logging widows.

The school had opened on schedule in a trailer that had been stripped of its traditional fittings and converted into an open single classroom. Fifteen children, including

Chris, from kindergarten through the eighth grade, shared the space with Marc and two mice in a wire-and-plastic cage.

The trailer was parked five miles from the cutting area at a trailer camp that had been established especially for the crew. The forest service had shared the expense of stringing electricity from their facility to the camp and billed John's company monthly. A bar was located a few miles beyond the forest service community, but few men were willing to drive by their families to get there.

Kathryn and John had discussed the arrangement and agreed it was adequate for the present. Chris was a leggy sixth grader, doing very well with his studies and showing an unexpected flair for creative writing and drawing cartoons. He had completed a collection of cartoons on logging life that had shown a surprising amount of maturity and humor.

John had stifled his initial reaction when Chris had tried his hand at poetry, but soon he'd displayed fatherly pride, pleasure and relief when the poems followed the style of Robert Service.

"Mrs. Brasher!" Amanda Duncan shouted from the art table where two third graders were working with papier-mâché. Amanda pointed toward Marc as he wobbled on chubby legs across the grassy yard.

"Marc, no!" Kathryn called, jumping from her chair and racing to intercept her son before he reached the open jar of red finger paint that had been left in the grass by two second graders. "Into the playpen for you," she said, kissing his cheek as she handed him a cracker. He grinned and snapped off a piece of cracker with his four pearly white, razor-sharp front teeth.

The playpen was a fenced area ten by fifteen feet that had been built by Swede one weekend. The weekend after he'd completed that task, he had drafted several other men and they had built a fence around the acre of land surrounding the trailer. The older children had held a class meeting and had agreed to take turns watching over the younger children when they were all outside.

The three sixth graders returned from the trailer where they had been working on a science project.

"We're done, Mom—Miss K—Mrs. Brash—" Chris grimaced and blushed, then shrugged and gave her a sheepish grin. "You know what I mean." His features had lengthened, revealing a promise of lean handsomeness that some of the older girls had already noticed.

She smiled. "I know, Chris. If you and Melissa will set up the video equipment, I'll bring the children inside, and we'll view the cassette we received from the library in town. It's all about the endangered species here in the Northern Rockies."

"Great," he said.

"There will be a brief test after the film," she reminded everyone.

Fifteen children groaned in unison.

LATER THAT EVENING, after the boys were asleep, John joined her in the bedroom of the trailer.

"Do you like changes, Kit?"

"If they're good changes. Why?"

"I was propositioned this afternoon in Bonners Ferry."

"Propos . . . ?" Uncertainty showed in her eyes.

"Remind you of the old hooker days?" he teased.

"Well, a little," she admitted. "You'd better explain."

"I was offered a job at the mill in Bonners Ferry," he said. "Leland Johannson is retiring next year, just about the time this timber sale winds down. What do you think?"

"But what about your contracting business? You can't do both."

"I know." He folded his arms behind his head and studied the paneling of the crowded bedroom.

She sat up in bed. "Would you really give up being your own boss? After all these years?"

"If you'd asked me that a few years ago, I'd have said no, but recently, well, I know you've never complained, but this trailer is a hellishly small place for a family. So I've been thinking."

"About?"

"About...selling off the equipment, liquidating the business, helping the men find other employment." He ran his fingers through his graying hair. "Sometimes I'm tired. Tired of all the pressure, the constant searching for more timber sales, fighting the bureaucracies of the forest service, the state, Uncle Sam. Oh, hell, maybe I just want to settle down in one place for more than a few years." He turned to her. "Want to settle down with me, Kit? We could build a home, a real home, large enough for that piano your mother's been keeping for you, with a dining room for all that china and crystal."

"Oh, John, I haven't mentioned any of those things for a long time. I'm surprised you remembered."

"You've been a good sport, Kit, exceedingly patient with me."

"But I love you, John. What would you expect of me? We've been together. That's what counts. But what about the school? We've just begun to work out the problems, and it's going so well."

"We have another year to decide," he said, sitting up. "Perhaps you can become a consultant for the state and the logging industry people on the subject of mobile schools."

"The children have loved the school, and I've received very favorable comments from the mothers," she said.

He nodded. "The men think it's great, too. We'll hold a parents' meeting at the end of the year to discuss it."

She dropped to the pillow and suppressed a yawn. "We still have more than a year to work it out. What about Swede Johnson? He's been with you for so long."

"Swede has been dropping hints about retiring."

She laughed. "Swede? Of all the workers on your crews, he's the one I'm positive has sawdust in his veins. What would he do if he retired?"

"He went to visit a niece who lives in Alaska during the last spring thaw," he said. "She wants him to come live with them and learn all about salmon fishing. She and her husband have written him several times since. I'm sure he would go if I can convince him he's not letting me down. Maybe there's a motive behind all these new ideas, sweetheart."

"You do what you think is best, darling," she said, reaching out to touch his side. "Where you go, I go."

"Then I think I've made up my mind," John said, lying back beside her and slipping his arm across her waist. "I'm going to build my schoolmarm wife a house, and we'll turn it into a home, with music and laughter and kids and room for Debbie and her family when they visit. Your mother said once you would make a marvelous piano teacher."

"Oh, I'd love that! I could stay home and give lessons when I wanted to and—oh, John, you're getting me all excited, too."

"Then it's definite. I'll tell the manager at the mill I'll accept. It's a management position, and I'll travel once in a while to other locations and to the home office, but mostly I'll be home every night like a loving husband and father should be."

Her hand grazed his bare chest. "Oh, you're a loving husband, that's for sure. You've proved that over and over."

"And I'll keep on proving it, too," John replied, his hand caressing her body beneath the silky green gown. "That's a promise."

"And I'll hold you to it," she said, drawing his face down to hers as she claimed his mouth in earnest.

Harlequin
Superromance

COMING NEXT MONTH

#226 CRIMSON RIVERS • Virginia Nielsen
Volcanologist Holly Ingram knows that it is her duty to
warn plantation owner Lorne Bryant when an eruption
is threatening Kapoiki. And she also knows that this
meeting will bring to a climax the rift that has alienated
them for eight long years....

#227 BEYOND FATE • Jackie Weger
Cleo Anderson thinks romance isn't for her—until she
encounters the charismatic Fletcher Fremont Maitland
at a summer camp in Georgia. Slowly love works its
magic, and the fate that first drew them together
becomes the catalyst for a lifetime.

#228 GIVE AND TAKE • Sharon Brondos
Performing a striptease for a group of women is
embarrassing for Kyle Chambers, but he'll "do
anything for charity." And no one is more aware of this
than Charity Miller. But the marriage and children he
wants to give her are more than she is willing to accept.

#229 MEETING PLACE • Bobby Hutchinson
When an arranged marriage brings the exotically
beautiful Yolanda Belan to a new life in the West, she
quickly discovers that exchanging vows is not enough to
win the heart of her husband, Alex Caine. But her
refreshing approach to life and her smoldering
sensuality soon have him behaving like a newlywed
should!

Harlequin *"Super Celebration"*
SWEEPSTAKES

NEW PRIZES—NEW PRIZE FEATURES & CHOICES—MONTHLY

1. To enter the sweepstakes, follow the instructions outlined on the Center Insert Card. Alternate means of entry, NO PURCHASE NECESSARY, you may also enter by mailing your name, address and birthday on a plain 3″ x 5″ piece of paper to: In U.S.A.: Harlequin "Super Celebration" Sweepstakes, P.O. Box 1867, Buffalo, N.Y. 14240-1867. In Canada: Harlequin "Super Celebration" Sweepstakes, P.O. Box 2800, 5170 Yonge Street, Postal Station A, Willowdale, Ontario M2N 6J3.

2. Winners will be selected in random drawings from all entries received. All prizes will be awarded. These prizes are in addition to any free gifts which might be offered. Versions of this sweepstakes with different prizes may appear in other presentations by TorStar and their affiliates. The maximum value of the prizes offered is $8,000.00. Winners selected will receive the prize offered from their prize package.

3. The selection of winners will be conducted under the supervision of Marden-Kane, an independent judging organization. By entering the sweepstakes, each entrant accepts and agrees to be bound by these rules and the decision of the judges which shall be final and binding. Odds of winning are dependent upon the total number of entries received. Taxes, if any, are the sole responsibility of the winners. Prizes are not transferable. This sweepstakes is scheduled to appear in Retail Outlets of Harlequin Books during the period of June 1986 to December 1986. All entries must be received by January 31st, 1987. The drawing will take place on or about March 1st, 1987 at the offices of Marden-Kane, Lake Success, New York. For Quebec (Canada) residents, any litigation regarding the running of this sweepstakes and the awarding of prizes must be submitted to La Regie de Lotteries et Course du Quebec.

4. This presentation offers the prizes as illustrated on the Center Insert Card.

5. This offer is open to residents of the U.S., and Canada, 18 years or older, except employees of TorStar, its affiliates, subsidiaries, Marden-Kane and all other agencies and persons connected with conducting this sweepstakes. All Federal, State and local laws apply. Void where prohibited or restricted by law. Winners will be notified by mail and may be required to execute an affidavit of eligibility and release which must be returned within 14 days after notification. Winners consent to the use of their name, photograph and/or likeness for advertising and publicity in conjunction with this and similar promotions without additional compensation. One prize per family or household. Canadian winners will be required to answer a skill testing question.

6. For a list of our most recent prize winners, send a stamped, self-addressed envelope to: WINNERS LIST, c/o Marden-Kane, P.O. Box 525, Sayreville, NJ 08872.

No Lucky Number needed to win!

**HARLEQUIN
HISTORICAL**

Explore love with Harlequin in the Middle
Ages, the Renaissance, in the Regency, the
Victorian and other eras.

Relive within these books the endless ages of
romance, set against authentic historical
backgrounds. Two new historical love stories
published each month.

HIST-A-1